T0267537

NIGHT JOURNEY

Greg Johnson

Regal House Publishing

Copyright © 2023 Greg Johnson. All rights reserved.

Published by
Regal House Publishing, LLC
Raleigh, NC 27605
All rights reserved

ISBN -13 (paperback): 9781646033911
ISBN -13 (epub): 9781646033928
Library of Congress Control Number: 2022949404

All efforts were made to determine the copyright holders and obtain their permissions in any circumstance where copyrighted material was used. The publisher apologizes if any errors were made during this process, or if any omissions occurred. If noted, please contact the publisher and all efforts will be made to incorporate permissions in future editions.

Cover images and design by © C. B. Royal

Regal House Publishing, LLC
https://regalhousepublishing.com

The following is a work of fiction created by the author. All names, individuals, characters, places, items, brands, events, etc. were either the product of the author or were used fictitiously. Any name, place, event, person, brand, or item, current or past, is entirely coincidental.

All rights reserved. No part of this publication may be reproduced, stored in a retrieval system, or transmitted, in any form or by any means, electronic, mechanical, photocopying, recording, or otherwise, without the prior permission of Regal House Publishing.

Printed in the United States of America

To my mother, Jo Ann,
and to the memory of my father, Raymond

The whole question is here: am I a monster,
or am I the victim myself?

- Feodor Dostoevsky, *Crime and Punishment*

To whom the morning stands for night
What must the midnight—be?

- Emily Dickinson

BOOK ONE

PART ONE

JARED

1

They stood at the window, staring, as the long black Cadillac churned up the rain-pocked driveway through the dusk.

"My God, it looks like a hearse," his mother whispered. She'd bent close to Jared, as though they were conspirators, parting the curtain a few inches with her slender ringless hand. That morning, before he'd noticed her makeup or her flowery cheap perfume or the white-trimmed blue polyester dress she'd dug out of the closet, his eye had darted to her left ring finger; he didn't know whether its nakedness pleased or repelled him. Now he stared at her hand instead of the window and the driveway beyond. Nothing she did or said made sense to him these days. Her dress smelled faintly of mothballs.

Together they watched as Aunt Billie and the two priests struggled out of the car, each preceded by the silent explosion of a black umbrella. The rain, near invisible in the dissolving light, had begun abruptly, splotching the Cadillac's dusty hood and doors. The car was only a few weeks old, a new 1991 model. This was the first time Jared or his mother had seen it, but already it looked worn, used-up. The whitewalls were soiled and the clumps of reddish mud clinging to the wire hubcaps and chrome fenders resembled dried blood. Here in mid-December the weather had turned warm and sticky. There were thunderstorms almost every evening at about this time, and people in town complained of the unnatural warmth and of how impossible it was to keep anything clean.

People in town complained about many things: for instance, Aunt Billie's having purchased this new Cadillac for the two priests who lived together at the rectory. Think of the poor people that money could have fed! The priests could have done with a compact, and there'd have been thousands left over for charity! The town's few Catholics were far more incensed than the Protestants, who were cynically unsurprised when the priests began driving the car. At his tiny parochial school, Jared endured crude wisecracks from his classmates, probably the same jokes their parents had made at home.

"Hey, Jared, which one is your aunt Billie after, old Father Brody or Father Zach? Bet she likes 'em young, huh?"

Jared ignored such remarks just as he'd ignored the far crueler jibes, earlier in the fall, about his father.

"Hey, Jared, what're you crazy McCunes gonna do next, start humpin' on the altar down at church? Maybe your mother and—"

That time, Jared's quick hot glance had silenced the boy, a tackle on the high school team who was half again Jared's size. Though he had a momentary surge of elation—this had been the first angry reaction he'd allowed himself to the taunts about his family—he'd felt strangely bereft when, after that, the ribbing had ended. During the last days of fall term Jared had walked through the classrooms and corridors sensing that an invisible circle had been drawn around him, setting him apart from the ordinary regimented life of the school. He had felt himself pulled back into thinking about his family and his oneness with them as into a dark hole bored into the earth and leading nowhere.

Lately Jared and his mother were uncertain with one another, self-conscious, the unthinking alliance they'd enjoyed before his father's hospitalization now turned awkward, not exactly contentious but pulling them nonetheless in random directions; as if perhaps they were unrelated, after all, left struggling in this peculiar atmosphere of politeness and intimacy. Now, listening to the echo of her poor attempt at a joke, *My God, it looks like a hearse*, Jared again had the unwelcome thought that neither of them really knew what they were doing or saying. These days his mother laughed readily at odd things, at odd times, because she didn't know how else to respond. And Jared knew no more than she.

He said nervously, "It's just a car. It'll get us there, won't it?"

Straightening, she let the curtain fall closed. Jared could hear the priests and Aunt Billie stamping their feet on the front porch, and their murmuring voices outside the door. His mother looked at him, frightened.

She said, "I thought you didn't want to go. Why didn't you?" "I didn't say that. I didn't say I wouldn't go."

What he'd said during their cold lunch of tomato sandwiches and cantaloupe was that they shouldn't converge on his father all at once; maybe Jared should wait at home. He'd thought she wasn't listening or couldn't quite hear. Lately she'd seemed vague, distracted, no longer the mother he recalled from his tenderest years. He could still picture that tidy, mild-voiced woman, smiling down upon him from a world of adult omniscience where everything was settled, known. Clearly she knew everything but would administer her knowledge lovingly, slowly, with the same prim confident smile she gave to men at the bank, the grocery store, the post office during the day, and to Jared's father when he came home from work at four o'clock. Maybe he idealized the woman his mother had once been but it was nonetheless true that she had vanished. This had become an irrefutable fact of his present life, and his father's illness was another such fact. Somehow these facts were related, though Jared couldn't know if his father's illness had caused his mother to abandon them or if it had been the other way around. The lives of these two people, about whom he thought constantly, were mysteriously entwined, confused. That was marriage. Somehow the youthful confident mother of his childhood had slipped away from them, from her family and her marriage, had separated cleverly in the way the soul leaves the body after death, unsullied, free.

The doorbell rang. His mother shot him a look that seemed both angry and full of longing, but this lasted only a moment. She looked tired, and very pale. Her eyes closed briefly and she took a deep breath. She was starting for the door when, abruptly, it swung open, and Jared could smell the humid oily turbulence of the air outside, could hear the rain clattering soullessly on the graveled driveway, could glimpse the swollen blue-black clouds. The last shreds of daylight were fading quickly. He simply waited there with his mother while the priests and Aunt Billie blundered into the house, uninvited.

2

In June they had taken his father away and since then his mother had seemed no less absent, moving through her chores like a sleepwalker and tending even to her son with that new vagueness of manner, her hands bumbling at his shirt collar before he left for Sunday mass, her eyes loving but hazy as though she were losing vision altogether. At night he no longer heard the hot vicious weeping behind her closed bedroom door and this new bewildered silence disturbed him far more than the noise of her grief had done.

He was reminded of those peculiar days last summer when, faced with the stifling reality of his father's absence, Jared's sense of relief had unaccountably changed to longing, a perverse nostalgia for the sound of his parents' arguments—the slammed doors, the screeching tires of his father's pickup as he made his angry escapes, the sickly sweet, smoky odor of his breath and clothes when he returned home. One day Jared's father had taken the small pistol he kept on the top shelf of their bedroom closet—"for protection," he said—and had brought it downstairs, held aloft in his hand like some parody of a cowboy's gesture, or the Lone Ranger's. He'd allowed Jared's mother to pry his fingers away from the gun and then Jared had seen, for the first time, tears standing in his father's eyes. But none of these memories seemed quite real. All that was gone, vanished, sucked down into that same dark hole.

Though he brooded constantly about his parents, he hadn't been able to imagine his father's recent life. He'd managed to shun the movie images of madness that tormented him those first few weeks, but then there was nothing to take their place. His mother, who had once been a nurse, assured Jared that his father wasn't psychotic but depressed, and depression was something they could treat nowadays. She told him that he should put ideas of straitjackets and padded cells out of his mind. They had wonder drugs now, she'd said, miracle drugs, and even when they used electroshock therapy, the patient was anesthetized and did not feel much pain. But the more they discussed the terrible things that were not happening to his father, the more absent and mysterious his father's present life became.

Sometimes he wished that his father might never come home.

He shared this wish with no one, of course. Certainly not with his mother, not with his two or three good friends at school, not even with Linda Hanratty, his girlfriend—or was she simply a friend?—for the past few months.

Linda was a tall, quiet girl who had moved to town this past spring with her divorced mother. Mrs. Hanratty had just knocked on the door one day, announcing that she wanted to get to know her neighbors, though it turned out the Hanrattys lived half a mile away. All the other women Mrs. Hanratty approached had rebuffed her, or so she claimed. She was as outspoken as her daughter Linda was shy, she laughed a great deal, she had "liberal" views and chain-smoked cigarettes and had an abrupt, strident manner that set her apart from the other women in town. During the summer, while she and Jared's mother were having what Mrs. Hanratty termed their "coffee klatsch," Jared would sit out on the front porch with Linda.

They'd had the immediate rapport that sometimes develops between shy teenagers—each had recently turned fourteen—and had talked idly and dreamily through a number of long afternoons. Linda loved books, and talked about poets and philosophers as if they lived down the street, but Jared felt intrigued rather than intimidated, and before long they were discussing what Linda called "ideas"—he'd never had such talks with anyone before, not even with teachers at school—and sometimes, though more tentatively, about their own mysterious lives. Linda said she had resigned herself to her father's disappearance when she was eleven (Kay had divorced him last year) but thought that as an adult she might try to look for him.

There were organizations now that could help you with that. Several times Jared had been tempted to talk of his fear that his father would never come home, either, and of his terror that he *would* come home but that their lives would be new and strange and unlivable. But the idea of having such a talk, and with someone outside the family, felt disloyal, and in any case the words would not form themselves clearly in his mind.

Thanks to the disability insurance and to a monthly "allowance" his rich aunt Billie doled out to them, his mother hadn't needed to get a job when her husband went to the hospital. She'd spoken about it, at first, but Aunt Billie, the priests, and of course her own conscience fought the idea, for Travis had insisted she give up her nursing career when they got married— she was pregnant with Jared a few months later—and now that he was hospitalized it would seem deceitful to go against his wishes. But every day when Jared would go out to do errands for her, or to visit Linda, or when a friend on a bike stopped for him so they could ride to get hamburgers or to a movie, he would spend his time away thinking and worrying about his mother alone at home, wandering the rooms, repeatedly dusting furniture or straightening pictures, as if somehow this constant maintenance of a near-empty house were occupation enough for a healthy intelligent woman still in her thirties.

Last week they'd learned that Travis was coming home. They'd been having a late breakfast of cinnamon toast and coffee—now that school was out for the holidays they both slept late, often past nine o'clock—when Dr. Hough called. Jared had stayed at the table, chewing silently, his jaw freezing now and then as he strained to hear his mother's words. Her voice seemed to waver, exuberant one moment but then halting, uncertain, almost inaudible.

He is? But when did—

Yes, of course, but I didn't expect—

But are they sure that he—what's that? Yes, I know that, I'm a nurse, but I—

Yes, doctor—

Yes, but I—

As he listened to these fragments of talk Jared's palms went icy, his breath came faster, the breakfast became a chilled lump in his stomach. His mother came back to the table and they sat in silence for a long while. His mother's fair, heart-shaped face was still creased with sleep, and she'd pulled her abundant reddish hair back with a rubber band. He'd watched her eyes. They were cast down as she finished eating, reporting in between bites what the doctor had said. Thanks to the medication, and the extensive therapy, his father's condition had improved. The doctors had agreed that it would be best for both Mr. McCune and his family if he could be released before Christmas. With further improvement, and provided he kept up his medication and therapy, the doctor saw no reason why Travis couldn't start looking for work soon after the new year.

Jared had stopped eating. He stared at his mother.

"What about—" There was no need to finish.

In the morning light his mother's pale green eyes had a clear, neutral look, neither contented nor distressed. "That's what I wanted to know," she answered slowly, "but they said he certainly hasn't drunk anything at the hospital. And supposedly, he's determined not to start again. They have a special therapy group for that, Jared, and he—"

"For being a drunk, do you mean?"

All at once he'd felt the need to say it.

After hesitating his mother said, "That's right," and she continued eating.

They hadn't talked about his father in months and hadn't quite known how to start again. During the summer, including the August day he'd turned fourteen, he'd gone with her for the weekly visit to the hospital, and invariably she would ask if Jared wanted to see his father alone, or should the three of them visit together, and always Jared chose the latter option. During these drives, and especially when he watched her interacting with the hospital staff, Jared became aware, and really for the first time, that his mother was a person separate from him and his father, from her family, from this town itself, and that somehow his mother had preserved the young nurse that Travis must have met that morning in Crawford Long Hospital in Atlanta, where he'd been rushed with an agonizing case of kidney stones. It was August 1976, and three months later they were married, and less than a year after that Jared had been born: but all through his boyhood the image of his mother as a young woman on her own in a big city, in nursing school and then her first full-time job, had seemed a mere romantic fantasy, disconnected to the rather shy and soft-spoken woman he knew.

Lately she had seemed to him fragile, pained, otherworldly in the cares of her loneliness and what must have been her relentless worrying about the future. Yet, visiting his father at the hospital, she spoke to the staff and the doctors in a forthright, friendly way, as if this were no crisis at all, nothing she couldn't handle; Jared had tried to imagine her as a very young woman tending briskly to patients, a starched nurse's cap set pertly onto that lovely mass of hair. Only when they got back into the car, a serviceable mud-brown Toyota that Billie had bought them last summer, did his mother return to the woman Jared knew: she would sit still for a moment before starting the car, her slender frame seeming to wilt, to soften, her eyes closing in the sudden release of tension. The former owner of the Toyota must have smoked, because the car had a faint ashen smell, and at times Jared imagined that a near-visible sheen, like fog, prevented him from seeing his mother clearly as she drove.

Yet one day she said, cheerfully enough, "He's getting better, don't you think?"

And Jared answered, after a pause, "Well, I guess he is. Yeah."

"Yes, I think he is," she said, gripping the wheel.

They'd said nothing else for the rest of the drive.

3

His mother once said that Aunt Billie entered a room "like gangbusters," and tonight was no exception. Though Father Zach came through the door first, with a quick embarrassed smile for Jared and Nina, he moved aside, held the door open, and at once seemed to disappear. Aunt Billie, a bulky splotch of maroon silk, erupted between the black-suited priests, and went to hug Nina, murmuring inaudible consolations into her ear.

The priests stood around awkwardly. Father Brody was a portly, big-jawed man whose smallish blue eyes were all but lost in the fatty ridges of his face. He'd always put Jared in mind of an aging pug. The old priest clamped one fleshy paw on Jared's shoulder, as a sign of affection or perhaps merely for support. Tonight he seemed wobblier than usual. People in town whispered relentlessly of his drinking, and as he drew near, Jared caught a whiff of minty chewing gum underlain by a sweeter, sicklier odor. The other priest, Father Zach, was young and dark-haired, sent down here two years ago from Minnesota. His build was slight, he had mild brown eyes and a fair complexion, but his jaw featured a dark stubble even when freshly shaved.

"Nina, are you and Jared ready?" his aunt asked. Her eyes grazed him and his mother quickly and then veered off. Devoted to the church, Billie had an officious, prepossessing air that, combined with her husband's money, made her something of a personage in the town, feared by most adults and, behind her back, ridiculed by the kids, who liked to call her "old Billie-goat"—among other, more vicious, nicknames. The oldest of the four McCune kids, Billie had left school in eighth grade to care for Jared's grandmother, who'd been ailing even then, and at seventeen she'd married Elton Fair, a land developer twenty years older, long known as the county's richest man. (Locally, the words *Elton Fair* had the solidity and luster that attach to the name of an institution, so that even Billie used his full name when she spoke of him.) Still infatuated with Billie despite her surgeries and her increasing weight—Jared knew he would never plumb the mysteries of romantic attraction— Elton had converted to Catholicism before their marriage and hadn't missed a Sunday or Holy Day of Obligation since. The very thought of skipping mass would have been unthinkable to Billie.

When Jared's mother had heard about the Cadillac Billie had bought for the priests, she'd merely shaken her head, smiling. Billie's domineering nature often expressed itself in curious bursts of generosity, which might be viewed cynically as a means of putting others in her debt but in which Jared could see, also, the rather sad, desperately awkward gestures of a frustrated nurturer. Many times, when Jared was younger, his aunt would thrust a twenty into Jared's palm, or stuff one into his pocket—always when Travis and Nina were out of the room. When he tried to protest, she would wrinkle her lip on one side and shake her head, frowning. Her relentless gift-giving seemed to embarrass Billie more than anyone.

"Yes, whenever you are," his mother said. She was trying to be polite but she sounded breathless, uneasy. Standing next to her in the middle of the old braided rug, and now exactly the same height as his mother, Jared felt that they must seem as out of place as Billie and the priests. They scarcely looked like mother and son, for Jared had inherited his father's glossy dark hair, sharp cheekbones, olive-pale complexion. And he had the McCune family eyes—a clear, startled blue—and eyebrows thick enough to provide a brooding look, and dark lashes as long as a girl's.

Father Zach glanced at Jared and the others, smiling. "A raincoat should be enough," he said pleasantly. He was holding open the closet door while Nina poked about inside. "It's still pretty warm," he added. "Hard to imagine that Christmas is two weeks away."

"Father, don't even mention Christmas!" Billie laughed, rolling her eyes. She'd crossed to Father Brody's chair and was helping him up. "I've barely gotten started on my shopping."

Aunt Billie made this statement often, though everyone knew she began her holiday buying in July.

Jared's mother was donning the shabby sky-blue raincoat she'd worn since his earliest memory, and which looked awkward, he thought, against the brighter blue of her dress underneath.

"Have you decided, Jared?" she said. "Are you coming along?"

"What?" Aunt Billie said, startled. "Of course he's coming."

So Jared had no choice but to follow.

4

The state mental hospital where they had taken Jared's father was in the next sizable town, a ninety-minute drive along a rutted, two-lane country highway. At first, both Billie and Nina had balked, since Georgia's "loony bin" had been for decades a place of legendary horrors, the butt of schoolyard jokes, a destination thought to be worse than jail or hell itself. Billie had offered to pay for private care in Atlanta, and Nina, eyes closing, had said thank you, thank you, not offering even a routine, perfunctory protest, but to their surprise their doctor overruled them. Travis would be hospitalized for such a short time that taking him so far would be pointless, perhaps even counterproductive. It was important that Dr. Hough be able to visit Travis, to oversee his care, and that would be impossible if Travis was shipped off to Atlanta.

At home, though they never talked about Jared's father when they were alone, Nina and Jared endured visits from Aunt Billie once or twice each week, and Billie talked of little but Travis's "difficulties," as she called his illness, and of the general misfortunes of her family. For her father, too, had suffered from depression, and had died in a shooting incident—he'd been out hunting, supposedly—which his family quietly acknowledged among themselves as a suicide.

This had happened in 1969, three years after his youngest daughter, Maureen, had suffered her terrible fall down the attic steps, for which her father loudly and repeatedly had taken the blame. The next-to-top step had needed repair, but he'd put it off. He knew that Rooney, as the family called her (her siblings had called their baby sister "Reeney" at first, but the little girl mispronounced it *Rooney*, which made everyone laugh, so they started using the name too) was an active, curious child, that she'd be into something the minute you turned your back, but he'd left the attic door in the hallway unlocked that Saturday morning after carrying some boxes of books up into storage. So the mishap had occurred though the whole family was home, Billie helping her mother with the laundry, Travis playing out back, Clyde upstairs with Rooney in the attic. While Clyde had found something in one of the boxes up there—an old stamp collection—that had absorbed his attention, the little girl had just wandered off, unnoticed, as sometimes happens in large busy households, and she'd rushed to the top of the narrow wooden steps and she'd lost her footing (they all assumed) on that broken step near the top and had fallen and bashed her head and, as a result, could not learn like other kids and could not even speak very well. She would never have a normal life, would always be *the spazz, the retard, Looney Rooney* as the mean kids called her at school. For three years after the accident their father had endured the guilt, seldom speaking to anyone, sunk in despair, and then one morning his own "accident" had happened after he'd gone out hunting by himself in the back woods, something he'd never been known to do.

Billie, who had adored her father and had been his favorite, was nearly grown by the time he died. The first thing she'd said to Nina after Travis's trouble at the plant and his hospitalization was that it "runs in the family," and by "it" Jared supposed she meant depression, or sorrow, or maybe just trouble in general, though to Jared's mind arose unbidden the image of some elemental darkness shooting through his family's blood, swift, amoral, featureless, and he'd stared at his own strong, well-molded hands—his father's hands, after all—and the slightly raised veins set thickly into the olive-dark flesh and wondered idly what sort of destruction these hands might perform.

During her unwanted visits Billie would talk also about Clyde and Rooney, who had lived all their adult lives in Atlanta and whom she and Elton Fair still supported, *Clyde-and-Rooney* who were the closest of the four siblings, Clyde having grown, since they were kids, fiercely protective of his little sister, taking her to doctors and psychologists, to daily "art therapy" classes, tending to all her needs such as helping to feed and bathe her and do the work that needed doing every time she went to the toilet. Clyde himself had led an erratic, restless life, working for a while as a store clerk, then as a carpenter, then as a handyman, studying for his real estate license but giving that up because he didn't like the instructor, working in a liquor store and then wanting to open his own wine bar but even Billie and Elton Fair wouldn't advance him the money for *that*, since Clyde tended to lose interest in anything—anything but Rooney, that is—after a year or two.

Now at thirty-two, as Billie joked ruefully, he was still trying to decide what to be when he grew up.

One day in August she'd stopped by Nina's house and had pulled a much-folded piece of notebook paper out of her purse. It was a letter from Clyde, and Jared had tried to peer at the letter as Billie held it, gesturing, the paper rattling in her hand. He hoped the letter contained good news, maybe even the news that Clyde and Rooney were moving back to town. He'd always felt admiration for his uncle Clyde, a small-boned but strong, sinewy, mustached man who had such energy in him—his sudden, reckless enthusiasms, his fierce love for Rooney, his notorious temper. Jared admired Clyde for taking care of Rooney, living with her, since without him she'd have been placed in an institution long ago.

When Travis went to the hospital, Jared had supposed that the same caretaker's instinct Clyde felt toward Rooney might impel him home to see about Travis and his family, but to Jared's knowledge Clyde hadn't called or written to Nina a single time. The only word of him came through Billie, to whom he wrote each month to thank her for the check and to report any news of him and Rooney. On that August evening when she'd brought his most recent letter Jared had only glimpsed the sheet in his aunt's gesturing hand, but he could tell that the letter was studiously printed, not written. Jared had the impression of large, rather childish block letters, and if the printing hadn't been so neat and orderly Jared might have supposed that Rooney had done it. He could have asked to see the letter, of course, but for some reason he always felt shy and vaguely inhibited around Aunt Billie.

Nor had he liked the way she had laughed, making fun of Clyde's news. "Can you imagine?" she said. "Working in an awful place like *that*?"

For Clyde had written that he'd recently started work at a funeral home. It was a small, family-run business, he said, and he joked that the family had gotten "stinking rich"—Billie gave a nipped smile at this joke, shaking her head—and that he was learning the business from the inside. The guy he worked for was a "cheap son-of-a-gun," Clyde claimed (though Jared suspected that Billie was cleaning up her brother's language) and paid him minimum wage, but pretty soon Clyde would have learned all he could in this job and would be ready to move on. For only a few thousand dollars, he said, he could get a degree in mortuary science at a school they had in Atlanta, and eventually set up his own business. He'd "make a killing," he said, joking again, and he hoped Billie would lend him the money to attend the school. Both Jared and his mother had laughed at Clyde's joke, which caused Billie to draw herself up and say that the whole idea sounded ridiculous, and very typical of Clyde. She'd rapidly refolded the letter and stuck it inside her purse.

"Well, you have to admit, Billie," Nina had said, "it's bound to be a good business. I mean, the demand is always going to be there."

Despite himself, Jared laughed again. He picked up his baseball cap and jammed it on his head backward, a habit he'd picked up from the older boys at school. He sat.

"But the point is," Billie said, "how long will he stick with it? I ain't gonna shell out thousands of dollars for this school, and then watch him drop out when he's halfway through."

Nina said, vaguely, "Yes, I suppose…"

"And it's just like him," Billie added, "filling the whole letter with his own self, and barely to even mention Rooney."

"Well, that's true," Jared's mother said politely.

Jared wondered what there was to mention. His encounters with Rooney during her and Clyde's few visits had coalesced into a single image, a single memory, for Rooney was as unchanging and predictable as her brother was volatile and restless. Like Billie, Rooney had grown into a tall, ungainly woman, and yet she put Jared in mind of an absurdly overgrown child, with her chalk-white moon of a face, fresh-looking as a baby's though she was almost thirty now, and her random bright smiles, all teeth and gums, and her careening gait, and the long silences in which she might sit slump-shouldered in a chair, staring for hours at nothing with her faded-blue doglike eyes.

Yes, exactly what—Jared had wanted to ask his aunt Billie—could Clyde tell them about Rooney?

Instead he'd said, rising, "Well, maybe you ought to help him."

Both women glanced at Jared, surprised. After collecting herself, Billie pretended to be amused.

"You think so, eh? You think money grows on trees? I'll tell him to borrow it from you, Mr. Money Bags."

Jared had smiled, awkwardly; he stood at the kitchen doorway, wanting to run out, perplexed by the sudden jump of anger in his chest, his legs. Trying to smile, he felt that he was contorting his face, but he didn't know why he should get so angry at Billie, who after all was a decent-hearted woman who'd always tried to do her best for the family.

He said, "Never mind, I didn't mean—"

"Jared, are you feeling all right?" his mother asked. She'd halfway risen from the table, too, and Jared saw those faint reddish streaks along her cheekbones that appeared when she was upset. But he couldn't answer her; he didn't know what to say.

Billie ignored them. She'd opened her purse, and with an angry laugh she unfolded the letter again and jabbed at the bottom of the sheet, where Jared could make out the large letters, *PS.*

"And listen to this, listen to what he says here," Billie spat out. "'PS, Rooney says to tell you she *loves you to death.*' Can you imagine?"

Billie paused, and for a moment Jared thought she might start to cry.

But she only said, "That poor, poor girl," shaking her head and returning the letter to her purse. After that, much to Jared's relief, she told them she ought to be heading home.

5

On their way out of town, Jared stared out the window, though he could glimpse only his ghostly reflection in the streaming glass, and beyond that a vague impression of the dark masses of trees lining the highway. He'd been forced to witness with his uncle Clyde's skeptical glare the shabby neighborhoods of white-framed houses, the few blocks of the "business district" with its ancient brick warehouses and tawdry glass storefronts, the churches (several Baptist, a Church of God, an Assembly of God) with their blaring marquees—"BUT *WHO* COULD OF MADE THE THINGS THAT EVOLVE? FOOD FOR THOUGHT!" one of them read—and their tarnished steeples, and the somnolent courthouse hulking silently in the middle of the square. On the outskirts of town there was a white-stucco shopping mall, which had arisen seemingly overnight like some grotesque mushroom, and a new public high school named after Robert E. Lee. This had caused a loud but short-lived ruckus among the town's Black community, but most of the state's growth was northwest of here, culminating in Atlanta; so Jared supposed that Clyde's calling their hometown a "backwater," the least coarse of the epithets he'd used, wasn't too far off the mark.

Because theirs was the only town in a thirty-mile radius with a Catholic church and parochial school, Jared had felt doubly sheltered, ignorant not only of the messy violent place called America that he glimpsed in bright, blaring, scarcely believable flashes when he flipped channels on their TV in the living room, but also of the local ethos of tent revivals, rodeos, livestock auctions, Friday night football games, church-sponsored youth camps, and the generally hard-bitten small-town conservatism that permeated the area. Even on their own street, the McCunes were known as "that Catholic family," and though not unreasonably disliked were left pretty much to themselves. This was just as well, Jared thought. He had only a couple of close male friends—boys as studious and thoughtful as he. He supposed he was glad that he'd met Linda Hanratty, but because the shy progress of their friendship had coincided with the eruption of his father's troubles it seemed a kind of distant, alien fact that he "had a girlfriend." Still, he saw her regularly, once or twice each week, and he'd kept up his perfect attendance record at school and Sunday mass with the same sense of maintaining a prudent but unexamined routine. This past Saturday, when she'd come over as usual for dinner along with her mother, Jared and Linda had sat on the front-porch rockers afterward, talking idly in this murky December warmth, and when Jared had told her about their going to get his father, Linda had offered at once to come along for "support." Jared looked at her strangely. The thought of bringing Linda or anyone into the airless tension and uncertainty that enveloped his family was unthinkable. He'd mumbled something polite and noncommittal, and then had changed the subject.

Entering the hospital lobby, he felt vaguely ashamed to be following his mother, like a boy hiding behind her skirts, for he had to shorten his stride to keep from overtaking her. A tall, dark-haired, striking kid—people would glance up, lately, when he entered a room, and when he and his mother were together people's eyes would now go instinctively to him, the male, rather than to Nina. Tonight for the first time he was consciously grateful for the priests. Father Zach had approached the reception desk and begun speaking quietly to the male attendant, who hadn't glanced at Jared or his mother. To Jared's surprise the man wore ordinary street clothes, no uniform, no crisp white jacket with a name badge affixed to the pocket. Waiting with his mother some ten feet away, watching Father Zach as he initiated their business, Aunt Billie and Father Brody flanking him on either side, Jared had the notion that the attendant might be a patient who had wandered behind the desk and begun impersonating a member of the staff.

The inmates have taken over the asylum... A remark Jared had heard from one of the nuns, as she surveyed the chaotic hilarity of the school cafeteria one day during lunch.

But the attendant was a slender, intelligent-looking, dark-skinned man in his twenties, his manner calm and self-assured. He gestured them toward the end of the hall, to the "recreation room." Instinctively Jared nodded his thanks, but the man never acknowledged him and returned to his paperwork.

Father Zach herded them down the hall, past the rows of doctors' offices and "treatment rooms." There were scattered attempts at decoration—white-wicker baskets of artificial flowers, desiccated hanging plants, cheap framed prints. Father Zach, whispering, repeated the words he'd heard from the attendant: they'd be bringing Travis down very soon.

They entered the large, beige-painted recreation room. To Jared's surprise, it appeared fairly modern: there was a pool table, a Ping-Pong table and, against one wall, a row of exercise equipment. Stationary bicycles. A weight-lifting bench. Along the back wall was a food-vending area, and the other walls were lined with bulletin boards, framed photos of administrators, and a large institutional clock exactly like the ones in Jared's school. The main areas of the room were filled with plain white Formica tables and chairs of orange- and yellow-covered vinyl.

Perhaps a dozen men and women sat at the tables, smoking and chatting. A few looked up briefly when Jared and the others entered but then they resumed their conversation. Jared felt a jolt of panic that faded almost at once. The patients looked so calm, so ordinary. Most were middle-aged, one or two were silver-haired, all were dressed plainly in slacks or jeans, old sweaters, tennis shoes. One of the older men wore a pair of new-looking slippers. At some of the tables patients sat alone, reading newspapers. Others sat daydreaming, or dozing.

Father Zach led Jared and the others to a large unoccupied table. "We'll wait here," he said nervously. "It won't take long."

Near them sat an old woman, knitting furiously at a sizable but shapeless piece of red wool. At the same table was a middle-aged man with his chin on his chest, dozing, his cheeks ragged with salt-and-pepper whiskers. Not far away, by herself, sat a young woman scarcely out of her teens who might have been pretty except that her face was blotched with what looked like a severe case of measles—a dozen or more circular, angry-red blemishes on her cheeks and forehead.

Jared glanced around at these people with mingled curiosity and dread. He'd imagined that the patients would be kept off to themselves, confined, for how easy it would be for them simply to get up, in unison, then proceed into the lobby and out the front door. That mild-looking young attendant could hardly stop them.

It seemed half an hour but was probably only five or six minutes before the old woman with the knitting caught their attention. She held up the piece of red wool and said, "Well, how do you think it's going? Am I doing all right?"

She sounded genuinely concerned, and Jared saw that she was addressing the scruffy-looking man at her table. He was still dozing, his head bowed as though in prayer. Jared would never be certain if his mother had looked over, too, or how she had reacted, or even the precise sequence of what happened next.

The old woman spoke again, her voice a bit sharper; groggily, her companion came awake. She said, "Do you think I'm doing a good job? Tell me what you think, Travis."

Jared looked over and saw that the man was his father.

The priests rose, Billie and Nina rose, and it seemed mere seconds before they were all standing awkwardly around the table, greeting Travis, shaking his hand and hugging him. A uniformed nurse had entered the room, too, and mumbled something like, "Well, I see you've found him," and stood waiting for the reunion to be over. At the appropriate time, Jared approached his father and they shook hands.

"Hey, Daddy," Jared said, though the cool, limp hand seemed

that of a stranger. The vacant blue eyes and ragged whiskers, the new thinness that showed in the sharpness of his brow, his cheekbones, even in the stained pale-blue sweater and jeans his father wore—all seemed unfamiliar, foreign. Yet this man had his father's voice, hoarse but recognizable, a dark-toned, somehow plaintive voice: "Hey, son, thanks for coming."

Jared smiled awkwardly. What bothered him most was his father's eyes, still that abrupt McCune blue and fixed on Jared, clearly recognizing him, yet something vacant in them, too, as if only a part of his father were greeting him. His clammy handclasp had held Jared's longer than necessary, but this seemed less out of emotion than mere forgetfulness, or uncertainty. Jared squeezed his hand a final time, firmly, and pulled his own hand away.

Moving his head slowly, Jared's father gave his pleasant, empty gaze to the others, each in their turn. That's when Jared, stepping back, collecting himself, understood that his father was drugged.

They're giving him things, medication, I think it's helping, his mother had said one day, after visiting Travis. *They decided against the electroshock treatment, did I tell you? It's just as well, really, I hate to think about...* Yet that's exactly how his father looked: as though he'd been shocked, permanently stunned by some horrific explosion, a searing blast of light. It was there in his father's eyes, which were opened slightly too wide.

Slowly, in bumbling but predictable stages, his father's release from the hospital was accomplished. (Where was Dr. Hough? Jared wondered. There seemed to be no physicians in attendance at all.) There were a couple of packed bags to be gathered, there were papers for both Travis and Nina to sign, there were instructions from the nurse about the medications she'd handed to Nina, in a plain white paper bag. Aunt Billie had tried to take the bag and she kept addressing stray remarks to the nurse, but the woman ignored her. Billie's countrified way of talk and her bluff, defensive manner often made educated people assume she was a fool, and at any other time Jared would have felt sorry for her. But his attention was fixed on his mother. She stood there looking bewildered, holding the white bag awkwardly and mumbling vague responses to the nurse's instructions.

"Two of the Prozac in the morning," the nurse repeated, "along with one Buspar, then another Buspar at night. The Dalmane as needed for sleep. Like I said, it's all written down—it's all in there." She gestured toward the paper bag.

"Everything's changed so much," Nina murmured, with an embarrassed glance at the nurse. "Those medications, I've never even heard of…"

"Heavens, Nina," Billie laughed, "even *I've* heard of Prozac. Don't you ever watch the TV?"

Jared studied his mother's face. The answer was no, she seldom did. Sometimes late at night Jared would turn on the set, and they might watch an old movie, but even that was rare. Nina preferred listening to music, or reading. Even now, Jared thought, she might be listening to music in her head, unable to give her full attention to what was happening.

Jared's father had stayed quietly to one side, as if someone else were the subject of all this fuss. Father Brody, seeming pleased and refreshed after his periods of dozing, now approached Travis and said for the third or fourth time how wonderful it was that he was coming home.

As they were coming back into town, Jared's mother quietly reached aside and patted her son's knee, as if she sensed his tension, his worry, but Jared did not credit this gesture. He felt she should be talking to Jared's father, paying him some attention. He supposed she didn't know what to say. Several times Jared had thought of leaning toward his father, making conversation, but the words would not come.

Only when the Cadillac pulled into the driveway did Nina seem to come alive. The moment the car stopped, she leaned forward and touched Father Zach's shoulder.

"Don't bother about coming in," she said quickly. Billie had already bent down, grunting, and retrieved her umbrella from the front floorboards. Outside the rain had lightened but apparently it had never stopped altogether.

"What?" Billie said, alarmed. With an awkward twist of her head, she turned to look behind her. "But I figure we ought to—"

"Really," Nina said, "you've done enough already, and it's such a messy night."

Beneath the firmness in her voice Jared could hear an edge of desperation. She must have been arranging these words in her mind, silently rehearsing them, all during the drive.

"Maybe she's right, dear," Father Brody told Billie. "We ought to let them alone—you know, the family..."

"But I'm family," Billie said, uncertainly.

Father Zach crooked his left arm, in a show of checking his watch. "It's not getting any earlier," he said mildly.

When Nina cracked open her door, the faint hiss and smell of the rain invaded the car. Jared did not know whether to feel relieved or alarmed that the three of them were going inside alone.

His parents exited the car, Nina opening her umbrella with a deft flick of her hand. Jared followed. Outside was darkness, rain, the unknown, and Jared had the sudden idea that they were skydivers exiting a plane, one by one, with no parachutes.

Inside the house, the awkwardness Jared had feared did not have time to develop. Nina rushed back toward the kitchen, talking brightly about making them something to eat. Travis glanced around the living room, as if making sure nothing had changed, and then followed Nina without saying a word to Jared. So Jared followed too. His father used a slow, shambling gait, seeming to move by instinct rather than any knowledge of the house. He walked with a certain heaviness, too; he might have been wading through water. Behind him, Jared felt weightless, insubstantial. He longed for the moment when they would all go to bed and this night would be over.

In the kitchen, Nina moved about quickly, taking out skillets and mixing bowls. "Hey, I've got an idea," she said. "How about pancakes? An old-fashioned pancake supper?"

Travis and Jared stood just inside the doorway, staring. The kitchen was square and plain, with an old dinette near the door to the backyard.

"I'm not hungry," he said. "Back there, they feed us early, five or five-thirty..." He sounded apologetic.

Nina gave him a brittle smile, then turned to Jared.

"Honey, what about you? Aren't you starving?"

"Nope," Jared said quickly. "I'll just get some cereal and go upstairs. I told Linda I'd call when we got back, and then I'm going to bed."

"Bed?" Nina said, glancing at the wall clock. "But, honey, it's not even nine yet. Don't you want to visit with—"

"Back there, they put us to bed at nine-thirty," Travis said. "I'm pretty tired myself..."

Nina lifted her hands to her hips, in a gesture of mock-exasperation. "Just listen to the two of you. You really know how to show a girl a good time, don't you?"

Jared smiled, glancing at his father, but Travis didn't look over. He was staring at Nina, dully, stubbornly, and Jared could sense his mother's distress. When unsure of herself, Nina would resort to the type of ultra-feminine, whimsical behavior used often by the girls at Jared's school. He thought again of Linda, so grown up for her age, who'd surely never behaved this way in her life.

Jared said, turning, "I'm going to call—"

"Oh, Travis, did I tell you?" Nina said abruptly. "Our son has a girlfriend now! He—"

"She's *not* a girlfriend, Mom." He'd made this correction several times before. "She's just a friend who's also a girl."

"Well, pardon *me*," Nina said facetiously, putting one hand to her throat. Jared felt uncomfortable when his mother acted like this. It was unnecessary, he thought, and it was beneath her. And it wasn't *her*.

Travis was smiling, vaguely. "That's good," he said, though whether he was answering his wife or his son, Jared could not tell.

"Well, it's been a big day, maybe we should turn in early," Nina said. "But tomorrow—"

Travis interrupted: with a dreamlike motion, a kind of lunge, he came forward and took hold of her waist and clamped his mouth upon hers. At once she began struggling, but his father seemed to have planned this move. He gripped her tight. He stood with his legs parted, as if for leverage. It took several long, agonizing seconds—agonizing for Jared, anyway, who felt a dreamlike paralysis though he wanted to bolt from the room—before Nina wrested herself away.

"Travis, for heaven's sake—" She couldn't keep the annoyance from her voice, though she was still trying—incredibly— to smile. To pretend this was all a game, a joke. Sullenly, Jared watched her.

Travis's arms were still held out, circling nothing. Nina had backed against the kitchen table, still with that bright wobbly smile that was awful to see.

"Okay, you go make your phone call, Jared honey—and, Travis, you get your things unpacked. I'll be upstairs in a minute."

She edged away from the table and toward the cabinets, Travis's dulled gaze following. She reached for the carton of eggs.

"I'll just put these things away, and I'll be up…"

Jared turned and ran out. He took the creaking stairs three at a time and, in his room, grabbed the phone and punched Linda's number before he had time to think.

He sat on the edge of the bed, looking out to the short hallway that led to his parents' room on one side and a small guest room on the other. Between them, at the opposite end of the hall from Jared's room, was the bathroom with its old claw-foot tub and cracking pale-green linoleum. It had been a mistake to leave his door ajar, for as the Hanrattys' phone rang—three times, four times—he sat watching his father rise out of the stairwell and into the hall, slow-moving and stolid but somehow ghostly, his very presence debatable under the weak-glaring hallway light. He paused, looking around with that same air of uncertainty, of not knowing which way to turn. But he didn't glance into Jared's room. He turned and shambled away, peered briefly into the bathroom, then veered into the bedroom and shut the door.

Jared understood that someone was speaking.

He felt the blood pounding in his chest, his ears.

"...Is someone there? Hello?"

It was Mrs. Hanratty. He waited another moment, for he'd hoped Linda would answer. Mrs. Hanratty unsettled him—her loud, ribald voice, her hectic energy that was so buoyant and carefree on the surface but seemed underlain by something darker, something Jared could not name.

Now her voice was lowered. "Look, who is—"

"I'm sorry, Mrs. Hanratty," he said quickly. "It's me, Jared. I—"

"What? Well hey, Jared honey, I was just thinking about you and Nina! Have you gone to pick up your daddy yet?"

"Yes, ma'am, we just got back—I told Linda I'd call. Is she—"

"Yeah, sweetie—hold on a minute."

Jared took a deep breath. He felt moisture on the receiver, and changed it to his other hand. He'd turned to the side, to avoid facing the hall, but from the corner of his eye he'd seen his mother there, passing like a sleepwalker toward the room where her husband waited. A few seconds later, his parents' bedroom door had closed.

When Linda came on the line, they talked in the quiet, rambling way of intelligent teenagers, Linda asking him questions, Jared answering her guardedly but, as usual, grateful for her interest. He always felt comfortable with Linda and could keep up his side of the conversation even when his attention strayed now and then. He thought he heard something from down the hall: voices. Raised voices. But this might have been background noise from the Hanrattys' television, which Linda's mother kept going day and night. "For company," she said. Nina had once whispered to Jared that Mrs. Hanratty was a lonely woman, that she had a few problems; Nina hoped that Jared would always be polite to her.

But politeness came even more naturally to Jared than it did to Nina.

"Jared, are you listening? Did you—"

"I'm sorry, I—I changed the phone to my other ear," he said awkwardly. "What did you—"

"I said, when did…" and Linda went on, asking questions, and he answered as best he could. But there was no longer any doubt about the voices. His parents were arguing. His mother sounded plaintive, angry, distressed; his father's voice, much louder, seemed familiar and foreign at once, bellowing like a gored animal, but because the voices kept interrupting one another and came blurred through the bedroom door, and because with part of his mind Jared was still listening to Linda (she was telling some anecdote about a girlfriend of hers, in the last city where they'd lived, whose father had "gone away" for a while, too, but was now doing fine) and because of the roaring of blood in his ears, his parents' voices seemed to come from underwater, from some other world.

He told Linda, "Yeah, but things here are different," and Linda paused as she always did when she felt thwarted.

"You just don't *want* to hear any good news, do you?" she said.

Jared opened his mouth to answer but at that moment he heard a screeching long syllable—it might have been "*No*"— and the bedroom door jerked open and his mother rushed into the hall. Her arms were wrapped tightly around her, mummy-like, as though she were hugging herself. She didn't glance toward Jared's room, though he was staring frankly through the doorway, the phone held to his ear like something forgotten. Instead his mother paused, her eyes closed, and took a deep breath. Then she loosened her arms and strode across the hall and into the guest room. She shut the door, so that now both the bedroom doors were closed.

Those loud but indecipherable voices, his parents' voices, now seemed distant and improbable as a dream.

Again Linda was talking. Complaining.

"Sorry, I need to go," Jared interrupted her. "I need to get back to them. But I promised I'd call you, and so…"

Linda talked for a few more seconds, sounding mollified, even contrite, and he listened dutifully and when she finished Jared hung up.

The house was silent.

He got to his feet. He felt unsteady, as though he hadn't walked for many days. The few yards down the hall to those closed bedroom doors seemed impossibly long. Now he felt as if he were walking through water, too, something stubborn and heavy that wanted to keep him back.

He knew what had happened, of course. But he did not want to know.

He remembered that Nina had taken fresh sheets into the guest room that morning, but he hadn't asked her about it, and hadn't even asked himself. He'd allowed himself to feel much younger, childlike, as though instructing himself that his parents were adults and moved in a sphere beyond his understanding.

Reaching their bedroom, he put his ear to the door. But his father, alone in there, had stayed silent. He heard a hoarse, rhythmic sound, his father's breathing, but nothing more. He pictured him lying alone on the double bed, fully clothed. He imagined his eyes opened wide, their sudden piercing blue that always took you by surprise, and the eyes were staring out at nothing, unmoored. But Jared chided himself for this. Probably his father was undressing, getting ready for bed, relieved to be home and thinking already about tomorrow.

Jared stepped across the hall and considered putting his ear to the guest room door too; he raised one hand to knock. But he felt a spurt of anger, that both of these doors should be closed against him, and so he took hold of the knob—he was no child, he was fourteen now—and went into the room where his mother waited.

Her hand flew to her throat, her eyes were bright with anger or alarm, but when she saw it was Jared she gestured him inside. She had glanced away. She sat in a chair near the bed, looking weary and disheveled, her hair disarranged on one side—had his father done that?—and her lipstick smeared. The chair was a small pink-painted rocker, and now she began rocking slowly, gently, as if consoling herself, her hands curled around the chair's wooden arms, like claws.

Jared said: "Mom? You okay, Mom?"

She tried for that girlish, reassuring smile she often gave him, but it wouldn't quite come.

"I suppose," she said. "I suppose I'm just tired."

"Are you—are you going to stay in here?"

The question was out before he'd quite known that he wanted to ask it.

"Yes. Yes," she said.

"But he's—"

He thought but did not say: But he's alone in there. But he's been alone, for a long while now. But he's the person you married, once upon a time.

"We'll talk in the morning, Jared," his mother said. "We all need some rest, I think. We—"

The sound, when it came, was insultingly brief, undramatic—not even like a firecracker, he would later think, nor like some ancient car backfiring. Nothing like the usual comparisons at all. The shot had been muffled, of course, by two closed doors and by the gauzy confusion of Jared and his mother's argument, if you could call what they were having an argument. (Yes, Jared would think, this was the problem—there were no words to identify what was happening, not any longer. But even this thought hurtled past in darkness, brief and pointless as the shot itself.) Jared felt his eyes lock onto his mother's for a brief soulless moment, as if they'd become unwilling conspirators and denying what they'd heard might be a possibility. Then her

hands went again to her throat; her eyes, the chilly green of
marbles, veered upward, her eyelids fluttering.

"Oh God," she said. She stood. Her face drained of color,
her hands held vaguely before her as though she were feeling
her way in the dark, she went to the neatly made-up bed and sat
on it, her feet barely reaching the hardwood floor. She was still
wearing her shoes—her one pair of "good" shoes, black leather
pumps with low heels that now glistened with drying mud. She
hadn't taken off her blue Sunday outfit. Jared stood halfway between the bed and the door. The sound still echoed in his head
and seemed less real all the time, but its fading released him
back to himself, to his normal good sense, to a world where
he stood perspiring and breathing fast and where his heart was
thudding madly.

His impulse was to run out of the room, to flee, but that
invisible heavy element like water that had impeded him before
had thickened, and he felt entrapped as in the paralysis of a
dream. He could not move. His mother, with seeming ease
and even grace, in her own dimension, now swung her legs
upward, muddy shoes and all, then lowered her shoulders and
head—moving sideways so that she stayed facing him, so grace-
fully!—and stretched out on the chaste-looking white chenille
spread. Lying down, as if for a nap, but her arms had reached
out to him.

The sound, he thought dully, had been like one of his friends
snapping his gum during class, loud and fast, the boy's mind on
girls or cars, maybe, but a million miles from here.

A quick snap, then silence.

A demand for attention, then an instant release of attention.
You could continue doing whatever you were doing.

His mother lay there, her arms stretched out. "Come here,
honey," she said. "Come here, let me hold you…"

Her eyes were dry, but her words were those of a drowning
woman, her voice half-choked.

He stayed rooted there, alive in the thumping of his heart
but his will paralyzed, too, or else departed altogether.

NIGHT JOURNEY   37

He began, lamely, "I've got to call—"

"No, I'm not ready, I'm not ready yet," Nina said. Her head on the pillow, she talked sideways from the bed, like a child. A stubborn, dreamy child. He knew she didn't mean ready for the police, the visitors, all the hubbub that lay ahead of them; she was backtracking. "I told Billie and Elton but they said his disability had run out and they weren't made of money and we'd all better pull ourselves together and—"

"Mom, stop it," Jared said gently, though what she'd said was news to him.

Her eyes, which had veered off again, now fixed on him. Again her arms jerked out, the pale slender fingers twitching lightly.

"Come hold me," she said. "He's out of pain, honey—but we need each other."

So he went. His leg muscles felt stiff but they weren't para-lyzed, of course, so he went and stretched out alongside her, at first keeping a careful inch or two between their bodies. Then he felt her arms grasp him tightly, one of her hands curling back over each of his shoulders. She felt damp, heated. She was trembling. Tears had welled in Jared's eyes.

"I told them I wasn't ready," she said, "that I was trying to get to—to the person I was when I married him, so I could coax him back there too. It was like a journey we'd be taking and I knew I'd have to lead the way. But I wasn't ready, not yet," his mother said, her breath moist and hot against his ear. "I told them."

"Never mind," he said. The tears had stayed in his eyes but had not increased or fallen, his mind veering from grief in the stunned awareness of his heartbeat. It kept going, sullenly, as he lay helpless and adrift and staring sightlessly past her shoul-der. The voice that told him he should get up, get to a phone, stop this madness, seemed to grow fainter and fainter, like the voice of a child being borne away through the night.

"Now, I guess we'll never get there," his mother whispered.

PART TWO

NINA

6

She stayed near the door, her hands clenched at her sides. He'd preceded her into the room, unhurried, casual, as if this were some ordinary night. He undid the top two buttons on his shirt, then his cuffs. She understood now what had looked strange, when they first recognized him at the hospital. She'd gotten accustomed to his unshaven face, its hollow, malnourished look, even the hangdog expression and that stunned glaze across his eyes. But never in the fifteen years she'd known him had he buttoned his shirt cuffs. Dressing in the morning—stiff white cotton on work days, polyester-and-cotton plaids for weekends—he would automatically fold each sleeve back once, twice, then tamp down the folded-over cuff so it stayed put. A masculine ritual, she supposed, folding back the cuffs just so, exposing his strong beautiful wrists and forearms with their glossy coat of fine black hairs. Tonight the long-sleeve shirt, so carefully buttoned (by someone else?), had turned him into an aged schoolboy, adequately dressed and sent into that grimy-floored recreation room not to play but to rot.

Now he was undressing as if none of that had happened.

"I—I put fresh sheets on the bed," she told him.

He exhaled, noisily. "Okay," he said, his back to her. His arms had dropped to his sides and he was looking out the double windows next to their bed. Outside it was dead-black now, and still raining lightly, and since Nina had forgotten to close the blinds she supposed the people next door could see them clearly through their own upstairs window if they cared to look.

Often he would stand for a moment at this window before bed, stripped to his briefs, still a good-looking man despite his crest of receding and thinning hair—its fine blackness somehow made what hair remained, combed straight back from his forehead, seem all the more imposing—and despite the paunch his drinking gave him, protruding over the front elastic band. He'd lift one slat of the closed blind and peer out, briefly, then let the blind fall. There'd been nothing to see, of course, and she'd never asked what or whom he might be looking for, or what he might be feeling. Boredom, anxiety, paranoia?—all of these? He wasn't avoiding her, she knew—*she* wasn't paranoid—for as often as not after snapping off the bedside lamp he'd rush his opened mouth and heated body close to hers, without hesitation, his sugary bourbon-breath overwhelming more than her sense of smell, having become in recent years the very element of their brief, wild, but pointless couplings, the prelude to her husband's motionless trance of sleep into which, the moment he rolled off her, he fell like a casket dropped into the earth.

The time had come for her to speak but she looked from Travis to the bed, where for six months she had lain suspended, wakeful, in a kind of renewed and perplexed virginity. How she longed now for that solitude, that luxurious permission to stretch her limbs wide without penalty, to be alive and awake and unsullied in darkness, herself, free. Making up the spare bedroom today she'd known this was only a gesture, a way of extending that pleasure of aloneness—or the illusion of it—for a few more days. Even during these past months, so acutely aware of Jared lying down the hall in his own perplexity, knowing herself a player in his insomniac drama, night after night, enduring the pressure filling the house like a gas from this son of hers who was undeniably male, and becoming a man…thinking helplessly of her son, she'd known herself not really alone, at all. Yet there was no chance Travis would appear at the door, a dark swaying silhouette, his breath reeking. There was no chance she would wake to feel his damp flesh pressing on hers, her patchy sleep turned abruptly to a wild tangle of limbs and groans and half-hearted lunges, from her, of protest and recoil. For months and months there had been no chance of that.

As though he'd seen enough, Travis pulled the blinds and

turned around, shrugging off the unbuttoned shirt in a gesture that, in a woman, might have seemed casual or even seductive, but in him suggested a habitual indifference. The shirt landed in a small heap at his feet. She saw that his paunch was gone, but his chest had gotten thinner, too, the skin a sickish white, the ribs too prominent. She wondered if they hurt. She wondered if he'd been underfed or had just refused to eat. Here was her husband beside whom she had slept for several thousand nights and she'd also wondered, recently, what he might still inspire in her, might there be some new surge of passion or affection or sympathy or pity?

"Well?" he said. "Here we are."

To her surprise and horror he tried to smile. Lifted one side of his dry-looking mouth, his whiskered cheek showing a ghost of that indentation she'd called a dimple when they'd first met—and that time in a hospital too!—and he'd given her that fast grin every time she entered his room. At night she lay in her bed, in her tidy garage apartment off Piedmont Avenue, unable to get that grin out of her memory, or to stop rehearsing their nurse-patient conversations that had seemed so innocuous on the surface—her professional coyness, his lazy sarcasm and playful leering—but that had been fraught with a forbidden excitement, putting thoughts in her head that she'd never before conceived for a patient. As Travis would later say, joking with friends after a few beers, *It was lust at first sight*, and it would have been hypocritical of her to feel offended. What else had it been, at first?

He said, "What's wrong? Why've you got your hands behind your back?"

The question had a child's directness; the old Travis, her husband, would never have asked it, or thought to. Nor did she have an answer. Often these days her hands seemed alien to her, like unruly birds, dropping things or fidgeting or flying to her throat or somewhere out of sight. Under a table. Behind her back. Now she brought them out and they seemed without her will to have formed an imploring gesture—held out to him, the palms upturned. She tried to turn this into a casual motion, again toward the bed.

"You'd better get some rest," she said, trying herself to smile. The effort felt hideous. It must have looked hideous. "I've got some things to do downstairs, and then I..."

"Then you'll what?" he said, but the question seemed neither childlike nor simple. His eyes were scanning her body, as if assessing her, figuring her out. She'd seen his buttoned cuffs, after all, and now he'd seen something too.

"Where're your rings?" he said.

He took a step toward her, and for an instant he seemed to lurch, lose his balance, exactly as if...but of course he'd had nothing to drink, not a drop for months and months. Still her limbs had tensed, and she'd felt that tingling at her nostrils and even, could it be, detected that overripe sweetness of the bourbon fumes assaulting her senses, wave upon wave... But this was only memory. This was only fearful recollection. As if to distract them both, she held up her left hand with the slender naked fingers splayed wide. Something on display, it might have been. An alien thing.

"The rings? Oh, I was getting ready to cook, just now. I must have slipped them off—"

"You didn't have them in the car, either. Or at the hospital."

"I'll look down in the kitchen," she said quickly, taking a decisive step sideways, unblocking the door. "They must be on the counter, next to the sink. Really, Travis, I think we both need some rest, for tonight at least. I made up the guest room, so I'll just stay in there."

Once the words were out, Travis seemed stymied. Focusing on the absent rings had given him energy, his eyes the glinting, fiery blue she remembered from his furious tirades of last spring and summer. When she'd thought of the rings herself—and really she wasn't sure where they were, it had been months since she'd worn or even thought of them—she felt again that vertiginous hurtling backward, to the earlier years of their marriage, when they'd been such different people altogether. Two weeks after getting out of Crawford Long, on only their second date, he'd thrust the ring box into her palm with mingled shyness and urgency, whispering something hopeful, tender, and anguished into her hair. She'd opened the box, and, she could not deny it, the first sight of her engagement ring— curling white-gold prongs, the modest but scintillant diamond trapped in their clutch like something alive and glittering in distress—had brought an insuck of breath, a knot of tears in her throat. She'd stood paralyzed in her moment of shocked, joyful protest, or protesting joy. So this would happen to her, after all.

She'd been only twenty-three and had begun to suppose that it might not. Her mother had married at eighteen, had Nina at nineteen, died of uterine cancer at twenty-two. Nina had begun to view her own life as comparatively slow-paced, and though she was, she supposed, fairly accomplished—her mother hadn't finished high school, much less thought of a "career"—when the time came for Nina to understand that she was older than her mother had been when she died, Nina felt odd to herself, vestigial, as if the rest of her days would become only a dulled repetition of work, of solitude that held neither grief nor joy, of occasional outings with unmarried women friends but a resolute turning-away of male attention. A life, in short, that became horizontal in its sameness, at once rigid and directionless, certainly competent, virginal, without surprises, and to which death would bring a mere stop rather than a conclusion.

Then, one day, she'd met Travis, just another young man with kidney stones, at first. He'd tried joking about the pain, after passing a stone during his first night in the hospital, and this jocular but uneasy exchange had been the odd beginning of their courtship. Kidney stones! Hadn't he even attempted some sort of pun about stones, later, while she sat enthusing over the diamond? She'd let the tears come freely by then, embarrassing them both (they had, she knew, an essential reserve in common, a discomfort with strong emotion) and she'd tried to laugh at the joke, which she'd scarcely heard in her confusion, her pulse-beat roaring in her ears.

Perhaps it was strong emotion that stopped him now, and for an instant she regretted that he could not have a drink, no palliative to calm or distract him. Instead he managed his rage (she saw his fists curling and uncurling at his sides) by pretending to be merely annoyed.

"What do you mean, the guest room? What are you talking about?"

"Travis, I—"

He advanced quickly, as he'd done earlier in the kitchen. At least, she thought, Jared wasn't here to see. He kissed her hard, rudely, and she felt the unaccustomed scratchy beard and the new smell of him, for that old liquorish sweetness had given way to a stale clouded odor that clung to him like an aura. He stepped back, but he'd taken hold of her elbow.

"If we're not staying in one room, then what's the point?"

Again that directness, his eyes that hotter, sharper blue as he watched her. She kept glancing off, her own eyes as unruly as her hands, feeling that her face under his scrutiny might turn to some other element—to water, to simple air. Now she saw so easily why he drank, how he needed to blunt that awful strength of feeling, his child's piercing sense of betrayal. Yet the grip clutching her elbow was hardly a child's.

"Travis, I just meant for tonight—"

"We've been apart for six months, goddamn it!"

His fingers had pinched past her flesh to naked bone and she winced in pain.

"I'm tired," she pleaded. "I'm just so tired…"

He wasn't listening, of course. She tried vague movements of her arm, this way, that way, to ease the pain—yes, he had the nuggety small bone of her elbow, caught like some poor mouse's neck in a trap—and in her distraction she didn't notice what he'd been doing with his other hand. He came close again, reaching up under her skirt and grabbing at the waist of her panties, as if wanting to expose her, too, and now he'd pinned her back to the door and with a curious deft precision had placed his opened mouth against her throat.

She squirmed against him. "No, Travis—I said *no!*" but then she thought of Jared and said, in a ragged whisper: "This isn't— We can't—"

He wouldn't listen. His free hand jerked at her panties with unthinking force—like the jutting violence of his penis, which bobbed between them, an overheated wand, at once fearful and semi-comical as it grazed several times against her inner thigh—and now it seemed only seconds before he would manage to enter her, no matter how numbed and dry she felt down there.

She knew her son was sitting on his bed, down the hall, talking to that sweet intelligent girl of his, that Linda, and how she hoped he couldn't hear.

Then she remembered the loaded pistol Travis kept on the top shelf of the closet but in a guilty lunge she pushed that thought away.

In any case, the closet shelf across the room seemed as distant from her reach as the unmarried life she'd led (which felt unreal now, like some earnest TV drama: lonely young nurse, big-city hospital) before she married Travis.

Now her body responded though her mind could not. Almost without her will, but with a kind of primitive volition, she closed and locked her knees and began rocking her hips from side to side, making each lunge more difficult for him, but only when she jammed her knee up between his legs, feeling his coarse bristly hairs against the skin of her knee did he groan in pain, bending over, stumbling back.

"Travis, I'm sorry, I—"

She listened to herself and understood his violence, his despair: he'd known before she had.

Now she didn't dare speak. Didn't dare touch him.

But her body worked despite her, again. Somehow it got away from this bent-over, gasping man and into the guest room where she slammed the door shut, a noise that again made her think of the gun; but in another way.

But no. Surely not.

Please go ahead, please do it please.

In horror she knew that her mind had gone awry.

When the door opened, panic stopped her breathing, perhaps even her heart. But it was Jared.

She was his mother, wasn't she. Nina sat in the chair, rocking. One glance at his face and it was clear that he knew everything but still it was only Jared and her relief blotted out everything else.

Even when the shot came, interrupting the tentative exchange between Nina and her son, she couldn't feel any guilt. Nor any sorrow. There was only that languid sense of relief and a child's need for comfort, for commiseration, so a moment later she had moved to the bed, lying there sideways with her arms held out despite her son's anguished look of revulsion.

He stood halfway between the door and the bed, staring.

She didn't know him, did she.

"Come hold me," she was saying.

Please.

7

Thank God, it was Billie and Elton who handled the funeral.

She supposed she could have, despite the sympathy cards and phone calls, the home-cooked casseroles and pies brought to her door by people from church, people she scarcely knew. She did not feel incapacitated, as these people with their watery pink eyes seemed to assume. The grieving widow, they thought her. Poor Nina, they were saying. Yet the Nina she had known and who had once seemed as permanent a self as any other no longer remained, except in memory. The girl raised by her long-widowed grandmother since the age of three, "poor Nina" even then she supposed—orphaned, isolated from other children on Nana's old farm west of Atlanta—but too contented in her unfettered childhood years (given free rein of the farm and its bordering woods, the object of Nana's sharp-eyed but kindly vigilance) to know that she was missing anything. This "deprived" childhood had resulted, she supposed, in the unthinking confidence and energy that had served her well in schoolwork, in teenage sports, in nursing school and then her first and only job, since for nearly two decades she'd felt energized as by an electric current whose source, her grandmother's firm embrace, was also her first conscious memory.

Then she became Nina McCune, or Mrs. Travis McCune, or Jared's mother, or the woman who, alone in the house, might stray toward a mirror and stand there wondering, daydreaming, for as long as she dared—which wasn't long. In the days after the funeral when the phone rang and a voice would say *Mrs. McCune?* or, less frequently, *Nina?*—she would pause as if unsure. When from another room she heard that familiar call *Mom? Mom, are you home?* she would pause and know that she did not know. She answered to anything people said because, she supposed, all the fictions were equal and she did not necessarily prefer one to the other.

For this reason, she avoided mirrors. Poor Nina had been told lately that she looked pale, or tired, but she did not care to check the visions of others against that fleeting reflection above the bathroom sink.

Bless me, Father, for I have sinned. And am currently sinning. And plan to sin again, in the future.

So she said, sincerely, "Thanks, oh thanks so much," when Elton phoned and offered to arrange the funeral, the legal details, everything. (She could hear Billie in the background, instructing him.) She said, grateful, "That's so kind of you," when Father Zach called and said of course there were no problems with the funeral service, for the Church's attitude toward suicide—at least, *his* interpretation of the Church's attitude toward suicide—had changed a great deal. There was more compassion now. There was more understanding of psychology now. Nina wondered if Father Zach were lying to himself or if he believed these consolations, but of course it did not matter. The Catholic funeral would please Billie and the church people and she supposed a ceremony of some sort would be good for Jared, and even for her—for hadn't she read that somewhere? A way of saying goodbye. A way of making an end.

That was very important, she'd read somewhere.

So Elton and Billie planned the funeral, evidently with Father Zach and, to a degree, with Clyde, who'd been in touch by phone and was driving down from Atlanta with Rooney. Every few hours Elton called with some bit of news or change in plans and invariably Nina said, "Yes, that's fine, whatever you and Billie think," nor did she consider it strange that Billie herself didn't call nor could she feel anything but relief about that, either.

And Jared?—he'd spent most of the two days after his father's suicide holed up in his bedroom, coming out only for their wordless meals together and then clomping back upstairs. Once or twice she'd paused outside his door, holding her breath so he wouldn't hear and from inside she heard a low continuous mumbling—even, muffled, monotonous as a dial tone, and she thought in horror that her son had gone mad, was talking to himself, but then to her amazement there was brief chortling laughter followed by silence, then a resumption of the slow even humming sound and she understood that he was talking on the phone. And she thought: Linda. He had someone then, not her but Linda, but that was all right, that was good, but whom did Nina have?

Soon enough they'd both have Clyde and Rooney. She spent the days before the funeral working on the house, since for some reason Billie (or so Nina presumed, though Elton made the request) had decided that Clyde and Rooney should stay here, never mind that Billie and Elton had four extra bedrooms and live-in help while she and Jared had only one room to spare. Clyde could have the guest room, and Nina had cleaned out the seldom-used storage room off the kitchen for Rooney. She'd unfolded an old army cot they'd used for camping a few times when Jared was small, softening the cot with an under-layer of blankets and fluffing the comforter on top, and she added some bric-a-brac and a couple of framed prints to make the room seem less spartan. Not that she thought Rooney would notice, really; she supposed these details were for Clyde, or for Billie if she stopped by after the funeral, to show them she wasn't heartless, that she cared; and besides, Nina liked or at least felt sorry for Rooney. And again she changed the sheets in the guest room, and swept the hardwoods all through the house; she plucked dead leaves and watered the plants; she dusted the dining room table; she scrubbed the old claw-foot bathtub; she walked through the house spraying air freshener, spraying until the can was empty for somehow a ferocious energy had surged up in her, verging on hysteria, and she thought how pleasant to go on cleaning this house forever so that she might never again feel lonely or forlorn.

Only Jared's room was spared the frenzy of cleaning. She didn't dare go in there. When the freshener spray ran out and she smelled the heavy oversweet air she took hold of herself. She'd bathed and changed but hadn't even thought about dinner when the doorbell rang and, glancing at her wristwatch, she saw to her amazement that it was nearly seven o'clock.

She'd started cleaning at two, after sharing a tuna sandwich and a plateful of pickles with Jared. They hadn't said much. They hadn't said anything. Jared had finished eating in under ten minutes and had excused himself.

But, when the bell rang, he came thundering down the stairs and had flung the door open before Nina had even composed her thoughts or her face, much less emerged from her room. Edging out into the hall she could hear their voices, Jared's polite and even friendly. As for Clyde, whom she didn't know well, his voice was deeper yet less distinct. So they drifted up to her as an awkward but consoling duet of male voices. She hurried downstairs almost as quickly as Jared had done.

"Hey, Mom," he said.

They stood in the living room as if contemplating whether to sit down or flee. The resemblance between Jared and Clyde startled her. Thanks to Jared's recent spurt of growth they were now about the same height, and both had that contained but well-muscled leanness of the McCune men, the sharp profile, the forbidding blend of darkness and silence in the way they looked at you, as though on the verge of passing judgment. Rooney, of course, might have been from a different clan, with her cap of lusterless dark hair, her sloping shoulders; she stood next to Clyde in a shapeless black raincoat, gazing downward so that Nina could not make out her face.

Jared's greeting had been for the company's sake, of course; when they were alone he seldom addressed her. To Nina's surprise her son had gelled and combed his hair, so it had the blue-black highlights of a forties movie star, and had put on some new-looking blue jeans (when had he bought them?) and an orange-and-blue plaid shirt he must have ironed himself. Every day her son seemed more handsome and more remote, starting to resemble closely that kid she'd met in a hospital room in

Atlanta, but she didn't know if the resemblance should bring consolation or terror.

Clyde smiled, or tried to smile. A compact, sinewy man, mustached, his forearms coated with dark hair, and ropy with muscle where Jared's were still hairless and smooth, Clyde had those deep-set McCune eyes that Jared had inherited from Travis, the same poise and inner silence, the same naturally serious or even scowling expression that a smile or courteous look appeared to violate. Still she could tell he was trying to be friendly, he just felt awkward and out of place, as they all did, so she smiled back recalling out of nowhere one of her grandmother's favorite admonitions, *A smile doesn't cost you anything, you know.*

Clyde began, "If we're getting here at a bad time—"

"No, not at all," she said quickly.

"I saw a Days Inn at the edge of town, so if you'd rather—"

"No, of course not!" She gave an odd, strangled laugh, not knowing why she should feel so alarmed.

Again Clyde gave that strained paltry smile. "We'd have gotten here sooner, but there was rush hour coming out of Atlanta. The traffic was unreal."

"Yeah, the goddamned traffic!" Rooney cried. She'd looked up, with her big wet-gummed smile.

Clyde said quickly, flushing, "Sorry, she's been going through a phase lately—repeating everything I say." Clyde gave his own sheepish grin. "I really have to watch my mouth, nowadays."

"You're like a goddamned parrot, Rooney!" Rooney cried out.

Nina smiled awkwardly.

"Come on back to the kitchen," she said. "You haven't eaten yet, have you?"

"Oh, we'll just take a sandwich or something," Clyde said. "Don't go to any trouble."

"How about you, Rooney?" Nina asked. "You getting hungry?"

She heard the false brightness in her voice, though she'd promised herself she wouldn't address Rooney as though she were a child. Really she didn't know how she should behave or what was "appropriate."

Rooney didn't answer. She'd turned her round mopey face toward Clyde, as though Nina had spoken in a foreign language and Clyde was the interpreter.

"Um, about Rooney," Clyde said, almost whispering; he might have been pretending that Rooney and Jared couldn't hear, though the four of them still stood together in a small circle, with the tentative look of people stranded in a lobby. "She can talk, you know, but she can't really—well, communicate very well."

"Oh, I wasn't sure..." Blushing, Nina smiled in Rooney's direction, but the girl was still gazing at her brother with her dull, suspended look, her pale moony face neither smiling nor displeased nor even expressionless, exactly, but just a blank.

"But she'll take a sandwich too," Clyde muttered. "She loves peanut butter and jelly. Anything sweet."

"Come on back then," Nina said, gesturing toward the kitchen. "Jared, how about you? Are you hungry yet?"

He'd already turned toward the stairs. "I need to get my jacket. Linda's coming over," he said, keeping his tone neutral. "We'll go get a hamburger or something."

So that explained his rush downstairs to the door. There was a hamburger place a couple of blocks away.

"A girlfriend, eh?" Clyde asked him, grinning. But Jared glanced off.

Nina said quickly, embarrassed for him, "She's a really sweet girl. Cute too. Bring her back to the kitchen, Jared, will you? To say hello?"

He mumbled something, hurrying up the stairs. Clyde had taken hold of Rooney's hand, as though to lead her from the room. Her face had come alive, her slit-like eyes looking wet and dazzled, reminding Nina of a girl at her first dance, that look of thrilled expectancy.

"She loves peanut butter and jelly!" Rooney cried.

8

They'd always been here, it seemed.

They'd become a family of sorts, as somehow Nina and Jared by themselves hadn't quite been, for now the household was noisy, in the way that families on TV were noisy. When Nina heard the clomping of footsteps up or down the stairs she couldn't be sure whose they were, at the same moment she might hear the refrigerator door opening or the kitchen tap running, so there was the confusion and profusion of a family, the noises of togetherness, the awkwardness of close quarters. A kind of family, she thought. A hobbled one, Nina supposed, but genuine enough, and there was even a single term—*the McCunes*—that could designate them all, leaving no one out, suggesting this was how things should be and here they were.

The funeral came and went quickly. A sparse gathering down at church, Nina and Jared in the front pew with Billie and Elton beside them, Clyde for some reason steering Rooney into the second pew where Nina could feel them just behind her through the service, that strange inseparable pair, Travis's siblings, Clyde and Rooney, *ClydeandRooney* somehow her attention strayed back there instead of to Father Zach at the pulpit delivering his monotonous consolations, or the glaring silver-toned casket, its lid discreetly closed, that rested on a bier not far behind him. Billie must have picked it out, Nina thought, for she couldn't recall having been consulted, and every few minutes Rooney would whisper something to her brother but she did it like a child, in stage-whispers, quite audible, self-conscious, impertinent—"What's he standing up *there* for?"—but that was just Rooney and everyone understood. Or Nina supposed they did. There was a scattering of people throughout the church, friends of Billie and Elton she guessed, most of the faces weren't familiar, or they might have been friends of Travis be-

fore he got married, before he became part of a family but now
they didn't count, they didn't belong to *the McCunes*, they were
back in the weakest fringes of her awareness, and the notion
seized her, too, that even Father Zach behind his podium and
even that silver-toned box they would soon drop into the earth
(how strange, when you think of it!) didn't count.

She didn't think of it. She listened vaguely to Clyde and
Rooney, the whispering and throat-clearing behind her, she
pondered Jared's stiff motionless presence to her left, so impossibly handsome she'd thought that morning when he came
downstairs looking shy, awkward, grumpy in his dark blue suit
and one of his father's ties, gray with navy dots. "Oh, Jared, you
look—" But he hadn't wanted to hear and pushed past her into
the kitchen where Clyde and Rooney were finishing up their
breakfast.

Nonetheless, she thought, Jared was one of them, he was one
of *the McCunes*, he belonged to her, with her, at her side during
the service and later at the cemetery when they listened to more
droning from Father Zach and watched the casket going down.
Jared was not only watching but really was present in a way that
she was not. She supposed his hunched dark-suited form must
contain a terrible roiling of sorrow and remembrance while
she felt little grief or sense of loss, nor even, any longer, that
discomfiting blankness where the overpowering grief and loss
should have been. What she wanted of Travis, she thought,
she kept stored somewhere, maybe her heart or her sex or in
the glazed-over mind that did not quite admit any of these
thoughts, rather they fluttered about it, like moths, like white
moths, but nothing was really wrong and there was little sorrow
(and as if reading her mind, Father Zach pronounced the word
at that moment, distinct as the toll of a bell, "sorrow") and not
even, any longer, any chagrin or regret.

You kept what was yours, she thought. You didn't lose things.

Across the gaping red mouth they'd dug in the earth stood
Billie and Elton, arms around each other, gazing down and
shaking their heads, and was thick-skinned Billie actually sob-

bing a little, or whimpering, and was Elton himself, big-bellied prosperous Elton Fair, was he misty-eyed as well? Yes, yes, they were family members and as if recognizing this privilege even the normally intrusive and fussy Father Brody kept a discreet distance from them, looking somber, pale, lumpen in his black clerical suit—looking entirely sober, actually—his near-bald scalp gleaming quietly in the winter sun.

But soon enough all this was over, too, and she understood that the priest's voice had stopped and the ceremony was concluded only when Jared squeezed her elbow, shaking it a little, and said in a low, irritated whisper, "Come *on*, Mom. Let's go."

So they went. And, at Billie and Elton's, talked with a stream of visitors, mostly friends of the Fairs' from church, along with a scattering of great aunts and second cousins whose names Nina couldn't recall. Father Zach stopped by, briefly, with Father Brody in tow, and noticing how the heavy-set priest eyed the liquor cabinet and the table heaped with food, Nina thought to herself how normal this all felt, how strangely predictable. For the first time she wasn't even particularly uncomfortable in this house, Billie and Elton's sprawling red-brick colonial that might have been lifted entirely from an Atlanta suburb and set down here, outside of town, their land still part of the countryside, really, and the owners still country people, too, never mind the three-oven kitchen and the six bathrooms and the expensive, rather formal clothes Billie and Elton wore, like packaging, with Billie's flag pin and Elton's diamond-studded Rolex for ornament, though the clothes sat rather oddly on their coarse, bulky frames.

Nina noticed such things and felt ashamed for noticing.

People came and went through the house, talking and eating, carrying Billie's china plates and crystal cups of raspberry punch, pausing to deliver their perfunctory consolations into Nina's face that must have looked receptive, even welcoming, for she elicited a clucking, sweet-voiced solicitude from the women and aggrieved moist-eyed silences from the men, who liked to grasp her small ringless hand and hold it firmly, and too long, as if imagining some current of nurturing sympathy must flow physically from them to her or else this fragile-seeming young widow might never recover.

After only a few minutes, Jared approached her and bent to her ear, whispering.

"When can we leave, Mom? Can we leave?"

"Jared, these people are here for us," she said gently. She glanced around. "Where's Linda, anyway? Did she and her mother—"

"They aren't coming," Jared said. "When we were leaving the church, Mrs. Hanratty told me. She said she'd call you later."

"All right, then, but where are—"

"They're out back," Jared said. "I asked Clyde, and he said they're ready when you are."

"Jared, we can't just—"

But Jared had gone out back again, to the flagstone patio and the winter-chastened lawn to which Clyde and Rooney had retreated almost as soon as they arrived—the afternoon had turned sunny, Clyde said, and Rooney really did better in open spaces, away from crowds of people—so Nina followed her son and in the slow bumbling way of such leave-takings the four of them gradually extracted themselves from the chattering well-wishers, and from Billie and Elton, who followed them into the side yard, to the driveway, to the car, watching as they opened their doors—Clyde and Rooney in front, Nina and Jared in back—as though Billie imagined that by talking she could delay from moment to moment the descent of a world in which she would be known most prominently not as the wife of Elton Fair but as the sister of that man who'd killed himself in such an abrupt and awful way.

"Thanks again, both of you," Nina said, lamely, wondering what else she could say, and at that moment Clyde gunned the engine. As Nina got inside, Billie bent low to the driver's window—Clyde didn't roll it down—and yelled, "Ya'll drive careful now, you hear? And listen, when you get home—"

Clyde backed out the driveway, fast.

9

Next morning, Clyde came downstairs and said they would stay until after Christmas—if that was all right. "Of course," Nina said, caught by surprise. She stood at the kitchen sink with her gloved hands in soapy water, Rooney beside her, ungainly but docile, drying with exaggerated care each dish Nina handed her.

"Of course, you're more than welcome…"

Never before had Clyde and Rooney visited for the holidays, or called, or sent a card, but here Nina stood nodding thoughtfully, handing Rooney another plate. The sides of Rooney's mouth twitched upward, as they did whenever Nina gave her any sort of attention. The moment Nina had come downstairs, around eight o'clock, Rooney emerged from her room, as if she'd long been fully dressed and waiting. She hadn't said a word as she "helped" Nina cook breakfast—holding the skillet handle while Nina poured pancake batter, as if otherwise the skillet might escape—nor was she talkative as they ate their meal with Jared, bumbling through their usual sleepy early-morning conversation about nothing, or next to nothing. Rooney was listening intently. But she hadn't spoken until now, seeing Clyde at the kitchen doorway looking boyish in a T-shirt and jeans, his feet bare, toes curling along the cold metal strip lining the greenish linoleum. Embarrassed, Nina saw that the metal strip was edged with dirt.

"We'll stay for Christmas!" Rooney cried.

Drying the plate, Rooney paused to glance at her reflection and gave herself a sideways, mischievous smile, then put the plate in the drying rack and stood waiting for another.

"I mean, it's probably not a good time to be alone—for any of us," Clyde said reasonably. He came into the room and opened the refrigerator, staring inside it, bending to scrutinize the lower shelves. He closed the door without taking anything.

"I'll make some more pancakes," Nina said.

"No, don't do that. I should have gotten up."

Rooney turned, smiling brightly at her brother.

"You're nothing but a lazybones, Rooney!" she shouted.

When Nina and Clyde glanced over, Rooney gave them a blank, startled look. Nina had just handed her a plate and this time it slid through Rooney's big plump hands and crashed to the floor, cracking into several large pieces.

Clyde lunged forward, one palm held up toward Rooney. "Don't move, honey, you don't want to cut your feet."

He bent over the shattered plate, carefully gathering the pieces.

"It's nothing," Nina said nervously. "I've been meaning to get a new set, these are all chipped and—"

"She could cut her feet," Clyde said, his voice edged with reproach.

Nina and Rooney both stayed silent while Clyde gathered the plate fragments and put them into the trash bag under the sink. He worked quickly but cautiously, as though performing an urgent ritual. This close, he looked quite different from Travis, though in the past she'd often thought how much they favored one another. The same thick black hair, the sharp-cut profile, the smooth olivish skin with a perpetual shadow at the jaw, even an hour after shaving. And those eyes: deep-set, watchful, a clear and unnerving blue. Yet Clyde was perhaps two inches shorter, his body lean-muscled, with an air of compacted power, of deliberate restraint and self-containment. When Nina strained to remember Travis she saw a man over six feet, swaying in a doorway, or at the bedroom window, his movements slack and a bit clumsy, his abdomen and even his face slightly bloated from drinking. She recalled a pale body, almost hairless except at the armpits and groin, whereas this younger brother's slim waist, barely larger than Nina's own, led her eye up along a slender, strong-looking chest, with matted black hair curling along the edges of his V-neck cotton shirt.

He looked both powerful and abashed, as if he didn't dare meet her eyes. His bare feet seemed vulnerable, she thought. Ever since arriving here Rooney had worn a thick-padded pair of house slippers, made of pink terrycloth with pink ribbons at the top. Her feet were large, splayed over the side edges of the slippers, whereas Clyde's feet were small, pale, bony, his toes twitching as he stood there.

As if to deflect Nina's attention from him, Clyde said to Rooney, "Okay, say you're sorry."

Rooney's face had a smug, stubborn look. "Say you're sorry," she repeated.

"Really, it's all right," Nina said. With her gloved hand still plunged in the water, Nina felt helpless, undefended.

"It'll have to be," Clyde said, his thin lips curling slightly. "That's the way she says it."

After breakfast Jared had run upstairs to call Linda, whose mother had agreed to drop them off at the mall outside of town while she and Nina had their weekly "coffee klatsch" at Kay's house; and now Jared's footfall thudded once more down the wooden stairs. Pausing at the kitchen doorway, he looked curiously at this strange knot of adults near the sink, his mother and Clyde and Rooney, giving them a brief, suspicious glare, as if he were the adult in charge. He'd put on his new-looking jeans and a windbreaker, and again had slicked down his hair with some of the pleasant-smelling gel the boys were using these days, so he had the air of someone older and fully prepared to encounter the world outside this house. Discomfited, Nina swished her hands around in the water, felt no more dishes, and said lightly, "Well, we're all done, I guess—are you ready to go, honey?"

Clyde gave Jared a sly, sideways look. "Going to meet the ball and chain, eh?" he said.

Jared stared at him, perplexed.

"Are you kidding?" Nina said lightly, peeling off her gloves. "He counts the hours until—" but she stopped. Jared was staring fiercely at the floor, his face hot with embarrassment. She always said the wrong thing, these days, as if her son had

become a prickly stranger with unknowable dislikes and pref-
erences. "Don't take it personally," Kay Hanratty had told her,
laughing. "Remember, he's fourteen. That explains everything."
But it didn't, Nina thought—not quite.

"Well then," Clyde said in a playful, leering voice, "I'd certainly like to meet her."

To Nina's surprise, Jared grinned, though he kept looking
down at the floor.

"Okay, let's go," Nina said quickly. Jared preceded her to
the front door, jingling the car keys as though he would be the
driver. For some reason Nina paused, looking back. She could
see Rooney still in the kitchen, standing there with her vague,
slack-mouthed stare, as though stranded. Clyde had come into
the small dining alcove and stood looking at her too.

"You and Rooney just—just make yourselves at home,"
Nina said awkwardly.

Clyde rubbed his jaw, smiling. "Will do," he said with a drawl,
trying to be funny. "Ya'll come back now, y'hear?"

In the days after the funeral, Nina performed the duties anyone might expect, writing notes to people who'd sent food or
flowers, taking the sympathetic phone calls that kept coming
from men Travis had worked with, women from church who'd
known the McCunes for years, even old high-school buddies
who told Nina mournfully what a fantastic guy Travis had been,
how they regretted not having gotten together more often…
As these people spoke Nina listened patiently, she nodded, she
said how grateful she was, she said yes, Jared seemed to be doing quite well, considering.

One thing cheered her: the weather had changed. Gone
were those soupy, foggy, oppressively warm days of mid-December, that odd spell of weather that struck her now as the
very atmosphere of sorrow and confusion. Late last night, after
flicking off the downstairs lights, she'd gone out to the back
porch and simply stood there, breathing in the fresh cold air

that had descended at last from the mountains north of Atlanta. In a few hours the temperature had dropped from the high 70s to the low 50s, and according to the paper they would have, tomorrow night, the first freeze of the year.

Yesterday a modest, single-column obituary had appeared on page eight, presumably written by the paper's editor, another school friend of Travis's; the article had been respectful but notably short on information, and of course had not mentioned the cause of death. This morning the change in weather led the news with bold, inch-high headlines: DEEP FREEZE ON ITS WAY.

Good, Nina thought, she welcomed the cold fresh air and made herself think about Christmas shopping for Jared, for Billie and Elton, for Kay and Linda. And now, she supposed, for Clyde and Rooney too.

She forced herself to think of what she must do tomorrow, and the day after that. The day after that.

One morning, a crisp cold Saturday, Clyde bundled up Rooney in some mittens and an oversized winter coat and they left the house to do "some errands," he said, with a boyish smile. Late that afternoon they returned with a miniature artificial tree they'd found at the mall outside town, at Sears, complete with bright ropes of tinsel, tiny balls of red and silver, winking lights.

"Do you like it?" he said, glancing hopefully at Nina. His cheeks were flushed from the cold. Rooney stood beside him, a bulky shopping bag in each hand, her nose reddened.

"Oh, it's—lovely," Nina said. "We can set it on the dining room table."

"Yeah, and the presents around it," Clyde said. "We can just eat in the kitchen until after Christmas—that okay with you?" He brought the tree into the dining room without waiting for an answer. "C'mon, Rooney, let's unload the loot," he said, and Nina watched in surprise as they opened the shopping bags and brought out gifts already wrapped, rectangular boxes of various sizes in red or green foil with elaborate silver bows. Clyde arranged them carefully on the table, around the tree, adjusting the boxes just so, like a clever photographer arranging a set. When he finished, he looked up as though awaiting her approval. "They're so—the giftwrapping is lovely," she said, quietly. But she was thinking of Clyde, not of the gifts. He appeared to have the confidence and decisiveness that Travis had lacked so woefully in his later years. Where Travis had become mean-spirited, Clyde seemed generous and resourceful; where Travis was focused on himself (his drinking, especially), Clyde took such wonderful care of Rooney and now seemed to display that same generosity toward her and Jared. She wished that he'd visited her and Travis more often: that she'd gotten to know him better. Something stirred inside Nina that had nothing to do with the funeral or Christmas or anything else that happened recently. She kept stealing glances at Clyde, admiring his apparent good health, his ready smile.

Clyde said quickly, "There's this place set up in the mall, they did them all in half an hour, it was no sweat. It's a little silly, all this Christmas stuff, but it has to be done."

She said, "Oh, I don't—" but she stopped herself. Of course, she agreed with him.

She'd never before enjoyed anything about Christmas: not the anxious overspending on gifts, not the tense family get-to-gethers—always at Billie's, since she professed to love the holidays—and certainly not the letdown when it was over, the sense of promises unfulfilled, the heavy descent of ordinary routine that hadn't seemed so onerous before. Even as a girl she'd felt this, although Nana had always overcompensated for what she called, in whispered phone conversations to her friends when she thought Nina couldn't hear, her granddaughter's "terrible loss," the girl's "deprivations." Every year Nana had crammed the space under their tree with boxes of all sizes and shapes, a dozen or more, some labeled *To Nina, with love from Nana,* the others marked *For a good girl—from Santa Claus!* Yet it seemed the more effort her grandmother put into the holidays the more depressed Nina felt. She would pause in the living room, just before bed, and stare dolefully at the glittering multicolored tree and the brightly wrapped packages, feeling bewildered and somehow bereft, wishing all this were over. But never, never could she have expressed such a wish aloud, though Clyde had said the words so bluntly, *It's a little silly, all this Christmas stuff,* as if speaking his mind were habitual with him.

And she liked this about him too. She listened closely when he said, forking off a wedge of Nina's meatloaf that evening at dinner, "Well, folks, I've been doing some thinking."

Nina looked up, startled by his frank, confiding manner. Even his appearance had changed: he'd gotten a haircut and had put on a starched white dress shirt, the cuffs rolled back on his sinewy forearms. Why hadn't she noticed? Already their meals together had settled into routine, the pleasant tedium of clanking plates and forgettable conversation. Clyde's attention was mostly focused on Rooney as he spooned out her helpings, cut her meat into child-size bites, adjusted the fork inside her pudgy, oversized fist. Nina would watch out the sides of her eyes, touched by Clyde's murmured promptings—"No, honey, this way"—and when Rooney's nonsensical outbursts of talk seemed directed at Nina she would smile agreeably, not knowing what other response to make. Did you treat someone like Rooney as a child, or as a quasi-adult? She was nearly thirty now, yet Nina had once heard Travis say that her brain development was that of a four-year-old, and that was on a good day. Nina had noticed that Clyde addressed his sister gently but straight-forwardly, as an equal, but then Clyde himself had struck Nina as a boyish sort of man, always wearing Levi's and sneakers, rotating the same three or four plaid flannel shirts. In his grave attention to Rooney's grooming he sometimes neglected his own, his coal-black hair looking snarled and uncombed, his bony jaw needing a shave. Yet Rooney was fresh-scrubbed and presentable, always. They were an unusual pair, she thought, but she'd begun to feel grateful they were staying through Christmas.

Nina felt surprised again when Jared looked up from his plate, matter-of-factly, and answered Clyde.

"About what?" he said.

Clyde looked at Nina, as though she had asked the question. "About us, about the future," he said calmly. "The fact is, I've been thinking of moving Rooney and me back to town here; I was considering it long before Travis started having his problems. Last week something happened that sort of—well, it was the last straw, you could say, and now that Travis is gone, and there's a new year coming, this just seems the right time to make a move. But the problem is, Nina, I don't have a job here, and it may take a while to find one."

He watched her intently, as though gauging her reaction; but what was he asking her, exactly? She gave a neutral smile and to buy time she handed the basket of rolls down to Jared. "Want some, sweetie?" she asked. Jared took the basket and Nina returned her hands to her lap, folding and staring down at them. She said, "But I thought—you were starting school in Atlanta? Mortuary science?"

"Oh, Billie wouldn't loan me the money," Clyde said matter-of-factly. There was no bitterness in his voice, but he added: "Guess she forgot to mention that. Part of the money's *mine*, by rights." Again he watched Nina, as if expecting some retort.

"I—I didn't know," she said vaguely.

"That money's mine!" Rooney cried, from across the table. She was chewing mashed potatoes and her open-mouthed smile revealed a mass of whitish mush. A dribble of gravy had reached her chin.

Clyde leaned across to her, touching at her face with his napkin. "Don't talk with your mouth full, honey," he said. He turned quickly back to Nina. "See, I don't know if you have the facts, I would think Travis had told you, but Mama left all her money to Billie, and to Rooney here. She claimed the reason was that Travis and I could fend for ourselves, being men, but it wasn't the same for her daughters. Now with Rooney, that makes sense, but Billie was already married to Elton, so she needed that extra money like a hole in the head. Plus, Mama made Billie the trustee of Rooney's money, too, even though I'm the one takes care of her."

Clyde paused and sat back, taking a swallow of his sweet tea. His voice had become emphatic, tense, but now he took a deep breath. He chewed at his mustache with his lower teeth—a frequent habit of his, Nina had noticed—and then came his quick grin as he glanced sideways at Rooney. "In fact, Rooney here is a rich woman by now, did you know that? She's worth a couple hundred thousand dollars. But Billie, she still doles it out to us, a whopping eight hundred a month. Sometimes Rooney's co-pays and prescriptions alone eat that up, and more."

Nodding in sympathy, Nina said, "No, I didn't know about all that," but this wasn't the truth. Billie had often talked about her "little brother," commiserating with Travis over some recent letter or phone call she'd received. Travis had always supported his mother's will, claiming he didn't need money and that it was best for Billie to hold the purse-strings for Rooney's inheritance. "Why, if I gave that boy access to her money," Billie said, "he'd have it squandered within a year," and Travis seemed to agree. She complained, as usual, that Clyde kept dreaming up schemes to invest the money, or finding some land he should buy with it; but Billie insisted on the safety of bonds, CD's, regular interest payments. "I know he takes good care of her, and he'd cut off his right arm before he'd let her do without anything, but where money is concerned that boy just don't have a lick of sense," Billie had proclaimed. "Well then, just tell him no," Travis answered. "Simple as that." Though neither of them asked her opinion Nina had agreed, too; she didn't know for sure if Clyde had poor judgment with money, but it would be tragic if somehow Rooney's source of support was lost.

Yet she thought it best if Clyde imagined her ignorant of all this. She could feel Jared watching her—he knew the truth, of course—but her son was far too tactful and cautious to say a word.

"Yeah, that's the way it's been," Clyde said. "Anyway, money being so tight, we can both live a lot cheaper here than in Atlanta. I went down to the funeral home this afternoon—that old man Tolliver's place—and he said he didn't have an opening

right now. Maybe in a few months, he said. I've been looking in
the paper, but I don't see much else that I'm fit for."

Again Nina smiled, in sympathy. So that accounted for the
haircut, his spruced-up clothes. And she did feel sympathy: he
spoke with such disarming bluntness, yet she could see the naked hurt in his eyes. If only people would trust him, he seemed
to be saying. If only they would give him a chance.

Of course, she understood what he wanted.

"So you'd like to stay here—a bit longer?"

"Yeah, if you wouldn't mind." He looked down at his lap.
"Probably just for a month or so. I thought maybe the situation would help you, too, since I could fix things around the
house—you know, things Travis would have tended to. And
I'll keep careful track of the food and such, and once I start
working and get us a place I'll pay you back."

"Oh, you wouldn't have to do that, I—I guess it's fine, that
is if Jared—"

Jared looked up, startled; she felt guilty for putting him on
the spot, but she thought it would be worse to ignore him.

"Sure, it's fine," he said, embarrassed. "I don't care."

For the first time, Clyde glanced at Jared. "Thanks, pardner,"
he said. Then he raised his voice into the lilting, kindly tone he
used with Rooney. "Your sister-in-law and nephew have invited
us to stay for a while," he told her. "What do you say to them?"

Rooney looked from her brother, to Jared, to Nina; she'd
been chewing her food, but now her jaw had stilled. There was
an awkward silence, but then a mischievous glint entered her
eyes. She swallowed her mouthful, then shouted, "I'm a very
good girl, and I'm rich!"

To Nina's surprise, Clyde seemed ill-at-ease, his cheeks
flushing, but after a moment he gave a sheepish grin. "That's
right," Clyde said. "You're a good girl, Maureen McCune."

Rooney nodded in her usual, exaggerated way, chin touching
her chest. Then her head jerked upward as though by strings.
But she said nothing. She reached for her milk with both hands
and began drinking, watching them all over the rim of the glass.

10

Christmas and New Year's had been accomplished quickly, more or less painlessly.

They gathered at Billie's on Christmas Eve for the usual exchange of gifts, a routine both Nina and Jared knew by heart. Elton played Santa Claus, looking ridiculous but merry enough in an old red cap, the snowball tassel bobbing against his big flushed face as he crawled around beneath the tree. "Let's see, we need one for Jared, this one is for Rooney but she's already opening one," he mumbled good-naturedly as he shoved one package aside and reached for another, prodded constantly by Billie: "Elton Fair, can't you find one for Clyde? Get that red-and-silver one, over by the wall—I'm pretty sure that's Clyde's…"

Billie glanced toward the sofa, where Nina and Jared were dutifully opening the gifts Elton handed them. "What do you think, Jared, will it fit? I never know what the kids wear these days, but the lady at the store said… Nina, honey, you're so *slow*—look at you, there's three stacked there by your foot that you haven't even opened! Elton, honey, you'd better hold off a minute, Nina's getting log-jammed, and I hate not getting to see what everyone…Oh, Rooney, sweetheart, look at you!"

Rooney sat in a wingback chair near the fireplace, her hands demurely folded and her smile a bit slack, her eyes not quite focused, seeming dazed by all this hectic activity "You need something to open, don't you—come on, Santa, can't you find something for Rooney?"

Crumpled wrapping paper littered the floor around Rooney's plump white legs, though she would only fiddle vaguely with each package Elton handed her. Clyde would finish unwrapping her gifts (a new bathrobe, some fancy gold-toned barrettes, a box of scented soaps), saying "Look, Rooney, look at *this.*" Rooney gave each opened box the same brief, measured scrutiny, her vague smile unchanged, her gaze shifting into the distance.

"She'll really enjoy this," Clyde said to Billie, repeatedly.

Nina noticed that Clyde, except when helping Rooney, appeared stranded and miserable amid all the commotion. She felt sorry for him. To say the least, Christmas at Billie's was overwhelming: the brightly wrapped gifts, the tiny lights winking on the oversized fir tree and along the mantel, the plates of speckled holiday cookies and almond fudge Billie had brought out, the cups of eggnog dusted with nutmeg, the jaunty tape of Christmas carols playing in the next room, and especially Billie's relentless busyness and good cheer. Nothing energized Billie like Christmas, there was no way to control her extravagant gift-giving, her insistence that everyone eat more, and drink more, and pose endlessly for snapshots; and her constant admonitions that everyone should smile and "have fun."

Christmas comes only once a year, she reminded them often, and Elton would push the woolen snowball out of his face and roll his eyes and say, grinning, "Thank God for *that.*"

Only Nina seemed to notice how uncomfortable Clyde looked: each time Elton handed him a package, Billie would watch his hands unwrapping the gift, as though curious and excited herself about what was inside, but she didn't watch his face. Clyde's deft, well-shaped hands opened each package meticulously, folding the paper and setting it aside, then slowly, almost ceremoniously, separating the tissue paper and lifting each gift for everyone to see. "Thanks, Billie, Elton—really, thanks a lot," he said awkwardly, again and again. A brown suede jacket, a set of car tools, a shoeshine kit, an envelope containing a check at which Clyde glanced briefly, embarrassed, before slipping it inside his shirt pocket. "Really, thanks so much."

Nina watched his face, wishing he would relax, but knowing he could not.

In the car, Nina tried to make light of it. "Well, you've survived a Christmas at Billie's," she laughed.

Clyde drove straight-armed, one hand gripping the top of the wheel; he tugged idly at his mustache with the other. Clyde looked handsome but exhausted. "Billie's like a kid," he muttered, "a big, overgrown kid. She just assumed we were all enjoying ourselves, but really the whole party was all for her."

"I think she means well," Nina said. "It's her way of showing—"

"It's her way of controlling us," he said flatly. "If she's using her energy, and talking, and herding everybody along, she's running the show—don't you think so?"

They'd come to a stop sign. In a sudden, angry gesture Clyde tugged the check out of his shirt pocket, ripped it neatly in half, then quarters, and threw the pieces out his half-opened window.

Nina's cheeks flushed with surprise. She glanced into the backseat, hoping Jared hadn't seen. But her son was looking out his own window, lost in his thoughts. Next to him, Rooney had assumed the odd suspended posture she used for car trips: her eyes half-closed, her face and body perfectly still as if she were meditating, or simply waiting for her life to resume. Nina said to Clyde, trying to sound pleasant, "You needed that check, didn't you?"

"Not as much as I needed to tear it up," he said.

"I mean, I don't know how much it was, but—" She hoped he didn't think she was prying. She couldn't help thinking, selfishly, that she'd soon be having money problems herself—the disability payments had stopped, of course, and there was no life insurance payment because Travis had committed suicide.

"More than I've got saved," he said, but he sounded defensive and, she had to admit, a little cocky. She had to admire his independence, the fact that he felt oppressed by Billie's largesse. In the past, she had felt the same emotion when one of her sister-in-law's "allowance" checks arrived.

By New Year's, his mood had improved. Fortunately, Billie and Elton drove over to Macon every year on New Year's Eve, invited by an old high school friend of Elton's and his wife for dinner and dancing at the country club, so Clyde took Nina and

Jared out for their own dinner—to a steak place down on the square that Jared loved—and when they got home he brought out a bottle of champagne and poured a flute for each of them, including Jared and Rooney.

Nina began, "Oh, Jared shouldn't—" but Clyde shushed her.

"It's just one glass," he said, grinning. He held his own glass in the air and in an elevated voice—Nina couldn't tell if he was being ironic or not—he said, "To the new year, and new beginnings."

They toasted; to Nina's surprise, Jared drank his down in a few long swallows. She thought instantly of Travis, then told herself not to be silly.

Jared smiled sideways at his mother. "Maybe I'll have another," he said.

"You certainly *won't*," Nina said.

"Hey," said Clyde, narrowing his eyes, "how come you don't have a date with that—what's her name?"

Jared shifted awkwardly in his chair. "I told you, we don't 'date,'" he mumbled. "She's just a friend."

"Not what I heard," Clyde said, a teasing lilt in his voice. He drained his glass and poured himself another.

"I think Kay and Linda are still in Atlanta, aren't they?" Nina asked, wanting to shift the attention away from Jared. "They go there every year for the holidays, to visit Kay's mother," she told Clyde.

He shrugged, still watching Jared. "She should have stayed here, so Linda could be with her boyfriend. Our party's a little hobbled, this way. More champagne, Nina?"

Nina found his good mood infectious; she held out her flute. She felt light-headed, almost giddy.

Clyde nodded toward Rooney, who kept putting her nose close to the rim of her flute, then smiling slyly to herself.

"Rooney likes the bubbles, don't you?" Clyde asked. He reached across and tweaked her nose. She ducked her head playfully, giggling.

Clyde had grown more animated, his cheeks flushed. He

laughed out loud, glancing around at each of them. "We're quite a crew, aren't we? No girlfriend for you, no husband for you, no job for me, and no"—he looked at Rooney, hesitating—"no nothing for you!" he cried. Again he lifted his glass. "So here's to the big nothing!"

"Oh, that's a cheerful toast!" Nina said, though she knew he was just playing around.

Nonetheless she lifted the flute Clyde had refilled, and Jared lifted his empty glass, and even Rooney played along, dipping her nose again to the bubbly champagne.

When she'd finished drinking Nina stood, abruptly. "Hey, anybody care for ice cream?" She was smiling at Rooney.

"Sure, ice cream goes great with nothing," Clyde said. "Bring it on."

So Nina spooned strawberry ice cream into bowls and Clyde kept pouring more champagne, making silly toasts: "To gravediggers, the unsung heroes of the modern world!" And: "Here's to Jared's first romance, may he somehow survive it!"

Nina said with a playful smirk that these were terrible toasts, but she drank to them anyway. Both Rooney and Jared started into the ice cream, ravenous, their lips turning pink, and Clyde kept raising the bottle and by the time the clock struck midnight the ice cream and champagne were gone.

January was almost over before Nina noticed that the phone had stopped ringing.

They'd settled into a routine: the four of them having breakfast together, then Jared leaving for school and Clyde, most days, going out job-hunting or sometimes spending the day in Atlanta "tying up loose ends," as he put it, while Nina stayed home doing chores. Slowly she disposed of Travis's things, giving the clothes to Goodwill and setting aside photographs and letters and her husband's boyhood possessions (a dirt-begrimed baseball, a black missal Travis had gotten for his First Holy Communion) in case Billie wanted them, and taking care of Rooney, a pastime she found strangely soothing, even enjoyable. More than once during her years with Travis, she'd thought it would be so wonderful to have a daughter: somehow, she thought, a girl would complete their little family. She knew this was sentimental and illogical but she did not care.

So she cut and shaped Rooney's hair in a softer, more flattering style, using rollers to add some curl along the sides of her face, where Clyde had just let her hair hang long and straggly. She put rouge and a bit of pink lipstick on Rooney, something Clyde evidently had never done, for Rooney had grown fond of the makeup as if discovering a new toy; Nina never applied enough to suit her. And Nina bathed her, using the scented soaps Billie had given her for Christmas, gently rubbing at Rooney's oddly tough, glaring-white flesh, trying but unable to imagine Clyde doing this night after night for how many years?—ten, eleven?—she'd asked him but Clyde couldn't remember. He just shook his head and said, as though Nina had brought up the issue, "She's *not* going to an institution—I'd never allow that."

Rooney enjoyed going with Nina to the bank, the grocery store, the post office, where Nina would introduce Rooney as "my sister-in-law, Maureen McCune," while the clerks or others within earshot, having either known Rooney as a child or having heard about her, made awkward pleasantries, complimenting Rooney on her lipstick or her hair while Rooney grinned sheepishly, showing her wet gums, or stared off into the distance. "Well, thanks very much," Nina would say, picking up her bags of groceries or pocketing her stamps, "we'll see you next time," and she and Rooney would turn to leave and the others would stare after them, feeling nonplussed or perhaps even annoyed but not quite knowing why.

The mornings were Nina's favorite time: late in the month a dome of clear frigid air had settled upon the town, the cold slicing pleasantly into Nina's lungs when she stepped outside in the mornings. It truly did seem a new year, a new time. *January, 1992.* No longer did she wait for the grief to strike her, she knew it would not come, for what had she to grieve, exactly? She'd done her mourning in the last sour years of her marriage, listening to Travis's stuporous mumbling in sleep beside her. She'd had to breathe the sickly sweet stench of bourbon on his discarded shirts, and that same smell was on his stale breath in the morning when he came near, sometimes roughly kissing her or even trying to start something while her stomach clenched with nausea, her throat closed as if she might gag, and she backed away, making some excuse, fleeing downstairs where the stale-sweet bourbon smell would greet her again, rising from unrinsed glasses, much fainter but somehow all the more sickening and sinister for that.

So she breathed thankfully the cold air of late January not quite able to remember that soupy stale overwarm air of last month before Travis had come home from the hospital and the future had seemed bearable only because it was unimaginable.

While Nina made breakfast, Clyde would sit at the kitchen table rattling through the paper, looking for jobs, circling promising ads with a red felt-tipped pen. Rooney and Jared sat eating their cereal—only Clyde liked a big, hot breakfast of scrambled eggs, link sausages, toast spread thickly with butter and jam—and after breakfast Rooney would go into the living room to stare at the TV and Jared would sling his backpack over his shoulder and rush off to school, leaving Clyde and Nina at the table, drinking coffee, idly discussing Clyde's prospects. He'd gone everywhere in town by now, it seemed, even applying for "the shit-jobs, though God knows I'll gladly take one" yet the managers said he was overqualified, too well-educated, too well-spoken; secretly Nina wondered if he was polite enough, "humble" enough during his interviews. His honesty could come off as brusqueness, and anyway for the good jobs there was always competition, often a family member or the son of an old friend and Clyde would claim that the ad had just been a ruse.

"They knew all along who they were going to hire," Clyde had said, furious, learning that an officer manager's job had gone to the nephew of the company owner's wife. "They've just got to meet the goddamned government regulations and interview x-number of women and x-number of men and x-number of Black folks, and then hire the blood relative they wanted all along. Letting me waste my money, getting the goddamned resumes printed up, my shirts done at the cleaners, not to mention my valuable time, and all the while knowing they don't have a damn thing for me."

Nina made vague, commiserating noises, but she felt oddly happy: surely it was an act of kindness to let Travis's younger brother stay here while he looked for work, surely it was a display of family feeling. And she had to admit, she cared for Clyde, a little. Yes she felt sorry for him but it was more than that, wasn't it? She didn't examine her emotions too closely. These days she was in the mood to enjoy whatever came along and not question it.

"Don't worry, you'll find something," she would say.

"But I feel guilty as hell, with Rooney and me in your hair like this."

"It's no bother, really, we appreciate the company—Jared does too."

Clyde gave a soft laugh, his blue eyes glancing off. "Jared," he said. "You know, I wouldn't be that age again for any amount of money."

Nina smiled. "I guess I wouldn't, either. But he likes having you here, really—I can tell."

Nothing in their new life surprised Nina more than the way Jared had come around: he'd quickly warmed to Clyde, and even to Rooney. He'd stopped holing up inside his room, he'd gotten talkative, even jokey, during meals, and after school he'd call out, "Where's Clyde?" the minute he burst in the front door, his book bag slung over one shoulder. In the afternoons Jared and Clyde took walks together around town, they arm-wrestled at the kitchen table, they swapped "horror stories," as Clyde called them, about having gone to Catholic school, and one Sunday morning Nina had felt oddly moved when she came downstairs and found them shining each other's shoes. Clyde sat in the overstuffed corner armchair with one foot on the old scuffed pale-orange vinyl ottoman, while Jared, on his knees, worked energetically at buffing Clyde's wingtips.

"Got another job interview tomorrow," Clyde told Nina, winking. "Guess I'd better try and impress the boss."

Then they'd switched places and Clyde had done Jared's shoes, while Jared sat above him laughing, striking an invisible whip as Nina stood watching them, her arms folded.

"You two are quite a sight," she said. She'd almost forgotten how Jared looked when he was happy.

But then something occurred to her.

Nina approached the TV and turned it down. "Did something happen, honey?—aren't you seeing Linda any more?" To her surprise Jared glanced down at the floor, blushing. Nina blushed herself at having asked the question so bluntly. "I'm sorry, it's just that I haven't seen Kay in a while, so I wondered—"

"I've been busy, Mom," Jared said. "Linda was just a friend, anyway."

Nina caught the "was," but didn't want to quiz him any further. She couldn't remember the last time her son had blushed. He'd always seemed so self-reliant and self-contained. At that moment Rooney, sitting cross-legged beside him, began jabbing frantically toward the TV set, yelling, "Cowboys and Indians! Cowboys and Indians!" So Jared picked up the remote and restored the volume, leaving Nina feeling set apart. She'd meant to add, "But what about church?" but she supposed that wasn't her business, either. Neither she nor Travis had attended at all, and in the six months since Jared had started going to mass with Linda; Nina had been relieved that she no longer had to take him since Kay now did the honors. Later in the day she mentioned it to Clyde, who said, "He's old enough to make up his own mind, Nina. The sooner he stops believing all that crap, the better. Just be glad the nuns didn't brainwash him."

She couldn't deny the truth: she *was* glad of that. She supposed that neither she nor Jared would bother with church again, though she hoped he'd keep serving at mass, once in a while. She liked the idea of Jared doing that, though she didn't quite know why.

A few days later, Clyde came home and told Nina that he'd found a job. He looked excited, boyish, his cheeks flushed, a dark thatch of hair fallen across his forehead. He grabbed hold of Nina's hands—his own were ice-cold—and led her to the kitchen table. Once they were seated, he rubbed his palms together briskly.

"Remember Earl Tolliver, the old guy who owns the funeral home? I've been going down there every few days, checking back with him, and this morning he said, 'Well, Clyde, it's your lucky day. I decided to get rid of Donnie.'"

"You mean—Tolliver fired Donnie Fredericks? So he could hire you?"

Clyde shrugged, his eyes narrowing as though he'd heard reproach in her voice. But Nina had known the fired man, slightly; his son Brian was in Jared's class, and Brian and his father had stopped by once or twice, last year, to pick up Jared for basketball games. She remembered a tall, friendly, heavy-set man, outgoing and talkative; Travis had mentioned that it seemed odd, Donnie's working in a funeral home. He hadn't seemed the type.

"I guess so," Clyde said. "He asked us not to tell anybody, but he said Donnie was a lousy worker. Came in late, took long lunches, that kind of thing. People like that, they deserve to be fired."

"Well, I'm—I'm glad for you," Nina said. "When do you start?"

"Tomorrow. So I can start paying you back right away."

"Oh, Clyde, you don't owe us any—"

"I owe you plenty. But there's just one thing—something I have to ask you."

All at once he grew serious, gazing at her intently. "Rooney and I will be getting our own place, soon as I've gotten a few paychecks, but I need somebody to watch her while I'm at work. Would you mind, Nina? It's just nine to five, and you're so good with her."

"Of course, but you don't need to rush about finding a place. I don't know what my own plans are, exactly, but for the next few months—"

"That's great, Nina. Thanks!" He stood and stretched his arms above his head. "In Atlanta, you know, I had to lock Rooney in our apartment when I went out to work, and I really hated doing that. Sometimes she'd give me the silent treatment when I got home." He laughed, remembering. "She'll be much better off with you."

"Sure," Nina said. "For a while—"

"Listen, I've got to get going. I'm driving over to Tolliver's to sort of get oriented and such. 'Office Manager'—that's my new title!" He grinned. "Don't tell Jared the news, okay?" he called over his shoulder. "Let me tell him."

He was out the door before Nina could reply.

11

Until Kay Hanratty called, later that same afternoon, Nina felt strangely alone, bereft. She hadn't expected that Clyde would find a job so soon. All around her, everyone seemed to be hurtling toward the future—Clyde and his work for Tolliver, Kay planning a move back to Atlanta, Jared getting taller by the week, his voice deepening, even a manly swagger to his walk that might have been amusing if it didn't tear at her heart. Everything was moving fast, too fast, leaving her breathless. She couldn't understand her own future, and she knew that to Clyde and Jared she was merely there, a fixture, unchanging, like Rooney sitting round-shouldered all day in front of the TV set.

She and Rooney had their coats on, ready for their weekly expedition to Kroger, when the phone rang. Rooney bellowed, "No!" Her heavy eyebrows drooped. She loved going to the grocery store—Nina always bought her some treat or other— and could have sudden fits of impatience (what Clyde called her "tantrums," though they were hardly that) when she felt thwarted.

"I'll just be a second, sweetie," Nina said. "You can go out to the car, if you want to. The doors are unlocked."

But Rooney waited by the front door, scowling. Sometimes when Rooney pouted Clyde would make fun of her, calling attention to the protruding lower lip, the dark brows knotted thickly above her deep-set eyes, but the more her brother teased the more adamant Rooney became, her ungainly body frozen as though she'd ceased to breathe, her eyes blank as a statue's. At such times, Nina knew, there was no reasoning with her. Waiting stubbornly for Nina, she stood with her black oversized rain- coat hanging askew, the belt dangling to one side. She'd tipped her head forward so that her dark straggly hair obscured most of her face. If Nina went upstairs and took a nap, returning in twenty minutes, or in two hours, Rooney would not have budged.

Nina paused over the ringing phone, tempted not to answer, but then she snatched up the receiver. "Hello? Hello?"

"Hey, you sound breathless. Am I interrupting something?" Kay's voice: amused, suggestive, a little snide. Nina couldn't help smiling though she felt agitated, not wanting to leave Rooney standing there, wishing she hadn't picked up the phone. For the past year Kay had been her best friend, she supposed; she liked Kay enormously and enjoyed their long aimless conversations, but somehow Kay had already receded into the past: Nina had little to say to her.

"No, I was just walking out the door," she said. "Could I call you back, maybe? Later tonight?"

"Well, I thought I'd just check on you, make sure everything was all right," Kay said breezily, ignoring Nina's question. "Based on what I've heard, you're doing just fine, but I didn't know for sure."

She paused, as though expecting Nina to respond. That sly phrase, *Based on what I've heard*, was just like Kay, but Nina didn't feel like playing along. And there was Rooney, standing frozen by the door.

"I've got to run, Kay. I'll call you back tonight."

"Listen, Nina, don't do this," Kay said, her tone changing so dramatically that Nina held her breath. "Don't shut me out. Please."

"Shut you out? What do you—"

"Look, you haven't been returning my calls, and I decided I wasn't leaving any more messages with what's-his-name. I called again yesterday and when he answered, I hung up. And now that I've got you on the phone, I'm *not* hanging up."

Messages? Had Clyde failed to give her Kay's messages?

"I'm sorry," she said slowly, "things have been hectic around here."

"Yeah, and around here too," Kay said, her voice edged with sarcasm, "but please don't give me the run-around, Nina. I really thought we were friends. I really wanted to help you."

"But—I had no idea you felt like this. Of course we're friends…"

Kay said hotly, "Just tell me what's going on, for starters. Look, I'll be straight with *you*. Linda says the kids at school are talking. About you and Travis's brother. You know Linda, she doesn't exaggerate or make up stories. So if the kids are talking, that means the parents are talking."

"You mean—just because Clyde is staying here? But he's family, Kay. He and Rooney are tired of the city, and he's just found—"

But she stopped; she didn't owe an explanation.

Kay said, "Talk to me, Nina."

"But—but what are people saying? It's ridiculous. It doesn't make sense."

"No, and it probably doesn't matter. You know how this town is, especially the women. Linda said she even overheard a couple of the nuns talking about it, outside of study hall one day. Good Lord—save us from the gossiping nuns!"

She laughed brightly. It was the old Kay.

"How—how is Linda?" Nina asked, wanting to change the subject. Her breath was coming quickly, whether in anger or panic she wasn't sure. People in town were talking?—about her and Clyde?

"Well, she's okay, but I guess she's a little hurt too. She hasn't been hearing much from Jared anymore. I guess you knew about that. Linda's got her pride, and I think it's bothering her more than she lets on. Jared was her first boyfriend, you know."

"I—I wasn't quite sure what happened. Jared says they were just friends."

"Yeah, but I guess Linda didn't know that," Kay said ruefully. "Anyway, it was just puppy love—she'll get over it."

"I'm sorry," Nina said. "Really."

"Well listen," Kay said, "I didn't want to intrude or anything, but I did want to get all this off my chest. I miss you, Nina. I guess you're not going to tell me, but if anything *is* going on with you and Clyde, and if it makes you happy, then I'm behind you one hundred percent. Just call me if you need me, okay?"

"All right, but really, Kay, nothing is—"

"I hope you'll call, sometime. I'd love to see you."

Her thinking dulled, Nina waited too long before replying: the next thing she heard was the dial tone.

Nina turned, determined not to dwell on what Kay had said. (People were gossiping about *her*? About Nina McCune?) She said to Rooney, "Ready for Kroger, honey? I'll buy you a Hershey bar, okay?"

Rooney stood in the same posture she'd assumed all during Nina's conversation with Kay: frozen into stillness, her head canted downward as though she were looking at a far corner of the room. She looked neither happy nor displeased. Her face wore no expression at all.

Then she stammered, "Hershey b-bar?"

Nina smiled. "Yes, and that's a promise. A Hershey bar."

Rooney stumbled forward impulsively, as she sometimes did when something made her happy, to give Nina an almost smothering hug.

When they got back from the store, there was an odd thing: Clyde's beat-up old Civic was in the driveway. Today was one of his "training days" down at Tolliver's, and normally he didn't get home until six or seven at night.

The day was frigid, the sky now in mid-afternoon a pale, opalescent gray. Nina and Rooney brought a gust of cold air into the small, tidy living room, and Clyde glanced up from where he sat slumped at the dining-nook table, staring down at his hands. Rooney hurried over and patted him twice on the shoulder, the sign she wanted him to pay her some attention. But he ignored Rooney's gesture. His mournful gaze had fallen again to his hands.

"Clyde?" Nina said, coming into the nook herself and taking a chair. "Is something wrong?"

Clyde pretended to study his nails, then fixed her with a pained look. His eyes were his extraordinary feature. A mineral blue, glistening, they grabbed you and compelled your attention. Those eyes could make the most ordinary exchange seem fraught with meaning, with an unexplained intensity.

He glared into Nina's face, then dropped his gaze to stare frankly at her breasts. He did this often and under his scrutiny Nina felt a chill at the back of her neck. There was no point, she thought, in denying her attraction to him; he was a younger, handsomer version of Travis, without the addiction and the frequent bursts of temper. She closed her eyes, not wanting to think along these lines, then opened them. He glanced at her again and said, in a flat voice, "I got sent home for the day."

Nina frowned in puzzlement. "Sent home?"

"Yeah."

"But—but what happened?"

Rooney kept patting Clyde from behind and this time he shrugged his shoulders to make her stop. And she did stop. She comprehended, Nina had noticed, when others were speaking of serious matters, and at such times Rooney herself went quiet, waiting in a kind of hushed anxiety.

Clyde said, staring at his hands, "I don't know if I told you, but old Tolliver, after firing Donnie, hired him back temporarily to help train me. Kind of an awkward situation, wouldn't you say? Anyway, I guess it's not surprising that Donnie was showing me some major attitude, and whenever I'd ask a question he deemed naïve or stupid or whatever, he'd raise his voice and act all pissed off at me."

"Clyde, I hope you didn't—"

"Yeah, I'd finally had enough, so I grabbed him by the collar, and raised my fist to him." Clyde couldn't help grinning at the memory.

Nina said, "Oh, God. You didn't hit him, did you?"

Clyde shook his head. "Naah, just had him in a choke-hold,

embarrassed him in front of Luther and Guthrie. So about then Tolliver walks in, tells me to go home and cool off."

"But what if Tolliver decides—"

"Oh, Tolliver likes me." Clyde grinned. "That's the main thing."

Again Rooney patted his shoulders and this time he turned around in his chair and put his sister's hand to his cheek. "That's the main thing, Rooney, isn't it?"

Rooney glanced at Nina as if for permission but Nina gave her a vacant look. Rooney shouted, "That's the main thing!"

Clyde rubbed his sister's hand along his cheek, then let it drop. "Inside voice," he reminded her.

Nina said, "But, Clyde, won't you need to attend mortuary school at some point? Back in Atlanta? I mean, I know right now you're just managing the office, but won't you need—"

"A degree? Oh maybe, eventually." He gave her a quick smile. "Don't get worried, hon, because *I'm* not. When Tolliver retires or dies, I'll take over the place—he's as good as promised me that. He has no kids, not many relatives. I can always hire mortuary staff, and focus on the business side—you know, running the place."

"Well, that's good…"

Clyde glanced up at her, sharply. He stood, the chair legs scraping against the scuffed hardwood floor. "I know you don't believe it, not now," he said. "You don't think I'll follow through. But just wait. I'm biding my time, but I'll get there eventually."

Charmed by this, Nina smiled at him. After all, she thought, he was only thirty-two, and many men were "late bloomers," weren't they? She wanted to believe in him. She did believe in him.

"You don't think I can, do you?" he said.

"Of course I do."

He came forward, took her fragile elbows in his hands, and pulled her close. He kissed her, full on the lips, and she felt her own response even as she knew she must look, to Clyde, unsure of herself. Clyde touched the little space between her eyebrows. "I'm going to make those disappear. Those two little vertical lines."

"What? You're going to…?"

"You're frowning, you just don't know it. I don't know if you're upset, or just surprised—or maybe a little afraid. But the next time I kiss you, those lines will be gone."

She asked, "Should there be a next time?"

"Hah!" he barked, and at the same time they heard Rooney's laughter, too, from where she sat slumped in her favorite corner of the couch. But she wasn't listening to them. She was merely reacting to some slapstick antics on one of her television shows.

Clyde and Nina looked back at each other, like indulgent parents. Clyde said, "Oh yes, there will be a next time," and to her own surprise, Nina said nothing. She was pondering his phrase, *The next time I kiss you.* For a moment she had felt uncomfortable, but only for a moment. For she'd wanted the kiss, hadn't she? She wanted more from him, didn't she? Her husband seemed so long departed, even after such a short time, and Clyde seemed so familiar, intimate, despite his recent arrival. Some seismic shift had occurred, allowing him to become her would-be lover, and any discomfort had fled as though to make way for something inevitable and perhaps valuable. *Be happy,* her nana had once told her, *and don't worry about what anyone thinks. Other people don't always have your best interest at heart, you know.*

She would try to follow this admonition.

She would follow this admonition, she thought, through the remainder of her life.

An hour later Nina lay in her bed, a sleeping Clyde beside her, thinking about her lost husband. Travis. *Travis McCune.* Only six weeks since his death yet his presence, his aura in this house was already weak, negligible. On the verge of disappearing.

How readily, she thought, Clyde had taken his place!—dif-

ferent as the two men were. Nina had felt, at times, faintly con-
descending toward her husband, especially as he sank further
into his disease, whereas Clyde had a strength and cunning
and confidence she admired and, she could not deny it, found
so appealing. Clyde was no victim, she thought. She couldn't
pinpoint the exact moment of transition from regarding him
as mere brother-in-law to sensing a stronger attraction, but that
Rubicon had been passed long before Clyde had led her, gently
but firmly, into her own bedroom.

Covering her breasts with one arm though no one was
watching her—she saw that Clyde was a hard, intense sleeper,
his eyelids clenched as if glued shut—Nina rose and drifted to
the large mirror above the old bureau Travis had inherited from
his parents. She stared at herself, and understood that the raging
anxiety of these past weeks had lessened. No, it had vanished.
Nina let her arm fall, and she stared at her small, pale breasts,
her abdomen, her silky-red pubic hair—behind which she felt
an unaccustomed soreness—and her long, shapely legs. Clyde
had whispered that she was beautiful. Clyde had whispered
urgently that her body was beautiful, cool to the touch yet the
loveliest thing he'd ever beheld, and then in their passionate
clutch he'd said other things, near-obscene things she did not
care to remember, though oddly she had not been offended.
No, not offended. That was the way men were, she thought as
she let her gaze drift back up her body to her face that seemed
shadowy and spectral in the late-afternoon light.

Now she heard an abrupt noise: the slamming of a door,
downstairs. Jared, she thought. Coming home from his job
at Nelson's, the small grocery store just a few blocks away...
She must hurry and get dressed, wake Clyde, go down to allow
Clyde time to get out of her room before Jared discovered or
even suspected what had happened.

But she hesitated a moment. She kept staring at her face,
without quite knowing why, and then she remembered: sure
enough, those two vertical lines between her eyes had vanished.
She was free of them.

She'd yanked open all the windows of her big upstairs bed-room as if performing an urgent and long-neglected chore, and her grief had flown out, like great unruly flocks of demented birds.

Part Three

Clyde

12

The first thing he noticed each morning was the smell. Tolliver had given him some of the grunt work like helping the others stuff bodies lately dead and some not so lately dead into the refrigeration unit against the back wall of the back room. Clyde hated this ritual. Cadavers that had been found in their bedrooms after several days tended to ooze fluids from every orifice and the skin was greenish and would slip and slide emitting some unguessed-at bodily fluid onto his hands.

Clyde liked his hands clean. On working days Clyde scrubbed his hands twenty or more times a day.

"Okay, boys, she'll be good for another day or two," Tolliver would say. He'd look from one to the other of his employees. Clyde the newbie and Luther Brown the amiable Black man who'd worked there more than twenty years and the other white guy with the inappropriate name of Chad Guthrie that was inappropriate because "Chad" was a preppy name and this kid of twenty-two was from the trashiest of white trash and lived in a tumbledown trailer park out by the city limits and had the intelligence of barnyard fowl.

That must be why everyone called him Guthrie instead of Chad.

"Uh, what should I do now," Guthrie asked Tolliver and the old man thought a moment and said, "Go vacuum the viewing parlors, make sure you do it right."

"Yessir," Guthrie said blankly.

He never did it right. There would be long swaths where the vacuum had cleaned but Guthrie in his dirty boots and confused stupidity would walk all over the swaths while he worked so when he finished the greenish carpet looked worse than it had before.

Clyde said, "Never mind—I'll do it. Let Guthrie here take himself a break."

Tolliver was quick enough to catch the witticism and to smile but he didn't smile. Inside the walls of Graceland Hills (a name that made Clyde laugh aloud and he laughed about few things) Tolliver was all business. The old man had to be pushing eighty but if you were white and dead, Graceland Hills was the only game in town so he hauled in buckets of money by upselling to poor whites who for some reason became pretentious when someone died and someday soon enough Clyde was going to take all this over and be rich as holy hell. There was no other reason he put up with this "apprenticeship" and kept company with the likes of Guthrie.

So Clyde went into the hallway off the viewing rooms and took the big Bissell out of the corner closet and methodically vacuumed around the dead folks, most of whose caskets were open so their families could come and say: "He looks even younger than he was!" and "She looks so natural!" Already he'd heard these phrases a hundred times. Why were most people so goddamned stupid? Why did they pay seven or eight or even ten thousand for a funeral that could have cost a few hundred if they'd just done a cremation and settled for a simple urn? But no. Pawpaw and Auntie Sue had to go out in style. As he vacuumed Clyde had the expression on his face of one who wanted to spit.

Sometimes he did spit. Right into the made-up waxy faces of the dead before he closed the casket lid for the final time.

But there were things he liked about the job. He could have done without the smell and the greenish ooze on his hands but there were things he liked. The vacuuming was one because it was mindless and he could think of Nina and Jared and even Rooney to a degree and know he had a jerry-built family back at home waiting for him. That was a good thing. His brother Travis he thought about less for fear he might feel a surge of guilt though seldom in his life had he felt a surge of guilt. Where his brother was concerned Travis had shot himself in the head and that showed weakness and if Clyde despised anything it was weakness.

Take Nina. He was going to make Nina stronger. She was not exactly weak but she was hesitant. She'd felt her share of guilt-surges as Clyde knew well because he could see them each time in her eyes. Jared he wasn't so sure about. A likable kid but a mysterious kid. From almost the moment Clyde arrived on the scene Jared had seemed attached to him which Clyde did not fully understand though he supposed he understood well enough. Father figure. Big-brother figure. Ah shit, it didn't matter—Jared was a good kid and part of the family and so Clyde had decided to love him, though in a far different way of course from the way he loved Nina. Sometimes Nina showed physical affection to Jared and for some reason Clyde didn't care for that although he said nothing. That would show *he* was weak. He thought of this all the time. Weak / strong. Weak / strong. He would rather walk in front of a Mack truck than be weak or cowardly the way Travis had been. Clyde kept vacuuming fiercely and methodically. He did a good job unlike that idiot Guthrie.

Then there was Rooney whom he loved with an irrational love. She was not weak at all. She was perhaps stronger than all of them put together but she was vulnerable. You could put her on a street corner and the tide of people would wash over her and she would be gone. Like that. Gone. Fallen down the stairs and hit her head when she was four and she'd stayed that age mentally and there was nothing to be done. Implacably her body had grown and become stronger. It had bled like any girl's. Her flesh was white and pasty like any girl who stayed completely out of the sun. But she was not weak. No. And he loved her with a hot wayward love that shot through his veins with such speed and ferocity that he wanted to take the vacuum cleaner and throw it out one of the viewing-parlor windows.

These were his people. These were his family. Other people you could get rid of. Tolliver would die soon, and the moment he did and Clyde took this place over he would fire Guthrie, and when Guthrie said, "How come?" Clyde would say, "Because you're a total dumbass." Sometimes he wondered if Tolliver was sucking Guthrie's dick or something because otherwise why employ such a moron? Tolliver did have a little mince to his walk. But Clyde shrugged. Didn't know and didn't care.

Clyde was occupied with these thoughts when he heard a slamming door louder than the noise of the vacuum and it jolted him. There was Tolliver coming into the room. With that limp-twisty mincing old-man's walk of his. Tolliver was a skinny fellow and always wore the same outfit like a uniform. White over-starched shirt with a string-tie. Navy pants. Black wing-tip shoes polished so you could see yourself in them when you looked down at the old man's feet. When a customer came he would retreat quickly to his office and don a navy jacket that matched the pants and there he was. Dressed-up. Presentable. Wearing his salesman's eager grin or if the customer was in tears wearing his salesman's deeply sorrowful and commiserating scowl. It didn't matter. Old Tolliver was a salesman either way and a good one.

Clyde had stopped vacuuming but the machine was still humming and precluded talk. Tolliver came over and flipped the switch to Off. He had a grin on his face but it wasn't over-eager or deeply sorrowful but oddly happy. Made Clyde uncomfortable while the two men stood there among the bodies in the deathly silent room.

"Meant to talk to you earlier, back in my office," Tolliver said.

"Talk?" Clyde gaped, as if not knowing the meaning of the word.

"But I reckon this is fine," Tolliver said. There was a mischievous glint deep inside his cloudy blue eyes. "Don't reckon anybody will overhear us."

Of all people Tolliver the funeral-home owner was always making dead-people jokes. Clyde pretended to laugh though he didn't find such things funny. He didn't find much of anything funny.

"Listen, I've been thinking about you," Tolliver said.

Oh. Shit. He wanted to suck Clyde's dick too.

"Me?"

"Yeah, I've been thinking it's past time you did more re-
sponsible work around here. You're wasted talent, vacuuming
the goddamn rugs." But he had an oily smile when he said
"goddamn" that softened the word. "I mean, what do I have
Guthrie for? He can do shit like that."

"Guthrie? He can't do shit of any kind." And despite himself Clyde smiled for he could sense where this was going. He'd
known it was a matter of time. He'd been working here for two
months now and knew the ropes and he'd done a goddamned
good job.

Tolliver then plunged into a little spiel he might have mem-
orized. Clyde was right smart and came from a good family to
boot. He was a nice-looking white man that customers white
and Black alike could trust once he donned a suit. And there
were records going back thirty years or more that Tolliver needed put on a computer in a modernized way (Clyde smiled at the
old man's phrasing) and he supposed Clyde could do that. Then
he told Clyde what Clyde already knew and that was about Tolliver's lack of a natural heir and how he'd like Clyde to take over
this place one day. He'd had odd-jobbers and even professional
mortuary science people work for him but they came and went
like circus people and you could not trust them. One had stolen
from him. One he'd caught fucking a fresh female cadaver in the
back room. But Clyde came from a respectable local family and
could be trusted. Besides Tolliver felt sorry about his brother.
Tolliver had personally embalmed the brother and knew what
kind of grief a thing like that brought to a family. He wanted to
help. He wanted to help give Clyde a future.

So he didn't want Clyde doing "grunt" work anymore. Besides Luther and Guthrie there were part-timers who could do
such work. Instead Clyde could work with customers and do
sales and oversee the various samples of human pond-scum
he'd hired over the years, and one day when Tolliver was gone

he'd inherit the place and what-all. Clyde was curious about the "what-all" and wondered if it meant Tolliver's five-bedroom ranch-house out on the edge of town built in the middle of a pasture and if it meant Tolliver's bank balances which Clyde had to assume were considerable. So what did Clyde think? Could Tolliver double his salary and make this a permanent situation with, as the book said, great expectations? Tolliver held out his hand and for a few seconds Clyde stared down at the age-freckled thing but finally caught himself up and shook.

"Deal?" Tolliver said.

"Deal."

"Don't back out on me now," Tolliver said, and glanced around at the viewing rooms. "We've got plenty of witnesses."

Clyde tried to laugh to be polite but it came out more as a phlegmy cough.

13

Really?" Nina said, drowsily. "When will you…?"

After he'd gotten off work Clyde had stopped at a nearby tavern and had several rounds of beers and he'd bought rounds for a couple of old drunks sitting at the bar as well. So he was lit. Not overly but comfortably lit. Clearly Nina had just woken from a nap because her hair was mussed and she had a pale sleepy-eyed look. She was trying to smile. They were in the kitchen where Clyde was scrubbing his hands, paying special attention to his nails for the umpteenth time that day. Jared and Rooney were in the living room watching a cartoon video together. In the distance he could hear "Pow! Pow!" and then surprised laughter from Jared and Rooney though they'd seen the damned cartoon a dozen times.

"Yeah," Clyde said. "Really." She was standing at the doorway that gave onto the dining nook, leaning against the doorframe as if still woozy from her nap. She was trying to give her timid smile but it didn't come off. He didn't understand.

"Aren't you happy for me?"

Nina yawned. "Sure I am," she said.

"For us?"

"Yes, of course…"

"You sure don't look it." He picked up the worn-out kitchen cloth and dried his fingers one by one.

"I'm sorry—I had a headache today, so I was just lying down…"

"You and your headaches," Clyde said. He considered headaches a weakness too and, though he'd had some raging ones, had never taken an aspirin in his life.

Her smile faltered. "It—it's a bad headache."

"Just ignore it," he advised.

"I can't—it's like my head is pounding, like a hammer is—"

"Think of something else," Clyde said.

She turned as though to leave him alone in the kitchen but he rushed forward and grabbed her thin shoulders.

"Look, I'm sorry," he said. "Sorry about your headache."

She was wearing an ordinary house-dress that was pale-violet and could have been made out of an old flour sack but nonetheless even with her mussed hair and part-closed eyes she looked lovely and forlorn. That was his type. Lovely and forlorn. He wanted to shake the forlorn part out of her until her teeth chattered but he did not really want that. No.

"Aren't you happy for me?" he repeated. He bent down to kiss her but she turned her face away.

"Of course," she whispered. "I said so. I already said."

"You did," Clyde said.

"It's a good chance for you," she went on, "and I know you'll do a terrific job, while Mr. Tolliver's still here and—and after."

"You mean after he croaks?"

"Don't say it like that." But she smiled.

"Why not?"

"Because he's being nice to you, giving you this amazing opportunity. Just think, someday you'll have that big house and you'll be a respected business owner in town and—" She kept talking but he quit listening. *Blah blah blah*. He'd noticed how often she repeated herself as if her real thoughts were elsewhere.

"We," he finally interrupted. "*We'll* have that big house."

"Yes," she said vaguely. "I meant 'we.'"

"No, you didn't."

Her cool green eyes had drifted off but now she looked back at him.

"I meant to," she said, senselessly.

"You meant to mean it?" Clyde gave a harsh laugh.

"Please, can't you understand? I just woke up and have a damn headache?" She was no longer smiling. She gave him something like a feminine snarl if there were such a thing. She rarely cussed even to say "hell" or "damn."

"That's my girl." Clyde grinned.

"Mama, what are ya'll talking about?" Jared yelled from the living room.

"Nothing, honey," Nina called back.

"Are we going to have supper pretty soon?"

"Yes, honey. How about salmon croquettes?" Clyde knew this was Jared's favorite.

"Yay," Jared said and then he hushed and the cartoon seemed to get louder again. There were cars screeching and cartoon characters yelling and muffled laughter from Jared and Rooney.

Clyde said, "The hell with cooking!"

"What?" Nina said, confused.

"You're sick," Clyde allowed. "And we need to celebrate besides."

"Celebrate?" Nina said.

"Celebrate!"

"Oh, of course…"

"Celebrate our good news," he said fiercely.

"Yes," Nina said in a placating voice. "The good news. Our good news."

"That's my girl." Clyde grinned as if acknowledging this response was facetious. He kissed her again and went to the living room to tell Jared and Rooney to get their coats.

If you'd been some fly on the wall, like the flies that sometimes lighted on the eyelashes of the cadavers at Graceland Hills Funeral Home, you'd have seen this cobbled-together family enter the Rainbow Café which was known as the "nicest" place in town. You'd have seen Clyde strutting in front like a family patriarch despite his youth and a revived-looking Nina trailing after him and the two risibly mismatched kids Jared and Rooney blinking at the candlelight and the white tablecloths and soft music that were such a jolt after their homely small living room and the cartoon noise they'd been imbibing all afternoon.

You'd have seen them stop at the table that the fake maître d' showed them (fake because he was an old country boy of forty-five or so whose whole family had burned up in a house fire thirty years ago, leaving him to do restaurant work all his life) and do an awkward minuet around the table trying to decide where they all should sit. Finally they got Rooney seated which was always the hardest part and then the rest of them quickly sat down and lifted their menus and started to read. For the McCunes this was "going out on the town." They were a family and each of their names ended with "McCune" and that pleased Clyde to no end because it supported his vision of them as *a family* and that was something no one could take away.

"Anything to drink?" old Roy Rittenhouse the maître d' asked. Slowly and hesitantly they began to order. Clyde wanted a dirty martini and Nina said she'd take some sparkling water so Clyde knew she was still nursing her headache and both Jared and Rooney wanted Cokes.

The closer you got to the table if you were that filthy buzzing fly you'd have seen more clearly that they were "dressed up" in the way small-town people do dress up, though Clyde would have denied that description "small-town people" since he'd lived for years in Atlanta and even their town here in southeastern Georgia wasn't all that small. He wore a starched white shirt with the sleeves tamped back to reveal his bony wrists, and he had on pressed blue jeans, and Nina still wore her violet dress but she'd added some violet-toned costume jewelry and a waist-length leather coat Billie had given her for Christmas, and the kids were presentable enough in Sunday clothes and with their hair combed. Clyde had made sure they'd scrubbed their hands.

He said out of nowhere, "Now this is the life!" The other three said nothing but they all smiled vaguely and looked around the candlelit restaurant with its brass sconces and dusty old portraits and pale lavender walls as if this were indeed the life. None of them had ever eaten at the Rainbow before. This was where city people ate when they came to town. This was where pretentious locals ate regularly or where ordinary folk came for special occasions. He supposed Billie and Elton came often enough, and earlier at the house he'd thought *Goddamn* it was time he and Nina and the kids went too. Why not? He was going to be rich one day and might as well get used to such things.

An idea popped into his head.

"I know," he said and smacked his forehead with his palm. "We're celebrating. Let's have us some champagne!"

Nina said quickly, "No. I'd better not have any. And of course the kids—"

"We'll get a bottle," Clyde said. He motioned to the waiter who'd filled their water glasses and said he'd be right with them.

He was a tall skinny fellow with sunken white cheeks but Clyde supposed he was a good waiter because he always seemed within earshot and kept his eye on the table and had that way of ambling quietly toward and away from the table so you hardly noticed him.

"Sir?"

"We'll take a bottle of champagne. Two glasses."

The waiter asked him what kind and he said the best kind.

"Oh no," Nina interrupted, perhaps knowing more than Clyde about the prices of champagne. "I don't even want any. I mean, I shouldn't drink any—" but she stopped herself.

"Sure you can!" Clyde cried, although he thought again about her headache. He was still feeling buoyant from the beers earlier but the buzz was fading and he needed a reinforcement fast. "The best kind," he repeated to the waiter.

"Excellent choice," the waiter said beaming and no doubt thinking (erroneously) that he would be getting his biggest tip of the evening. But as a precaution he whispered, "That would be our Dom Perignon, sir. One hundred twenty dollars for the bottle but worth every penny."

Clyde blanched. Clyde stared. He had maybe a hundred dollars in his pocket and no credit cards.

"I don't care for that brand," he said.

"Well, sir," said the waiter, loftily, "we have a very nice Moët for twenty-nine dollars," and Clyde grinned and said quickly, "That's my brand. Bring us that."

"A very good 'brand,' sir," the waiter said, with a faint condescension Clyde could barely register because his ears had a roaring in them that came from his momentary embarrassment.

Once the waiter had gone Clyde looked around at the others. "Hot dog," he said.

Nina was fretting with the napkin in her lap.

"You'll love it," Clyde said. "Twenty-nine a pop and you'd *better* love it."

"Can I have a sip?" Jared said.

"Yeah, can I have a sip!" whispered Rooney. They'd taught her to whisper in public places because the alternative was a loud excited screech and since she was being good Clyde patted her hand.

"Sure you can, honey," he said. "Both of you can."

But his gaze kept shifting toward Nina. A damn fly was buzzing around the table creating a blue confusion in the candlelight and Clyde reached out to swipe the damn thing but missed.

"Just have a sip, won't you?" he said in a placating tone.

Nina smiled and looked around appreciatively. "Okay," she said. "It's all lovely. I love that we came here."

"Once you try it, you'll like it."

"All right, I'll try it," Nina said, giving him a seductive smile he knew better than to take seriously. He knew a plug nickel when he bit into one.

But the second their faggy waiter poured the champagne to let Clyde taste he was back in his buoyant mood again. "Damn that's good," he said. The waiter smiled and filled both glasses and then set the Cokes down in front of Jared and Rooney.

Rooney sipped her Coke and turned red and whispered, "Damn that's good."

They all laughed. Soon afterward they ordered and the food came quickly and they all seemed happy. Clyde had ordered a steak and potatoes and Nina had ordered salmon and Jared asked for a cheeseburger though that wasn't on the menu ("I'm sure we can manage it," the waiter had said) and for Rooney they'd ordered baked chicken because chicken was the only kind of meat she liked. "Could you put some mashed potatoes and green beans on the side?" Nina had inquired.

"Of course," the waiter said.

But before they started eating Clyde had raised his flute and watched as Nina lifted her own flute and he'd said, "To the McCune family and its bright future!" Nina put her glass to her lips but Clyde said, "Not yet. You've got to make a toast as well."

Nina thought a moment and said pleasantly, "To happiness. To happiness for all of us."

Clyde drank and liked the taste so well he drank again. He could feel the alcohol warming his gut. Nina sipped once at the flute and then put it back down.

"Dig in!" Clyde told the others and they did just that.

Halfway through the meal someone tapped his shoulder and he glanced up. He was surrounded by what looked like dark angels in black cloaks and veils. But then he recognized Father Zach. He hadn't seen the junior parish priest in years. Father Zach was smiling at him. The dark angels were smiling at him too but of course by now he'd realized they were nuns. Father Zach said, "So good to see you all. Clyde, Nina. Maureen. Jared." Clyde thought disdainfully that the man didn't have to say all their names. They all knew who they were. The priests were all politicians fundamentally. They needed your money and that kept them smiling and winking. Father Zach had winked at Jared.

"Nice to see you, Father," Nina said. She put down her fork. "Sisters," she added.

Father Zach introduced the nuns. Sisters Irene and Yvonne and Justine. He said they were teaching nuns from a mother house in upstate New York but were here looking into the possibility of setting up a small parochial school in the next town. He said they were meeting with civic leaders and contractors and of course with Father Brody and Father Zach. They'd arrived just today and Father Zach had decided to show them a good time at the Rainbow. His smile faltered as soon as the phrase "show them a good time," with its slight sexual connotation, slipped out but he kept talking and soon that was forgotten.

"It's nice to meet you all," Nina said to the nuns. "Perhaps we could all sit together? A bigger table…?" She did not look as though she meant it. Her face was pale and covered with a thin film of sweat despite the cold draft that swept over the table whenever someone entered the restaurant.

"No, no, we'll let you eat in peace," Father Zach said. He eyed the champagne. "Are we celebrating?" He smiled.

"Sort of," Clyde said, but he didn't want to go into details and he hoped Nina would not.

Father Zach waited as if for an explanation. Clyde saw that he'd gained a bit of weight in the years since he'd seen the young priest. Now he had the beginning of jowls and a waist that pushed at his black belt and pants. Living off the fat of the land. Letting others work to support him. At least the nuns taught and *did* something but Clyde had never liked priests. He was relieved that evidently they weren't going to accept Nina's invitation. Nina kept toying with her glass but she hadn't drunk more beyond that first sip.

And that's when it came to him. The knowledge popped into his head the way the champagne cork had popped out of the bottle and suddenly horribly, tragically he knew.

Father Zach was talking but Clyde could barely listen. "…so we're driving over to Macon to speak to the bishop tomorrow and I'll be showing the sisters some of the sights and then…"

Clyde stared at Nina. She stared back with a dismal smile. She knew he knew.

"So, Jared," Father Zach was saying, "I guess I'll see you at altar boy practice this Saturday?"

"Yes, Father," Jared said. His gaze fell just slightly so he wasn't meeting the priest's eyes.

"Good, good," the priest said. "We'll be talking about Easter service, isn't that amazing? Already? It's still so cold but it's already time to start thinking about—"

"Thanks, Father," Clyde said. Apropos of nothing.

Father Zach's politic smile faltered a bit but then he said, "I understand you're working over at the mortuary, Clyde. We're so glad to have you back in town. We'd love to see you down at church sometime"—and he glanced at Nina too—"all of you. I know the family has been through a rough patch, to put it mildly—"

"Thanks, Father," Clyde said again, but this time there was an unmistakable note of dismissal to his voice. The nuns were backing away. Roy stood waiting to show Father Zach and the nuns to their table. But Father Zach could not quite let go. He must know that Clyde had not been to church since he was a teenager.

"Clyde, if you'd ever like to talk—"

"Appreciate that," Clyde said. "*Thanks, Father,*" he added and then even this determined priest backed off with a wave of his hand. "God bless!" he called. "Enjoy your dinner!"

Nina smiled after the priest and nuns longingly. "Oh, wasn't that nice," she said. "Jared, when are you serving mass next? I'll come watch you, if you want."

"That's all right," Jared said. "I'm quitting soon, anyway."

"Quitting? Really?" his mother said.

Out of nowhere spiraled down the big fly that had been harassing them but it landed on Clyde's wrist bone and with his other cupped hand he killed it. There was nothing but a bluish-green mess on his forearm.

Nina touched his other arm. "I'm not feeling too well, and the kids have cleaned their plates. Can we leave?" she said.

Clyde thought this was a good idea. "Yeah," he agreed. "Let's get the hell out of here."

14

As time passed there was a new urgency and even desperation at the speed of its passing. Every time he glanced at Nina's stomach he felt it more acutely. February and March, gone. April, gone. Now it was early May. Middle of springtime. Even clients stumbling into the mortuary with Kleenex wadded in their hands had something to say about springtime. Sky sure is blue. Weather sure is pretty. Are you done embalming cousin Sheila yet? Could we look at her? Clyde stood there with his slight bow-legs in the front viewing room with the woman client and her two sniveling kids but he was thinking of other things. "Sure," he said and cocked his head. "She's right over there."

New death and new life. What a kick in the gut. Nina had considered getting an abortion but he'd said no. Hell *no*. There would be no aborting any child of Clyde McCune's.

"But people will…"

"The hell with what people will say."

"But Jared will get kidded, at school. He…"

"Jared's a strong kid. Don't worry about him."

He hovered around in the other viewing rooms while cousin Sheila's family gawked and wept and he did busy-work like dusting off a lapel here, fixing a woman's eyelid that had started to come apart there. You would think otherwise but the dead kept you busy. He remembered that an old man named Peyton was due for his closed-casket service later this morning so Clyde grabbed the half-lid and gave the old geezer a final cold-eyed stare and that was it. Slam.

"Mr.— Mr. McCune—?" said Sheila's cousin.

"Yep." He returned to the cousin's room.

The woman had taken a pink-gemmed necklace (rhinestones?) out of her purse. "Would you mind if we switched this for the—the other?" Clyde came over. He saw that the dead woman was wearing a pearl necklace that might be worth something so he understood. "Sure," he said. "You can get some money for that." He didn't need to add these words but did so because he was feeling harassed and this pasty-faced young woman annoyed the hell out of him. Not to mention her little boy and little girl with their noses running like faucets. But the woman ought to be ashamed. Looting her own cousin. "Oh no, it's not that," Sheila's cousin said. "It's just that our grandmother gave her those pearls, and I'd like my little girl to wear them one day. Besides, this pink necklace was Sheila's favorite." Clyde was already reaching around the stiff's neck to unclasp the pearls. He took the pink necklace and clasped that in place and the deal was done.

"There you go," he said.

The woman held the pearls as if she thought Clyde thought they were thirty pieces of silver.

"Ought to be able to get a bundle for those," Clyde said gratuitously and turned on his heel.

"No, but it's not that…" but bedeviled by his own concerns he'd stopped listening and left the woman with her guilty conscience never to see her again and passed out the door to the back room where Guthrie and Luther were "working." Luther held a broom at least, but Guthrie had been frowning at his nails and now quickly shamefacedly opened one of the refrigerator doors and peered inside so it looked like he was doing something. Clyde tiptoed around behind him and said, "Boo!" Guthrie jumped a mile and a half and Luther chuckled agreeably and Clyde laughed aloud.

"That old booger's gonna *get* you," Clyde said.

Of all people Guthrie the mortuary worker was scared of dead bodies. He could assist at an embalming fairly well and he could witness the most gruesome raw cadavers that ever came into the place (suicides with their heads part-blown off and kids beaten past the last inch of their lives and bodies so eaten up with cancer they looked like fifty-pound human prunes) and he could even help stow them body by body into the refrigeration unit but he always looked vaguely queasy and you could scare him if you caught him off guard. This tickled Clyde to no end. Once he and Luther had leaned an iron-stiff cadaver behind the door to the viewing area, waiting for Guthrie to enter, and when he did the cadaver fell and knocked him down and Guthrie screamed like his guts were on fire. Clyde laughed every time he thought about that one. They didn't joke around while old man Tolliver was there but otherwise it was open season on poor Guthrie.

"Let's look busy at least," Clyde told the two men as he wiped his eyes. Clyde wept when he laughed and he hated that but it happened every time. "Old man'll be here any minute."

So Luther commenced using the broom and Guthrie got out cleansers and utensils to tackle the work table. The smell of the bleach warred with the stink of the embalming fluid. The coroner was sending over a suspected murder victim from the next town and he didn't want anybody else's DNA getting mixed up with hers. It was a rape case too. They'd taken their blood samples and done their rape kit but sometimes bodies were exhumed if more evidence was needed. Clyde looked forward to seeing the girl and hoped she wasn't in too rough a shape. A naked girl's a naked girl. Once all this was in motion he went through another small doorway into a book-and-paper-crammed cubbyhole of an office where on a rickety table Clyde did the daily computer work of admission sheets and invoices and such and also where he made his private phone calls. He punched Nina's number.

"H-hello?" Always sounded like she'd just woken from a damn nap or if awake didn't quite know where or who she was.

"Me," Clyde said. "What-cha doin'?"

Nina paused. "Just some—some dishes. Washing dishes." He knew this wasn't the truth. She'd been lying on the bed hoping when she woke this madness would all be over. But he decided to play along.

"Can't Jared do that?"

Nina made a sharp tsk-ing noise. "Jared has a *job*. It's my job to do the dishes."

"Can Rooney help you…?" He was playing with her now.

"Rooney's sick," Nina said. "She's on the sofa but doesn't even want her cartoons on. She's got a runny nose and she's coughing a lot."

Clyde felt a jolt of alarm and sat up straight in his chair. "Sick? Rooney?"

"She's sick," Nina repeated.

"Give her some aspirin or something. Does she have a fever?"

"I—I don't think so. But she did clutch her head like she had a headache. I'll give her some aspirin now."

"Good—that's my girl," he said.

"I'd better go," Nina said. "I'm making her some oatmeal and some hot chocolate."

Those were her favorites. Clyde approved. He thought a moment and said, "You call me if she gets any worse." His voice softened. "Will you?"

"All right," Nina said.

"Call me—please," Clyde said gently and hung up.

15

Five minutes later he called Nina back and told her something that should cheer up Rooney. He'd seen an advertisement in today's paper for "an amusement fair" starting this weekend. He'd taken Rooney once before to Six Flags west of Atlanta and she'd loved it. *Six fags! Six fags!* she'd crowed for days afterward with that lopsided smile of hers and that had tickled Clyde to no end. He laughed and wept. He laughed and wept. So when he saw the ad about the fair he'd made a mental note. Now that she was sick Clyde thought she needed something she could look forward to when she got well. The fair was just the thing. Sawdust-covered walkways and Ferris wheels and bumper cars and ring-toss games and dozens of other distractions that would cheer her up and make them look (he thought incidentally) like a real family. And if that wasn't enough to cheer him up, now Clyde heard the unmistakable whining engine of the hospital morgue truck bringing him that female murder victim. Hot damn.

But that wasn't his reaction finally. No hot damning with Luther and Guthrie as they stared at the woman's naked body. In fact the second he'd glimpsed *Maggie Trainor* as her toe tag read Clyde had shushed the boys out of the room. "I'll handle this," he told Luther and Guthrie. "This is a murder case. Maybe." It might have been a suicide. There was a bullet hole in the woman's head. Looking disappointed Luther and Guthrie shuffled out the door to the viewing rooms where they could goof off in peace with lots of company. Though nominally their boss Clyde really didn't give a shit.

The more he examined the bullet hole the more he was convinced this was no suicide. The cops had already taken their pictures and done their analysis so Maggie Trainor's hair was pushed back all around the entrance wound and Clyde could see (surely even the numbskull cops should have seen) that it was far toward the back of the head which was an impossibly awkward location for a suicide. She'd have had to wrench her arm back to take the shot and why would she have done that? No. This was an execution. Maggie Trainor had truly pissed off someone and for her trouble got a plug of lead through her brain.

Clyde's body had chilled as he examined the wound. Chilled with anticipation for he knew that in a moment he would be paying no attention to the wound at all. Now he took her matted hair and arranged it down and around the entrance wound to cover it fully. He took a small wetted cloth and wiped the blood from her forehead and cheek and by the time he had finished Maggie looked almost normal. She might have been a sleeping woman—albeit a very pale one—whose cheek he might brush with the backs of his fingers and she would come awake. She would come awake and smile at him.

Now he did what his chilled body and soul had been anticipating he would do. He straightened, threw the soiled cloth aside, and merely stared at her as if he were one of her mourners. He *was* one of her mourners. The chill sensation in his brain and body was replaced by warmth and by something like affection. Maggie Trainor was a woman in her early thirties with dark unkempt hair and unearthly white skin. Her skin was the color of those toadstools that spring up overnight and just as damp as they were and, though he had not really touched her yet, he knew Maggie all down her body would feel like the vulnerable skin around a woman's vagina. That soft. That tender. Though Maggie was naked he did not glance even briefly at her vagina but rather kept his gaze on her lovely white face. She wore no makeup. She must have been killed in her sleep for sleep is the only time a woman looks this plain while at the same time unbeknownst to herself so naturally and stunningly beautiful. Clyde stared. He stared and stared.

He allowed his fierce hot eyes to trail down from her face toward her narrow sloping shoulders. To her smallish breasts with their nipples purple as bruises. To her waist and finally toward her vagina and he felt the stiffening at his crotch but he tried to ignore that and simply do nothing. For some reason he thought of Nina. Sometimes he woke before she did and he'd lie there staring at her. He supposed there were similarities between his lover and this girl Maggie for Nina too was slender and had soft curling hair that would become disarranged by sleep, and Nina too rubbed hard at her makeup before bed so that her face looked denuded, as if somehow the soul and personality had fled her features altogether. Of course this woman Maggie was not breathing but he could always hear Nina breathing slightly, and he couldn't help but think how easily he might reach over with his strong adult male hand and take hold of her neck and quickly enough squeeze the life out of her. Why would he do this? He had no reason. Not really. But still he could have done it.

Someone had spared him the trouble with Maggie. She lay wholly vulnerable and as it were served up to him. So he thought. So he thought without guilt or hesitation. He decided to touch her and he touched the side of her face. Cool to the touch of course but not that plastic coolness of the embalmed. God knows he had to feel that every day as part of his job. But this was different. She'd been dead for less than a day. It must have been last night that some asshole lover had gotten pissed off watching her sleep likely because she'd said something hurtful just before they went to bed and that seed of anger had sprouted fast until it became a quivering tree of rage within him. So he'd taken the gun and his eyes had been swimming with lust and fear and sorrow but he had done it anyway. He'd shot her clean through the head with a trembling index finger.

Clyde's own index finger was trembling now as it brushed along her cheek and then took a strand of her hair and curled it around the finger tight and hard so they were bound indissolubly. Then he unwound the hair and pushed the hair back again to uncover the wound. He touched first his little finger and then his index finger against the wound and then he began to push. He pushed a little more. His finger was inside her near the first joint and then he kept pushing and was astonished by how warm and intimate it felt. He could not stop. He pressed his finger deeper until it was fully inside the woman's head up to the knuckle and then the finger was there entirely. Inside her. Feeling the warmth of the bullet's trajectory. He was breathing heavily. He was panting. He kept one ear cocked in case one of those fools Luther or Guthrie decided to wander back here again but he heard nothing. Then in a sudden lunge he withdrew the blood-covered finger and stared at it. So it was done. It was done.

He stood there trembling. He could not believe how beautiful she was. Though deceased and pale and her lips pulled back unattractively from her teeth still Maggie Trainor was beautiful. He imagined her in life. Lifting a cocktail to that mouth with a smile, a laugh. Lying in her bed and looking upward longingly toward her murderous lover. Or simply crossing a room to draw the blinds and look out as an ordinary woman would do on an ordinary day. His heart twisted and squirmed. He took a sanitary wipe from a cart beside the aluminum table on which she lay and he wiped at his finger hard until it was clean. His penis had stiffened almost unbearably. That raw pushing desire behind his penis had never seemed more urgent. He dared to glance again at her vagina and now he carefully, gently, reverently brushed his fingers along one side and then the other. So smooth. So tender.

Abruptly he stopped and glanced behind him. He thought he'd heard something but he had not. He knew Guthrie and Luther were sitting out on the brick wall that ran alongside the mortuary. They were having a cigarette and laughing even though old man Tolliver was expected back soon. No doubt they were making jokes about Maggie Trainor. But they did not understand. To them she was just another body. Another corpse. A once-living thing they'd soon have to eviscerate and embalm and put inside one of those refrigerated drawers with all the others.

Then came a shrilling sound. The telephone. It was Nina telling him that Rooney seemed better and was well enough to be excited about the state fair. She had asked about the Ferris wheel. She had asked about the clowns.

"That's good," Clyde said, not taking his eyes off Maggie.

"Clyde, are you—okay?"

"Yeah. Fine," he said.

"But you—you sound funny."

He paused. "I'm sorry, hon. Just busy with work."

She could have laughed or gotten annoyed and she chose the latter. "When are you getting home? It's almost—"

"I know. I may be a little late."

"But it's almost dinnertime—"

"I'm sorry, hon. I really am."

"All right. Fine," she said. And then, "Bye, sweetie." She hung up.

Clyde forgot the phone conversation the moment it was over. He glanced toward Maggie and let his soulful gaze trail from her hair to her breasts to her vagina to her feet. He noticed the damn toe-tag and decided to remove it for now. He placed the tag onto the cart, his heart hammering. He crossed to the door to the viewing rooms on which there was a deadbolt and he locked the door just in case somebody decided to wander inside. He pressed his ear against the door and heard nothing but the sleep of the dead. All was well. All was well. He thought this as he turned with his fierce eyes moving hotly onto Maggie once again. *All was well.* Yes. Yes. He began unbuttoning the top button of his shirt.

16

Happening upon that advertisement about the fair had been a form of serendipity or maybe pure blind chance but it didn't matter to him. Rooney had stayed sick for a few days with some kind of flu-like bug and going to the fair was her reward for suffering through that and Clyde who was head of this little haphazard family was determined everyone would have a good time. That included his pregnant soon-to-be wife Nina and her son Jared, who'd become like a son to him. On the drive over to the makeshift fairgrounds it occurred to him that life was good and that besides being enjoyable in itself the fair was an excellent escape from the mortuary.

He couldn't believe he'd been working at that place for four months already. Since Tolliver had promoted him he rarely dealt directly with the bodies but mainly with the live customers whom he had to upsell as far as the customers' stupidity would take them and with Tolliver's chaotic books which Clyde was putting onto the computer. Though it was already 1992 Clyde didn't know as much about computers as he'd let on but he'd gotten some business software and was doing the best he could. For sure Tolliver wouldn't know the difference and once Clyde left he didn't care what his replacement thought.

He daydreamed often about quitting. Did he really want to run a mortuary the rest of his life? No matter how rich it made him? Again and again he imagined taking Rooney and Nina and Jared out west somewhere and starting over in some place like Santa Fe or San Diego. But he needed more money first. He had a few thousand saved by now but he needed more because four people with all their little wants and needs ate up the money fast. He reasoned that out west nothing changed or at least everything changed at a slower rate than here in this fusty-smelling town where he'd found himself living after his brother had shot a slug of lead into his head. Clyde still considered that Travis had been a coward but he tried not to think about this. Especially now at a happy time when Nina and Jared seemed to have gotten over Travis's death and allowed Clyde to replace him in their lives and let Rooney come along for the ride. And anyway how could anyone not love Rooney?

The fairgrounds were coming into sight. He had the car window rolled partway down and he could already smell the sawdust they spread along the walkways and the sizzling hot dogs and the faint odor of animal dung from the farming exhibits. It was dusk of a cloudless evening and the sun was a faint lowering golden coin overlain by pink and blue scrims of cloud. Mixed with the smells of the fair was the fresh breeze that blew through everything and filled the car and helped enliven the four of them with anticipation. Of course it was Rooney who pointed first at the Ferris wheel.

"Look!" she crowed. "Ride!"

Nina and Jared had been telling Rooney about the rides over their dinner of chicken fried steak and mashed potatoes. One of the meals Nina made tolerably well though Clyde didn't want to be cruel. She tried. She did the best she could. Occasionally she'd tell him about her past life as a nurse in Atlanta but this seemed faintly unreal but perhaps no less unreal than her work as a housewife here in the brand-spanking-new McCune family. Travis McCune was dead and that was no less a fact than the occasional stinking corpse that would arrive at the mortuary after lying in bed unfound for a week or more. Clyde thought there was a pleasant symmetry to his having assumed Travis's role in the family. And pregnant Nina had taken on her role as *Mrs. Clyde McCune* (soon as they got around to getting married she could call herself that) and Jared was their fine-looking son and Rooney at last had a complete family she could call her own. So it had pleased him when Nina and Jared had told her about the hammer-claw and roller-coaster and Ferris wheel over dinner earlier. Now she yelled, "Ride!" again before any of them had the chance to answer her the first time.

Jared grinned and said, "Yeah!" He sat in the backseat with an Atlanta Braves cap mashed down backward on his head. "That's right. We're gonna do the rides."

"You bet," Clyde said. "We're gonna have fun." He made this sound like a fiat.

Nina looked at him with her pale heart-shaped face that he loved to frame inside his smooth fingers that might have been handling an oozing corpse only hours before. But Clyde was meticulously clean and he knew his hands smelled not of rank cadavers but of the lemony-scented hand cleanser he used both at home and at work.

Nina said, "Do you think I should...?" She glanced down at her abdomen for his benefit.

Clyde had slowed the car. The parking lot was nearly full, even though this was a school night and the fair would be here through the end of May. Now he took a moment to smile at Nina. "Sure," he said.

Rooney, as she often did, cawed like a parrot. In many ways she *was* a parrot. "Do you think I should? Do you think I should?"

Obviously Nina had helped Rooney get ready for this outing for Rooney wore some pale-pink lipstick and a bluish-silvery eye shadow so faint and skillfully applied it might have been the natural color of her eyelids. Wearing a new white seersucker dress Nina had bought her, Rooney looked almost pretty, despite her full-moon face and her melting-away chin that Clyde acknowledged as her worst feature. Rooney's lips were always wet with spittle and when she spoke she sometimes bathed her listener with a faint spray of saliva. For some reason Clyde thought of her fall down the attic stairs when she was four. To this day she soiled her panties and Nina heroically dealt with that and all the other small indignities associated with a brain-damaged individual. Clyde thought with approval that Nina seemed to know that this was woman's work. He was glad as hell to have

Rooney's shit and menstrual periods off his hands. Working at a mortuary he witnessed enough human sleaze in the course of a day without having to change his adult sister's underwear and wipe her butt when he got home.

He put this out of his mind. "We're all gonna have a good time. No doubt," he said cheerfully.

Nina brushed a swath of her pretty auburn hair out of her eyes. Once Clyde had rolled down his window a bit earlier, Nina's hair had begun blowing about her head. Now she was looking at the Ferris wheel that had just stopped, eliciting screams from the people swaying back and forth in the topmost cars.

Nina laughed. "Yeah, sounds like fun, doesn't it?"

Clyde decided to change the subject. "How about some cotton candy for our dessert? Or a snow-cone?"

Jared and Rooney both piped up from the backseat. "Yeah, a snow-cone!"

"Snow-cone! Snow-cone!"

Jared added, "I like the blue ones."

Clyde grinned at him in the rearview mirror. "Blue snow-cones it will be."

They spent more than two hours at the fair. First they came to the bumper cars, and when Clyde pointed to Nina to precede him she made a gesture of pulling out her hair. "Did you happen to remember that I'm expecting? I'd miscarry in the first minute if I got into one of those things."

Clyde said, "Sorry, hon. I wasn't thinking."

So Clyde and Jared and Rooney all got into their own cars and soon enough were careening around the rink. They crashed into one another. Sometimes on purpose and sometimes not. Rooney screamed in delight. Clyde laughed harshly like a silent-movie villain and drove his car straight at Jared's. "Take that!" Jared's head jerked backward with the impact. All three of them bumped into strangers' cars too, and sometimes it was accidental and sometimes not but in either case everyone laughed politely. It was all a game. There might be some sore necks in the morning but it was all a game.

After the bumper cars they wandered through a hallway lined with funhouse mirrors. Clyde saw himself grow taller and skinnier while Rooney looked almost inhuman as her made-up face went wide and then normal-sized again. She started to whimper. "It's just a mirror. Don't worry about it, sweetie." Clyde hurried her off and let Nina take her turn and then Nina apparently saw her belly grow twice the size it already was and she gave a little intake of air… But Jared was enjoying the mirrors. He was already thin and now looked like a sliver of spaghetti with the stupid baseball cap distorted into a red-and-blue foreign object atop his head. He didn't look real. None of them looked real. Even Clyde was relieved when they came away from the mirrors and were themselves again. Now they remembered who they were or at least who they were supposed to be.

"Uncle Clyde! Look!" Jared yelled over the oddly cheerful organ music ubiquitous throughout the fairgrounds. Though Clyde had asked him politely not to call him "Uncle" but rather "Dad" there was no point in badgering the kid. What else could he do? Rough him up for calling him what he literally was?

Jared was pointing to a sign that said "Test Your Strength!" There was a huge sledge-hammer and a metal plate you hit to make the machine register what kind of a man you were. "Puny." "Average Joe." "Muscle Man." "SUPERman." These were some of the indices you could hit if you dared to play the stupid game.

Clyde pointed at Jared and said, "Go ahead. Knock yourself out."

Jared picked up the sledgehammer and slammed it down on the plate and the ball shot up in the register and almost reached "Average Joe." Clyde whistled. "Hello there, Average Joe! Not bad for your age." Jared fed the machine another dollar and said: "Watch this! I was just getting warmed up."

Clyde narrowed his eyes and grimaced. "Ha ha. Get higher than 'Average Joe' and I'll stuff that mallet up my—" But he stopped himself. He glanced at Nina but she hadn't seemed to notice.

Jared lifted the sledgehammer and swung it down again. To Clyde's surprise this time he got halfway to "Muscle Man."

"Hey, did you see that!" Jared sounded like a much younger kid.

"Yeah. I saw it. Now step aside."

This time Clyde took the sledgehammer and brought it down like someone chopping off another man's head and he went past "Muscle Man" and halfway to "SUPERman."

"Yay! Look at Uncle Clyde go."

Clyde put another dollar in the machine and slammed the hammer down again. This time just short of "SUPERman."

"Good going. Did you see? Mom?"

Nina nodded. Clyde couldn't tell if she was impressed or not.

Another dollar. Another slam. Then another dollar and another slam and then more money and Clyde kept slamming the plate even after the machine had stopped registering because he couldn't be bothered to feed dollars into the machine, and his face had turned red as a tomato, so overripe it might explode, and his lips had become an angry snarl and still he kept slamming and slamming down on the metal plate until a man with a cigar hanging out of his mouth approached Clyde and clamped his hand down on Clyde's shoulder. "Hey there! What the hell you think you're doin'?"

Clyde dropped the sledgehammer and his face was sweaty and contorted, and he turned to face the man as though the two were about to fight. The man backed off one step. Then another. "Be careful with that machine. That machine cost—"

Clyde got up in his face and said, "I don't care what the damn machine cost. You're talking to SUPERman here. And don't you forget it."

"Yeah? I didn't hear no bell. If you hit 'SUPERman' you get a free ride ticket but I didn't hear no bell."

Clyde turned away with a derisive whistle and left the man to ponder that.

As Clyde got off the "Test Your Strength" machine he realized his stomach felt queasy. He'd had only a bite or two of Rooney's pink cotton candy and a caramel-covered apple he'd bought for himself but still he felt queasy. God it would be embarrassing if he threw up in front of the others. Especially Nina. *She* was the one four months along. *She* had the right to feel queasy if anyone did. He could imagine her regarding him and her nose lifting slightly at the stench. "I'm the one who's supposed to be pregnant." Or she'd come up with some other witticism. She'd gotten more and more sarcastic during the pregnancy. He didn't like that. He liked her feminine and malleable, the way she'd been when they'd first met and when he'd first fucked her and she'd hardly moved at all. Lately she did move. She moved a lot. Clearly she wanted him. Her wants and needs scared him a little. So did her sarcasm. It made them equals and he didn't like feeling merely equal to anyone and especially not a woman.

But God he loved Nina. He understood now why Travis had spoken about her with that tender voice, a boyish glisten in his eyes... This memory calmed him a little and his stomach felt better. He didn't throw up. He took deep breaths as he walked and though he knew his face had turned pale he felt a little better. They were almost past the Ferris wheel when Rooney pointed at the thing and cried, "Ride! I wanna ride!"

Like the bumper cars the wheel's cars were red and blue and yellow and green. Bright primary colors appealing to someone childlike as Rooney, who had trouble deciding which car to get inside. Finally she cried out, "Green one! Green one!" The gruff-looking wheel operator waited until a green one came along and she got in with Clyde. The wheel jerked slightly and behind them Jared got into a blue car by himself. Nina stood watching some distance away. She didn't look unhappy but a certain wistfulness in her expression made Clyde think she wished she wasn't pregnant and could ride.

The wheel jerked again and this time it kept moving. Clyde

instructed Rooney to hold on to the bar and as soon as they started ascending backward she pointed to the car ahead of them and cried, "Yellow one! Yellow one!" Clyde remonstrated with her but she kept crying, "Yellow one!" though he'd told her she'd made her choice and it was too late to change cars. The wheel started going around. Thankfully Clyde's stomach had settled. The wheel arced gently backward and up, until it began rising and Clyde could distract Rooney a little by pointing out the town lights and the cars with their zigzagging headlamps and the moon high overhead. Though Rooney looked obediently wherever Clyde pointed, she could be stubborn when thwarted and she'd started jerking at the metal bar and yelling ever more loudly, "The yellow one!" The people up ahead in the yellow car heard her and peered back at this strange large woman with her pale moon-face and pale puffy legs in the white seersucker dress screaming like any four-year-old.

"Sweetie. Listen." Clyde attempted to calm her and even tried his authoritative voice, which he hated to use because he loved Rooney more than anyone on this earth but she refused to listen. "Yellow one! Yellow one!" She grabbed hold of the bar and pushed and pulled the thing until Clyde was afraid it would break and Rooney would be sent tumbling down through the darkening sky. They were rising higher. Higher. Almost at the apogee and of course now the ride operator chose to stop the wheel and let a few more folks get on. Rooney screamed. Rooney howled. Abruptly she stood up and the car lurched back and forth until Clyde was sure they would both be lost, though he'd grabbed her waist and stepped up his attempts to console her. "Honey! It's all right!" It seemed fitting that she would cause the death of both of them but he thought *No* he wasn't ready to die so he kept hold of her waist and held the bar fast with his other hand and endured the swinging and lurching of the car as best he could.

Then all at once she calmed. She took some raggedy tearful breaths and she calmed. She sat back down and let her brother put his arm around her heaving shoulders. She was crying still but it was crying of the kind she did when she was unhappy for no reason he could discern. Just ordinary crying. Sometimes Rooney just needed to cry. Now he glimpsed Nina's face upturned down below, looking delicate as a flower with an expression of concern on her features—evidently she'd seen everything that had happened—but Clyde smiled at her and winked as if everything was okey-dokey. That was something his big brother Travis, the eventual suicide, used to say when they were younger. Everything was okey-dokey. *Okey-dokey.*

Finally the wheel started to circle back down and when in hearing range of the ride operator, Clyde yelled, "We want off! We want off!"

The man looked displeased but he stopped the wheel and let them off. Jared got off too and asked Clyde if he and Rooney were all right but Clyde brushed this aside. "We're fine. We're fine." He looked around at the other three. They looked exhausted and demoralized.

Clyde just laughed.

On their way out of the fairgrounds they saw the sign for a small dilapidated building called "Freak Show" and Rooney pulled her brother's arm in that direction. A sign promised a bearded lady and the fattest man on earth and a sword-eating man along with other assorted freaks but Clyde said, "We're enough of a freak show on our own. Let's move along."

To his surprise Rooney acquiesced without yelling or whining but she became excited again when they passed a booth that held a ring toss game. The back of the booth was stacked with large teddy bears in different colors. "Teddy bear! I want one!" Rooney shrieked. So just to hush her up they wandered over and the man inside the booth greeted them amiably. "Three tosses for a dollar. Get all three and win a teddy bear. Three tosses for…" He seemed to have been reciting these words all his life. His arms were muscular and tattooed with mermaids whose tails ended at his wrists like tiny bows. Somehow Clyde wanted to best the man so he bought three wooden rings and started tossing them at one of the small posts. He landed one and two but missed the third one. Damn.

"Come on, Uncle Clyde," Jared said. "Try again."

"Honey, I'm getting pretty tired," Nina complained. She held her arms wrapped gently around her abdomen.

"Teddy bear!" Rooney yelled. He wasn't sure himself if Rooney understood the relationship between landing the rings and getting a teddy bear but he doubted it. Nor did he really care.

Clyde pointed. "Three more rings."

"Three tosses for a dollar," the tattooed man said, handing Clyde the rings once more. "Get all three and…"

"Listen. I've got your spiel," Clyde told the man, whose eyes had an amber cloudy look and never quite met Clyde's.

This time Clyde got all three, though the third one spun for a moment and fell off. "Give me my teddy bear," he said.

"Sorry, fall-offs don't count," the man said, but he saw the look in Clyde's eyes. He paused a moment, then turned and grabbed a teddy bear the color of Pepto-Bismol and handed it to Rooney.

Though the tattooed man was a couple of inches taller and maybe twenty pounds heavier, Clyde reached across the counter and grabbed his food-stained T-shirt. "Now listen, you overgrown parrot," he whispered fiercely. "My sister here wants *that* teddy bear." He indicated the pastel blue-and-white bear she'd been pointing toward the whole time. "And you're going to let her have it. I'll give you either ten dollars or the roughest beating you've ever had in your life."

Clyde's words seemed to wake the man up. He hesitated and then looked at the others and then back at Clyde.

"Winner on post number one," he intoned. "Winner on post number one!"

"For the young lady," he said, and he took back the pink bear and gave the blue one to Rooney.

Clyde handed the man ten dollars and nodded to him.

Rooney clutched her teddy bear all the way home from the fair.

17

When they got back to the night-shrouded white-frame house Clyde saw that the red button was blinking on his answering machine. He mashed the button.

"Clyde? This here's Tolliver. I need you to meet me down here this evening. Call me back."

The call had come just after seven p.m.—long after Tolliver normally left the mortuary—so Clyde knew that something was up. It was eight-thirty now and he debated whether to return the call and while he was thinking the phone rang.

"Clyde McCune."

"Clyde? Get my message?"

Tolliver didn't sound pleased. So Clyde decided to sound as pleased as the old man did.

"What do you need? It's almost nine o'clock…"

"Don't give a flying fuck what time it is. I need a meeting with you. I need it now."

Clyde grimaced. The last thing he wanted was to drive over to the mortuary and listen to a bunch of complaints from his cantankerous employer.

"Can we meet on the phone? I'm pretty bushed."

"Come down here. See you in ten minutes."

"But—"

But the old man had hung up.

Clyde told Nina where he was going and pecked her on the cheek. "You okay?"

He asked because she didn't look okay. Her face was still pale as if *she* had been on the Ferris wheel with Rooney and might throw up any second. For Clyde's part, his stomach had mysteriously settled but he could use a drink. He remembered he had half a flask of J.D. in the glove compartment.

"I'm fine," she said in that wistful way she had that pulled at his balls.

"Be back soon!" he called as he walked out.

Nina mumbled, "Okay," and he was gone.

Another old saying of his brother's was "fit to be tied." He thought of this because when he got to the funeral home Tolliver was fit to be tied sure enough. He was pacing up and down his office. Somehow Clyde had expected this, which was why he'd fortified himself with a couple swallows of the J.D. as he drove through the town's quiet streets to the mortuary and parked his car next to Tolliver's beat-up pink Eldorado. He'd gone inside expecting a fight.

Tolliver had pointed Clyde to a visitor's chair in his cubbyhole and Tolliver himself sat at his battered roll-top desk. "I'll get right to it." He swiveled in his chair to face Clyde. Behind him the desk was covered with papers. Death certificates. Invoices. Around the back of Tolliver's head were bookcases stuffed with everything from textbooks on mortuary science—of course the old man never consulted these any longer—to filthy ashtrays for Tolliver's wet cigars and the old man's own flasks and little Styrofoam cups of half-drunk coffee that he never tidied up. Thank God a cleaning lady came in once a week. At least she took care of the ashtrays and the Styrofoam cups. She was instructed never to touch or move any of the books or papers.

"Looks like you've got your work cut out for you," Clyde said.

He gestured toward the mess on Tolliver's desk. He was deliberately ignoring what the old man had said and hadn't liked the sound of it. But finally Clyde relented. The old man was glaring at him.

"You wanted to see me?" Clyde said.

Tolliver coughed and said, "Folks're talking. You've been fooling around with Travis McCune's widow."

Clyde was taken aback. He hadn't expected anything like this.

He said, without thinking, "I'm Travis McCune's *brother*. All his property belongs to me."

"Property? Property?"

"I meant—"

"I know of two funerals we've lost to Jenkins down in Savannah because of this." Tolliver looked as though he were about to spit. "People wonder what kind of operation we're running here all of a sudden. With you living in sin with that poor man's wife."

Clyde's glaring-blue eyes shifted left and right. He said, "That's family business."

Tolliver slammed his gnarly brown fist down on the desktop. "It's my goddamn business! You're going to run this place into the ground."

Was that supposed to be a joke? Clyde felt that familiar hand of anger rise up the back of his neck. What did this old pecker have to do with whether Clyde and Nina were sleeping together or not? Why couldn't the narrow-minded townspeople (especially the old church biddies he knew were behind this) keep their mouths shut? Why did they give a bullcrap where he slept at night?

But they did care. He knew better in his gut.

"Now you've been a good worker around here, Clyde. People like you." Tolliver paused to let loose one of his wet phlegm-filled coughs. "They like you and until now they've respected you. Far as I can see, you've started to put this place in order and I've begun to feel you're like a son to me." Then he added, "Almost." Tolliver was staring just past Clyde's head to the opposite wall. "Enough so that I'd done made that new will I told you about that leaves you this place and my place out on the highway so you'll get everything soon as these cigars and that there bourbon"—he gestured toward his leather-covered flask—"get me once and for all. But I'll be damned if I ain't gonna change the will. I'll be damned if I'm going to allow—"

"Allow!" Clyde clenched his fists to keep from going into one of his rages but he saw that Tolliver noticed the fists. "What I do when I leave this place at night is *my* goddamn business."

The old man's forehead had bunched up into a mass of

wormlike wrinkles. "I'll be damned if it is. I should be damned for thinking you McCunes were a decent family... Your brother was all right, far as I could tell, but your daddy and granddaddy weren't no good and I see one apple that ain't fallen far from the tree. A lady I know saw Travis's widow at the bank and said she sure had gained some weight, but only in her stomach."

Clyde was sweating. He stood up. "You take that back about my daddy and grandpa."

Tolliver said, "Ain't gonna do it."

Now Clyde reached out and grabbed the old man's collar. Tolliver's string tie got in the way so Clyde paused to throw it neatly back over the man's skinny shoulder.

"Apologize." Clyde gave him a fierce look.

Tolliver stubbornly repeated, "Not gonna do it."

Not that Clyde had any special veneration for his father or grandpa. Clyde's grandfather died of drink and his father shot himself so maybe it was true they were no good. But it was the principle of the thing. You didn't go around bad-mouthing another man's kin. Especially to his face.

Tolliver said hoarsely, "Now let go o' me! You son of a *bitch!*"

"What do you mean by—"

"Let go of my—"

Clyde pulled the old man's head closer, then debated for a moment and finally decided the hell with this. His inheritance was lost. Everything was lost. Out of nowhere he thought of the Ferris wheel with its rainbow-colored cars and how it went around and around senselessly. He thought of poor Rooney screaming her head off because she'd gotten onto the wrong-colored car. Didn't we all go round and round without meaning and didn't we always choose poorly and besides that, how was he going to support his sister and his pregnant wife-to-be and their teenage son if the old man changed his will? If he was no longer the heir to Graceland Hills Funeral Home and the old man's residence to boot and no telling how much cash he'd gotten stacked up in the bank by now? Clyde tightened his grip on the old man's collar—after all, he was "SUPERman!"—and slammed Tolliver's head down on top of the desk. That felt good and right so he did it again. Then he sidled around so he could get a better purchase on the old man's neck and he took both hands and squeezed until the old man sat up straight in his chair in panic and his little dry tongue poked out between his lips like a corpse's. Clyde squeezed harder. A minute passed. Two minutes. The sight was harrowing so Clyde's hands abruptly went limp and he watched dispassionately as the old man's body fell to the floor. Unfortunately he'd landed face upwards and Clyde saw that his sunken cheeks had turned a purplish-blue.

He thought about what he had done and looked at the body and thought some more. "Shit." For emphasis he said again, "*Shit.*" And for good measure he kicked the old man in his stomach. Tolliver's little gray-blue tongue still poked out of his mouth.

But Clyde wasn't one to fool around so he got busy. His adrenaline pumped fiercely as he dragged the skinny old pecker into the prep room and found a body bag and with some effort stuffed him into the bag feet first. Then he opened one of the topmost refrigerator drawers and stuffed the body inside where it would keep (he reasoned) for at least a week and where perhaps for that long nobody would think to search for him. Then he turned and began looking around the place for giveaway signs of struggle and returned to the old man's office where he lifted up Tolliver's chair that had fallen over and rearranged his papers just as they had been until the office looked ordinarily messy as always. Luther would open the place tomorrow morning and not think anything was amiss. Clyde would write a note for him. Unless somehow he got to fiddling around in the refrigerator drawers (which was unlikely) Luther wouldn't find Tolliver anytime soon. Luther just wasn't the type to poke around. He minded his own business. Clyde took a sheet of computer paper and wrote a neatly lettered message:

Hey, Luther, Tolliver went to visit some sick kin in Montana and wants you to run the place for a few days. So it's double pay for you and Guthrie and we'll settle up when we get back. There's just old lady Maxwell's funeral pending and you know where she is. All by herself in the viewing room. So you'll have an easy time of it. Clyde McCune. PS If neither of us is back by Monday then you just run things on your own for a day or two. Pay will be double. And turn away any new business. Just say the boss is "indisposed."

If Clyde hadn't been so worried, and if his adrenaline hadn't been pump-pumping, he'd have surely smiled at his cleverness. But he did not. He did another thing; he went to the safe and punched in the code. Tolliver had given it to him not long ago on a tiny piece of paper and Clyde had put it in his wallet but hadn't used it yet. Now he got the shock of his life—there was a bulky manila envelope and he knew what was inside before he even touched it. Something about the shape. Something about the smell. He opened the envelope and started counting the money. His hands were trembling. His body was trembling. There were stacks and stacks of hundred-dollar bills and each stack was held together by a rubber band. He lifted one and removed the rubber band and impulsively threw the dozens of bills up into the air. He allowed himself a "Hot damn!" But he'd embarrassed himself and so now with a grim smile he picked up all the bills and stuffed them back in the envelope with the others. Then he made a phone call and shut off the lights and left.

Ten minutes later he came in the front door to Nina's house and told her they were going on a trip. She had been cleaning up the kitchen. "A trip? Sweetie, what do you mean? We can't just—"

"Sure we can. Know what Tolliver wanted?" He pulled out a single wad of the cash he'd taken from the safe—he hadn't counted it all yet and had left the rest in the trunk—and shook it in the air. "Wanted to give me these Ben Franklins as a bonus and told me to take everybody on a week's vacation. Hot damn! We're going out West!"

Nina kept giving him a blank look. "But—but Jared has

school tomorrow. And Rooney, she can't go, I can't take care of—"

"Rooney's staying at Billie and Elton's." That was the call he'd made: to Billie. Billie had recently suggested that Rooney could come stay for a while—generous Billie—and Clyde had the sneaking thought of how much simpler life would be without his needy sister. Then he'd pushed the thought away. A moment later he'd pushed his guilt away. Now that he'd gotten rid of Tolliver it was essential that he travel light and quick. Having Rooney along would give him away for sure. And besides without her Nina and Jared would be happier—this he knew. He had to think of them and not just of Rooney. Besides his sister would be safe and happy at Billie's and he'd decided in a snap. To Billie's she would go.

Nina looked miffed. "How long have you been planning this?"

"For about forty-five minutes."

That seemed to mollify Nina. She smiled faintly. "But really, what about Jared's school? He can't miss a whole week. It's almost time for exams…"

"I just called Father Zach and told him what we were doing." This wasn't true but it sounded right. Wasn't that what mattered? "He said Jared was such a good student that he could make up the exams when he got back and for us to have a great time."

"But—out West?"

"Sure. I've always wanted to visit Santa Fe, haven't you? I love that kind of country and that kind of weather. It'll be cool and dry—not muggy as a swamp the way it is here."

Nina seemed stymied. She had run out of arguments.

Clyde said, "Now let's get started. And pack a suitcase for Rooney."

Jared and Rooney were upstairs and heard none of this. When Clyde and Nina stopped into Jared's room and told him, he looked blank for a moment and then said, "Yay." Clyde grinned. That's all the reaction you had when you were a young teenager: Yay. Then they crossed to Rooney's doorway to find his sister playing with the big teddy bear Clyde had won at the fair. She appeared to be trying to force the bear to hug her but Clyde did not stop to ponder this except to think: Good luck.

"Want to visit Aunt Billie and Uncle Elton?" he asked her.

"Aunt Billie...?" Rooney said.

"Sure, remember from Christmas? They bought you all those presents?"

Rooney cried, "Visit Aunt Billie!"

Nina smiled and stepped forward into the room.

"We'd better pack your things. We're leaving in the morning, I guess."

Clyde corrected her. "No. Let's leave tonight."

"Tonight? But, Clyde, it's after ten o'clock."

"I love to drive at night. We'll stop in Atlanta first. We'll spend a day or two there. If the weather stays nice, we can have a picnic in Piedmont Park. We can visit the botanical gardens—"

"But Clyde, I'm so tired..."

"Hon, you can sleep in the car."

He could see that Nina was smiling again. A little "hon" or "sweetie" worked every time. She seemed to have worked through her patch of sarcastic behavior and had begun smiling more. And he could tell she liked being told what to do. A women's libber would choke on that but it was true. Something in her was always waiting for him. Listening for his voice. His guidance. And just now something in his tone of voice had settled the matter.

18

They packed furiously. Nina asked if they were taking too many clothes for a week's trip. Didn't they have laundromats in Santa Fe? She'd noticed that Clyde had packed not a few but *all* of his shirts both long-sleeve and short-sleeve.

"Why so many?" she asked him.

"I go through them like you wouldn't believe."

He'd always lied to her to some extent but now every word out of his mouth seemed to be a lie. He felt no qualms of conscience about this even when he thought of old Tolliver's corpse in the prep room refrigerator.

Nina couldn't know this but they were never coming back.

As Nina packed her clothes Clyde fussed about her working so slowly. She rose up from her suitcase with her elbows jutting out. "Is there a deadline?" But she was smiling.

He gave her a relenting look. "I'm sorry. I guess I'm just excited."

He bent to her. They kissed.

Again her wan smile. "Give me ten minutes, can you? Ten little minutes? And in the meantime you can go help Jared and Rooney."

So Clyde did that. He packed one large bag for Rooney— he knew that Billie would buy her all new things—and a gym bag for Jared with two pairs of jeans and four shirts. Nina was right: laundromats were everywhere. What he'd said to Nina about being excited was a dramatic understatement for he felt his head might explode. By the time somebody discovered old Tolliver's body they would be out West. Free as a flock of birds. Free as the cool dry air itself.

Somehow they managed to fit everything into the trunk of the Toyota and the four of them (the five of them if you counted the gigantic teddy bear) were inside and bumping in reverse along the graveled driveway toward the street. Then Clyde said, "Damn. We're low on gas."

Jared whistled in a way intended to make fun of Clyde. "There's tons of all-night places on the interstate."

Clyde grinned back at him. "Sure there are. Sure there are."

When they pulled up in front of Billie's house Clyde paused a moment and then told the others, "Kiss Rooney good-bye." Jared kissed her first and then Nina met Rooney halfway from the front seat and they kissed. Clyde's heart was slamming in his chest. He gave his sister a peck on the cheek that didn't begin to express what he was feeling. He'd been taking care of her for so many years he couldn't count them. It was like someone was sawing off his leg.

But he said, "Jared, walk Rooney up to the porch. Billie's expecting her."

"Me? Why me?" Jared said.

"Just do it for me. You carry her bag because she's got that teddy bear and all."

"Yes, master," Jared said.

Clyde and Nina waited tense and silent while Jared got Rooney's suitcase out of the trunk and then walked her up the sidewalk. Rooney zigzagged as she walked because of the weight of the teddy bear she still held as she poked along. The sight of her tore at Clyde's heart but he said nothing.

Nina said, "Are you sure you don't want—"

And Clyde said, "No."

Naturally Billie would want Jared to come inside but as soon as the door opened Jared had started backing away as if obeying some psychic command of Clyde's. Good boy. Good boy. Finally Rooney stumbled inside and then Billie came back to the doorway. She was wearing a velour bathrobe and had curlers in her hair. She waved hesitantly. Nina and Clyde waved back.

Jared kept backing away from the door, and when he reached the stairs he turned and went down them two at a time. Then he was in the car. The three of them glanced up toward Billie who wore a bewildered look, and they waved one last time. Billie waved back with the air of a person who does not know exactly what she is doing.

Rooney was no longer visible in the opened doorway.

They would never see her again.

☙

Clyde had almost choked. He'd had to swallow his emotion. But he knew she was in safer hands than his and once they were on the oiled highway out of town and heading toward the interstate he felt better. Not much but a little better. A couple of times Nina had cast him worried glances and patted his kneecap but Clyde did not respond to this. She could not possibly understand. But, yes, he did feel better. He called over his shoulder to Jared, "Atlanta here we come."

"Hey, Mom, Clyde," Jared said. "Can we visit the Hanrattys while we're there?"

Clyde said, "Sure. We can do whatever we want."

"I miss seeing Linda," Jared said wistfully.

"I'm sure you do, honey," Nina said.

Clyde said suggestively, "I'm sure you *do.*" And Jared slapped him on the shoulder. Clyde said, "Ouch." He grinned.

They had reached the interstate and sure enough there was a Shell station with its "Open" sign lit in red neon. Clyde rifled through his wallet and found a twenty and handed it to Jared. "Fill 'er up."

"Yes, master," Jared said again.

While he was filling the car Clyde and Nina sat tensely together. She glanced at him once or twice but he did not want to see the look she gave him. He knew she was skeptical. She did not know what was happening but one thing she knew was that she didn't believe a word he'd said and probably never would again.

Clyde said, "Don't worry."

Nina said nothing. She stared through the windshield.

When Jared got back into the car Clyde gunned the engine

and they pulled away from the station. Here was the interstate to Atlanta. Clyde pulled onto the right lane slowly and almost ceremoniously.

He thought: This is the beginning.

He thought: Whatever happens next is beyond my imagining.

Jared sat forward with his arms crossed on the seat back like a much smaller child. "How far to Atlanta?" he said.

"Three hours. Three and a half."

"It won't even be morning when we get there."

"Nope."

"You like driving at night, Uncle Clyde?"

"Yep."

Finally Jared eased back into his seat and brought out some gadget or game he'd brought along with him in that flaking leather satchel of his. He'd had it for years. The inside of the car grew quiet but it was an ominous quiet. Clyde and Nina certainly heard it. Probably even Jared would hear it if he paused in his game to listen. But he continued playing the game, which made a faint clicking sound.

Finally Clyde looked over at Nina. "You okay?"

Nina said dryly, "Sure I am." She kept staring out the windshield at the highway and the star-filled night sky above.

"We'll see your friend Kay. You can call her tomorrow."

"Sure," Nina said.

She didn't seem inclined to say any more so Clyde didn't either and that forbidding silence filled the car. Clyde drove about fifty and knew he would not get pulled over. They looked like a normal white-bread American family and it occurred to him that's what they were. All families had secrets. All families lived together inside a silence they all heard but would not acknowledge. It filled the car. It strained the car to bursting. Clyde nodded. It didn't matter and would not get them pulled over.

They drove without stopping all the way to Atlanta.

BOOK TWO

PART FOUR

JARED

19

W e're going on a trip, bud."
That's what Clyde had said. He'd spoken the words casually, as though saying they were going out for a pizza or a movie. Yet somehow Jared was not surprised. Clyde was known for sudden whims, spontaneous adventures. One Sunday morning he'd taken them all out to the lake south of town; Jared and Nina had helped him pack a picnic lunch of tuna salad, potato salad, pickles. Though the day had been fairly chilly, they'd had an excellent time, Jared thought. There was that word everybody used. But he liked that idea, *he was like anyone else*, though knowing it wasn't true.

It was Clyde who was always insisting that Jared was special in some way. That he was "a good kid," "smart as a whip"; that he was going to "make his mark in the world, you bet." Jared showed nothing but inside he writhed with pleasure at such praise, not caring if Clyde's words were true or not. For his own part, he didn't think he was anything special. There was always a part of him sitting back, observing, judging, and he judged no one more harshly than himself. It didn't matter what innocent, early-teenage thing he was doing—shooting baskets in the school gym, thumbing through the newspaper pretending to be interested in the movies or sports, fiddling with his computer or with his Rubik's cube, which he could "solve" with startling speed and efficiency. There was always a part of him set back in judgment, wondering at this kid pretending to be a kid, presenting a front to the world that seemed healthy, normal. That's what he craved: normalcy. Even now, hurtling through the late-night darkness in the Toyota with his strange uncle and his quietly rebellious mother, that mismatched couple in the front seat, he thought himself and his family more normal than at any time in the past. It seemed as if his deceased father had been a cancer in his family's well-being and now that cancer, that infection, had been excised, so they could go forward again, healthy, free. Such thoughts buoyed him even as his fingers worked hectically and he cried, "Got it!"—then handed the perfectly aligned puzzle up toward the front seat for Clyde's inspection.

Clyde gave a low whistle, impressed. His mother looked back and smiled tensely. "Smarty pants," she said.

Clyde glanced over to her, winking. "Told you," he said.

Jared's mother said nothing. Ever since Clyde had announced, so excitedly, that they were going on a trip (late at night, yet) his mother had seemed skeptical, though she'd packed as Clyde instructed her and had pulled her hair back in a ponytail as, oddly, Clyde had also suggested, claiming he'd always wanted to see her hair that way. It accented her face, he said. It accented her beautiful skin, he said. It didn't take long for Jared to detect his mother's strategy—simply do what Clyde wished, no matter how eccentric his wish might be. It was easier to acquiesce than to question or object, after all, and Jared supposed to an extent he had copied his mother's behavior, quietly packing his clothes and toiletries as though they'd be gone for a long while. When he asked Clyde how long, his uncle had said, "Maybe a week— maybe longer," but he would be no more specific than that. And Jared did not question him further. Jared had taken the Rubik's cube out of the satchel he'd brought into the backseat with him, had grasped it in one hand as though it were a token of security, something he could always solve in a time of uncertainty or distress. And in fact since they'd left town he'd worked the puzzle three or four times, pleased that he could still solve it so quickly, that he could create out of his fast-working fingers the correct pattern, the perfection the game demanded. *Maybe a week—maybe longer.* But the game he was playing gave him an answer that was precise, known. It was something at which he could not fail, the opposite number of his future that seemed as murky and ill-lit as the backseat of this car.

Clyde had glanced back at the clicking sound of the game Jared had executed yet again, so Jared held the solved puzzle up toward the front seat so his uncle could see. Clyde grinned. "Got it. You got it," he said. This time his mother did not glance over and Jared pulled the plastic cube back and dropped it into the satchel. He felt foolish—like a child. What kind of pathetic approval was he seeking from Clyde that he could not provide for himself? After all, he was a teenager. In some countries, kids his age went into the military, left their homes forever, and here he sat in the backseat playing a game like a much smaller child. This was something he'd noticed about himself—he was fourteen but he was much older, mentally, so he often found himself impersonating a kid of exactly his age. He hated this impulse in himself. Someday he supposed he'd be grown up like Clyde, who seemed so definite, self-contained, sure of himself, but he could not quite imagine that time. He could not yet imagine the man he would become.

As though to confirm his childishness, he asked Clyde, "How far to Atlanta?"

His uncle laughed. Even his mother turned her head and smiled slightly.

"Lord," Clyde said. "That question again."

"How far?" Jared repeated. He might have been eight years old.

Clyde made a show of checking the trip odometer. "We've gone one-ten," he said. "So another hundred, I guess. Maybe a little more."

Jared looked at the dashboard clock.

"It'll be around five when we get there," he said, "not even morning yet. We can't show up at the Hanrattys that early."

"Honey, you've already asked about that," his mother said, and of course she was right. He wanted everything to be logical, to make sense.

"Like I said, we'll stop at a motel." Then Clyde added, fancifully, "And behind the desk there'll be this sad, pot-bellied night manager, with a dead cigar hanging out of his mouth."

"Dead?" Jared asked.

"Unlit," Clyde said. "Use those smarts of yours, kid. Anyway, he'll show us to our rooms."

"We—we'll have separate rooms?"

"We'll have separate rooms," Clyde affirmed, glancing at Jared's mother. "You can solve your little Rubik's cube all night, every night, if you want to."

This sounded demeaning so Jared went silent. He'd finally gotten used to Clyde and his mother sleeping together, sharing a bed—after all, his mother's pregnancy was beginning to show—but he didn't care to sleep in the same room with them. When he thought of this matter he felt a sinking in his heart, as though he weren't really a smart kid, a good-looking kid... But he tried to put this out of his mind.

"Then what?" he said. "We'll go to Mrs. Hanratty's?"

"No," Clyde said, fancifully again, "then we'll go get a haircut and have breakfast."

"A haircut?" Jared said.

"Honey, enough questions," his mother said gently.

But Jared didn't need a haircut, he thought, puzzled, and neither did Clyde. He'd gotten one a few days ago.

"Okay," he told his uncle. "Then what?"

"Then your mom here will get on the phone and call—what's her name, honey?"

"Kay," Nina said tersely.

"Yeah. Kay. Kay Hanratty."

"And then?" Jared asked.

Jared's mother turned back to him. "Sweetie, we're hoping Kay and Linda won't mind if we stay with them for a night or two. Before—before we head out of town."

Clyde added, "Motels are expensive, kid. We've got to watch our funds."

Jared had held his mother's gaze, as though hoping to see there some sign of what they were doing, what it all meant. But her eyes held that same dreamy look he'd glimpsed in them when she was packing, methodically, skillfully as though performing an action dictated by some alien voice inside her head. Then she blinked at him, and smiled.

"Don't worry, Jared. It's just a little vacation."

"But why didn't we bring Rooney with us?"

Clyde bristled at this. "In the way," he said. "She would have been in the way. Besides, if anything happened to—"

"But you don't care if something happens to *us*?" The question had come from nowhere; he hadn't meant to ask it, hadn't been aware of the words forming in his mind or the way they sounded when spoken. He saw that his uncle's narrow shoulders had stiffened, like his grip on the steering wheel; Clyde didn't like being questioned, and Jared knew that he was being an annoying kid, once again impersonating that boy of a much younger age… "I mean—it's just that—" Jared stammered.

"It's all right, don't worry about it," Clyde said evenly, but still Jared could tell he'd seriously annoyed his uncle and he hadn't wanted to do that. "Look, Kay is good company for your mother, and Linda is good company for you. Don't you want to see Linda?"

Jared hesitated. "Sure."

"Sure? That's all? Earlier you seemed—"

"Yes—I mean, sure, I want to see Linda." He'd taken on the same zombie-like tone his mother had used.

Nina said, "She'll be thrilled to see you, I'm sure. It's the weekend, so you can do some things together—take a walk around the neighborhood, find a place and get something to eat. You'll want some time alone with Linda, won't you?"

Jared answered honestly. "I don't know."

"Sure you will," Clyde said. "And your mother will want to catch up with Kay. Meantime I'll be figuring out what to do."

Jared said, "What to do?"

Clyde said, "That's right, goddamn it. What we're going to do next. Where we're going to go."

Santa Fe, Jared thought. You said we were going to Santa Fe… But Jared knew finally it was time for him to shut up. He looked out the window at the relentless passing of the darkened trees and fields. Here was middle Georgia. He knew that if it was daytime he'd see the deepening green of the trees leafed out here in late spring, and the occasional barbed-wire fence enclosing a field with cows all facing in the same direction, chewing their cud with meaningless energy and a soulful emptiness in their eyes. But it was night and so he saw only the clustered trees passing incessantly, their branches tipped in moonlight, and the occasional whitish gleam of a farmhouse set far back from the highway. All this bedraggled scenery, he thought, stayed basically the same while they rushed along, hurrying to Atlanta for no purpose he could understand. He thought about Linda Hanratty—her slender, graceful body, her dark hair in girlish pigtails hanging over each collarbone, her intelligent conversation about books and school. Yes, he did look forward to seeing Linda, their nightly phone calls had stoked his attraction to her... He could imagine that wondering, questioning look in her eyes when she asked, as inevitably she would, what the McCunes were doing in the city, and Jared would have to look back at her and shrug his shoulders. He didn't know. He really had no idea. But he would say nothing, of course. After mumbling something about a "vacation" he would simply change the subject.

That's what Clyde had done, Jared noticed, when he'd gotten angry at Jared a few minutes ago. He'd started talking of something else, as if not wanting to explode, to say something that couldn't be taken back. Clyde was unpredictable that way—you didn't know what might anger him, set him off. The other night at dinner, just as they were starting to eat, Clyde had carried his plateful of food and emptied it into the trash, uneaten, then had come back to the table and just sat there staring into space. Offended, Nina had asked, "Was there something wrong with your dinner? Why did you *do* that, Clyde?" Clyde had simply glared at her and said, "Because I wanted to." When Rooney made a move to lift her untouched plate, too, Clyde slammed his fist down on the table and moved the plate back into place beneath Rooney's rounded, perplexed face. He said to her, "Eat.

Eat." And she ate, and then Nina and Jared ate, and nobody said anything more for the rest of the meal.

Most of the time, though, Clyde was good to him, and to Nina as well. He and Nina had their arguments, spurting like a suddenly lit match in a darkened room, but then dying down again, dying out altogether. To Jared's knowledge Clyde had never struck her. Certainly Clyde had never struck *him*, though Jared knew that at times he sorely tested his uncle's patience. What was this need in Jared always to know, to question, to badger the two adults who ran his life—was this part of getting older, becoming a teenager, or was it some trait peculiar to him and his family's peculiar life? He didn't know, and he supposed he didn't care. He was still too young to openly defy either Clyde or his mother, so he merely asked questions in his dully repetitive, almost whining way, wondering when he would truly grow up, when his maturity would match the lowering tone of his voice. His mother and Clyde both kidded him about the "deep" and "manly" voice he'd acquired during the last year, and for the occasional squeakiness of his voice as he went through puberty. But he'd always turned away, embarrassed. He couldn't help any of this, he thought, so it was best just to ignore it all, to turn his back. Someday he supposed he would be a grown-up male, like Clyde, and such teenage anxieties would be far behind him, scarcely recalled.

He longed for such a time.

As Jared had predicted, they began seeing the rosy-lit sky above Atlanta around five o'clock; they had already exited onto the interstate that led into town. Jared felt his heart beating erratically, excitedly. He'd been to Atlanta only a couple of times, though the last time was years ago, and he remembered his father's admonition that they stay "north of Interstate 20"—that is, in the whiter areas of town. The south side of town was mostly African-American, evidently, and Jared could hardly imagine it. He knew only the tall buildings of midtown, the skyscrapers of north Atlanta—the Buckhead area—as they flashed in the sunlight. Here were the fancy malls—Lenox

Square, Phipps Plaza—where they'd gone shopping that last time, lingering in Phipps to have lunch and see a movie at the cineplex; it was a movie starring Mel Gibson, he remembered, an action-adventure film of some kind, but other than that his memory failed him. He'd been only seven or eight years old... This was before his father's drinking had become really bad, before he'd lost the energy to go anywhere with his family.

How different life was with Clyde, he thought; despite the uncertainty and occasional turmoil, how grateful he was to be part of *a family* again, even though Clyde had not married his mother—not yet—and even though Jared was almost old enough, or so he thought, to strike out on his own. As much as he enjoyed his uncle's company, and his mother's, he thought how daring it would be to sneak away from the motel where they were headed, to hitchhike somewhere, maybe go north toward Chattanooga, or Nashville, or anywhere else, some strange city that was only a word to him, with no associations or memories attached. But of course he would never do this. He remembered that he was a "good kid," and even—to borrow a term they'd learned in theology class this past year—"an ethical kid," and he wouldn't be able to worry his mother like that. To run away would be a wholly selfish act, that was a certainty, and Jared wasn't capable of that.

Clyde, who knew the city well, made a series of turns in an area he told them was "midtown, not far from the park," and finally pulled up to a beige-stucco building with neon signs. The vertical sign over the front entrance, lit in blue neon, said "Vacancy."

"Well, here we are," Clyde said, easing into a guest parking space. "Home at last." He added, "For a day or two, anyway."

Nina touched his arm. "I'm sure Kay will have a spare room," she said. "And Jared can sleep on her couch."

"Gee thanks," Jared said, in an amused tone to let them know he wasn't serious. A couch would be fine with him.

They came through the entrance and sure enough there was a sole night manager, but he wasn't fat and there was no cigar in his mouth. In fact, one of the first things Jared had noticed was a sign behind the desk that read NO SMOKING. And the manager was a tiny, wizened-looking Black man, his dark arms (he wore a sleeveless shirt) covered in tattoos that he meant, evidently, to display proudly. There was a sense of display, too, to his manner, his gesturing the McCunes inside, telling them, "Welcome!" in an overdone loud voice, putting together some paperwork behind the desk exactly as if he'd been waiting just for them. "Come on in, don't be shy," the man said, and it was true that the McCunes, even Clyde, were hanging back a little, as if unsure how you checked into a motel room. But Clyde found his voice. "Couple a rooms," he said curtly. "One for my wife and me, an adjoining for our son here." Nina and Jared both glanced at him, and then at each other, but neither said a word. They'd both learned that you did not contradict Clyde or you would pay and pay.

"Yes, sir, let's see…adjoining, hmm." He shuffled through more papers. "We're having a busy few days just now, so I may have to put you and your wife in a second-floor room, the boy just beneath you. How would that—"

"No," Clyde interrupted. "I said adjoining. Adjoining rooms."

Jared didn't see why it mattered but he said nothing. Nina stood with her head slightly bent, as though the men were speaking a language she could not understand.

"So they have to be adjoining rooms," the man said. "Adjoining, let's see…"

Finally the clerk's eyes, with their pronounced red veins running through the yellowed whites, seemed to light up. "All right, all right—I think I've found the perfect thing for you nice people. It's a pair of rooms in the back of the building. Now, I'm afraid they're not near the pool, but at least they should be nice and quiet and—"

"That's fine," Clyde said. "So long as they're adjoining."

The clerk nodded fervently. "They are, they are, and we always aim to please our customers," he said. "Now, if you'll just show me your credit card, and sign here, and here."

Clyde signed the papers quickly. "No credit card. I'm paying cash."

"Cash in full?" the clerk asked. "In advance?"

"That's fine."

So the man waited patiently with his pink-skinned palm turned upward as Clyde doled out the amount he had requested. Several twenties, a ten, a few ones.

"Thank *you*, sir," the clerk said. "Shall I show you to your—?"

"We'll find them," Clyde said sharply. But then he stopped, reached back into his wallet, and pulled out another ten. "Here you go. Thanks for your help."

It wasn't the first time Jared had his breath taken away by Clyde's generosity. It was like him to be brusque and then open-handed like this, as though compensating for his near-rudeness. Jared didn't quite understand, but in a way he did understand. That was Clyde. That was the way Clyde was. *Because I wanted to.*

The three of them hobbled down a corridor toward the back of the building, each carrying a bag or two, and found their assigned rooms. After opening the first door and gesturing Nina and Jared inside, he said, "Ta da!" This was ironic, of course, as the room featured a worn carpet of some faded shade of green, a couple of beds with lightweight bedspreads, and some "paintings," cheap reproductions, over each bed.

"Home sweet home," Nina said dismally.

"C'mon, it's not that bad," Clyde said.

"It's only for a night or two," Jared said. "Right?"

"Depends on your mom's friend. Whether she's hospitable enough to invite us to stay."

"Let's hope she will," Nina said, uncertainly. "I just hope she has a guest room. If she has only a two-bedroom, of course, Linda will be in the second room...so I'm not sure."

Clyde said, "Hope is the thing with feathers."

"Feathers?" Jared said.

"Sure, kid. That's poetry. Don't they teach you anything in that school of yours?"

Jared shrugged. He still held on to his satchel, waiting for Clyde to unlock the room next door. "Guess not."

"It perches in the soul," Clyde said, cutting his eyes toward Nina, who ignored him.

"Okay," Jared said.

"Come on, you two!" Clyde said. "It's the first day of our vacation—I know we're a bit sleepy, but let's get into the spirit, okay?"

Jared said, in a monotone, "Yay."

Clyde reached across and slapped him on the butt. "Smart ass." He looked to see if Nina was smiling; she wasn't.

"C'mon," Clyde told Jared, "let's go next door. I'm sure your room will be much more exciting."

"Yeah. I'm sure," Jared said, in that same monotone.

Again Clyde swatted his butt, and Jared went out the door. Clyde followed him, then unlocked the adjoining door, which revealed a room almost identical to Clyde and Nina's.

"Here you go, son," Clyde said. "Two beds in here, too, so you have a decision to make. A very momentous decision."

"You're funny," Jared said flatly.

"You're screwed," Clyde said, and began chasing him around the room. Jared jumped onto one of the beds, followed by Clyde, and soon enough they were on the other bed, wrestling strenuously. Jared managed to get Clyde in a headlock, and Clyde said in a strained voice, "Let go, you asshole," and in case Clyde wasn't kidding Jared did let go. Immediately Clyde laughed aloud and put Jared in the same headlock. Jared tried to say, "*You're* the assho—" but he could not speak. He could not breathe. Finally, laughing, Clyde let go, while Jared took several deep, lunging breaths.

Then Jared began laughing too.

Clyde stood up from the bed, adjusted his clothes, and said, "Now make yourself presentable, kid. We're going to get a haircut."

Jared frowned. "Hey, why are we—"

But Clyde was already out the door.

❧

Nina was staying behind at the motel, saying she needed to unpack and take a shower. "I'm filthy," she said.

"So what does that say about Jared and me?" Clyde said.

"You're filthy too."

Clyde shrugged. "We'll shower when we get back. Come on, hoss," he said to Jared. "We'll let your mom have some time to herself."

Jared followed Clyde outside. The last thing Jared wanted was to get back in that car, with its smell of road dust and fast-food containers, but something in him wanted to obey Clyde, even in this case when what Clyde wanted was ridiculous. The last thing either of them needed was a haircut, and this was the oddest time imaginable for them to get one. So he tried again.

"Hey, why are we getting a haircut?"

"Hey, you ask too many questions."

"Your hair looks fine, and I don't need one, either."

"Is that a fact."

So Jared gave up. They were driving along a street called Cheshire Bridge, and at eight-thirty in the morning, the sun already bright and warm, the area looked pretty seedy, with its abandoned dirt-stained store fronts, single-level strip malls, porn shops, "smoke" shops. Clyde made a turn off Cheshire Bridge, then a second turn, and Jared saw another strip mall where there was, sure enough, a glass window with "BARBER SHOP" emblazoned on the front, and an old-fashioned barber pole just outside the front door.

Clyde pulled into the graveled parking lot and stopped. He turned to Jared and said, "Don't fight me, now."

"Fight you? I'm not going to fight you, I was just asking—"

"Just remember what I said. Don't fight me."

Jared shrugged. He thought to tell Clyde, I'm fourteen, not four—why would I fight you? But he didn't bother. As though they were playing chess, Clyde was always one or two steps ahead of him.

"No problem," Jared said.

Clyde laughed. "No problem," he repeated. "That's my kid."

Jared couldn't help thinking of his father and that night they'd picked him up at the state hospital. *He* was the one who'd needed a haircut.

They went inside and since one of the two barbers, a young dark-haired fellow, was just finishing up a man in a blue-and-white seersucker suit, they were both available soon after Clyde and Jared sat down in a couple of sagging chairs with ripped orange vinyl. "We'll have ours done at the same time," Clyde had said to the middle-aged barber with half-glasses, who'd been lounging in one of the padded barber chairs, reading the paper. "Once your colleague here gets done…" Within about five minutes, the young barber had finished and the man in the seersucker suit paid and left. Jared noticed that the man tipped the barber a single dollar bill. Clyde would do better.

Minutes later Clyde and Jared were sitting in their barber chairs, side by side. The smells of disinfectant and sweetish pomade were almost overpowering. Jared felt a roiling in his stomach, like the onset of nausea, but he liked old-fashioned places like this. He recalled that his father and even his grandfather had gotten their hair cut in a similar place, just off the town square. And there was a smaller, even dingier barber shop on the outskirts of town, which his grandfather hadn't cared for because it catered to both whites and Blacks… But no "hair salons" for them; the nearest such fancy place was probably in Macon, anyway. Jared had grown up with old-school barber shops like this one, with their dirty-greenish floor tiles, their dust-balls in the corners, the red-faced barbers in their starched but stained white smocks.

Jared sat nervously in his chair, his sneakered feet twitching against the dirt-encrusted footrest. He felt sick, that kind of apprehension that something bad was about to happen. His cheeks had turned pale, he could feel that, but most of all his stomach was upset, churning, as though filled with hot rocks… Clyde had whispered something to the two barbers, both of whom had nodded, and now he said, "Me first."

"Okey-doke," said the younger barber. He took his electric razor and, beginning in the front, began cutting Clyde's hair off, all the way down to his scalp. Three, four, five long strokes and the job was almost done. Jared had not turned toward his uncle but was staring at him in the mirrored wall across the room, noticing that Clyde had a glum but self-satisfied look on his face. Clyde said, "Start on him," and Jared felt paralyzed, his heart hammering wildly, the moment he heard the middle-aged barber's electric trimmer start and felt it make a deep swath through his thick dark-brown hair. Right down the middle. Right down to the scalp. Clyde's hair had been short, so for Jared it took longer for the haircut. Jared kept his head very still ("Don't fight me") but let his eyes drop, and he saw the enormous swaths of his hair drifting down on the black smock the barber had swung in a circular motion, like a matador's, to protect Jared's clothes. He felt hair tickling his nostrils but he didn't dare take an arm out from under the smock to wipe it away; he felt he was going to be sick. His stomach churned. Some if not most of Jared's hair drifted to the floor. He didn't dare look up to witness his and Clyde's bald heads, even after the barbers had trimmed the sides, run their fingers across their scalps, and said, "Okay?"

Clyde said, "Okay," and Jared looked at his uncle first. Uncle Clyde, with a bald head! His first impulse was to laugh. If he'd been sitting in the waiting chair, still with his full head of hair, no doubt he would have laughed. But as he felt the breeze of the lazily turning ceiling fan across his bare head he knew there was nothing funny about any of this. He sat there with a glum look similar to his uncle's, but he did not feel self-satisfied at all. Instead he felt ridiculous, ashamed.

"Now," the older barber said, tapping Jared's shoulder, "you can start growing it back again."

Finally Jared's gaze lurched over and in the mirror he saw his own unrecognizable head. The barber had done his work well: there was not even a bit of stubble left. After cutting Jared's hair, the man had rubbed some lotion along his scalp, which felt cool but not really soothing. He noticed craters and bumps in his skull that he hadn't known were there.

"Well, kid, what do you think?" Clyde said, winking at his own barber in the mirror. "I guess your Miss Linda Hanratty will be surprised, won't she?"

Jared's stomach kept writhing. About fifty miles outside Atlanta they'd stopped at a fast-food place and Jared had ordered egg sandwiches and a glass of milk, and now he wondered—had that meal made him sick? Or was it the aura of this smelly old barbershop, where he'd been made to look so ridiculous? He didn't know which, and now he supposed it didn't matter. His stomach gave another painful, writhing lunge, and Jared bent his head and threw up all over the black smock. He was very careful, since that was his way, to lift the sides of the smock so none of the vomit would hit the floor, the chair, or the barber's shiny black shoes.

20

Nina had covered her face with her hands, her shoulders shaking. Was she laughing? Was she crying? Jared couldn't be sure. He and his uncle stood there by the door and Nina, fresh from her shower, dressed in an outfit Jared hadn't seen before—navy-and-white striped blouse, white wraparound skirt—kept her palms over her face for what seemed like several minutes but must have been a few seconds.

She breathed, "Oh—oh my God…"

Clyde tilted his head this way and that, preening. He looked like a different man—as an afterthought, he'd had the barber shave off his mustache too.

It turned out that Jared's mother had been laughing. But there were tears in her eyes. There was something extreme about her reaction that troubled Jared. His mother usually didn't behave this way.

"Stop it, Mom," he said.

Clyde glanced aside, irritated. Then he said, "Oh, let her have a good laugh."

Nina was shaking her head. "I'm sorry, I—I didn't mean to—it's just that—" She came over to Jared, tentatively running her hand over his bald head, and down to his ears. "My poor baby! His beautiful hair…"

"We thought we'd surprise you," Clyde said, though Jared wasn't sure what he meant.

Nina glanced at him, irritated. "Well, you did that. You surprised me."

"Why're you all dressed?" Clyde asked. "We need to sleep. We've been up all—"

"Sleep?" The way his mother spoke the word, it had a foreign sound. "I thought we were going to Kay's. I want to see her, and I know that Jared wants to see Linda…"

"Would everybody stop saying that?" Jared said, with an uncharacteristic truculence that must have had something to do with his haircut, his extreme self-consciousness.

Clyde laughed. "He's chafing at the bit, that's for sure."

"I'm *not*—"

"But we need to sleep," Clyde said. "We'll visit this evening. These rooms are paid for, we might as well use them."

Nina blinked her eyes, slowly. She said, "All right…"

"That's my girl," Clyde said. He picked a key with its small plastic attachment off the desk and handed it to Jared. "Here you go, bud. See you in a while."

But Jared was staring at his mother. She looked so fresh, her auburn hair pulled back again in that unaccustomed pony tail; he hadn't liked the new hair style at first, or the idea that Clyde had insisted she adopt it, but he had to admit that she looked better, younger, almost like a college girl. Her complexion was pink and clear, and from her mild green eyes you wouldn't know she wasn't rested. He wanted to say something to her, issue some protest, but he couldn't quite put his uneasiness into words.

Grudgingly, he took the key from Clyde. "Okay," he said. He glanced at the bedside clock and saw that it was only 11:15. "Around five, maybe? We could invite Linda and her mother out for dinner."

"Great idea, bud. Now get next door and get some sleep."

Clyde shut the door in Jared's face.

Minutes later, all at once feeling very tired, Jared had just closed his eyes when he heard something, a sound from next door. The sound was muffled but familiar, and then he understood they were laughing. Clyde and his mother were laughing. He could picture them lying side by side on the bed, each with one hand on the other's side—were they fully clothed, only their shoes kicked off, or had they undressed entirely?—and one of them, probably Clyde, had made some intimate joke, and so they were laughing, not thinking how the sound would carry to next door where Jared lay alone (*he* had not undressed, had not even removed his shoes and socks) with his knees pulled up toward his chin. What was wrong with them? he asked himself. Sometimes, in recent days, they behaved like children, so that Jared felt like the adult in the family. They were always joking together, snickering. Now he heard something more like a shout, it was definitely Clyde's voice raised in an amused shout of surprise or delight, and then there was more of that muffled, throaty laughter, and after a minute or two Jared, mercifully, felt his eyelids drooping and he stopped hearing altogether.

Kay and Linda Hanratty lived in a tidy yellow-bricked bungalow on Highland Avenue, which Clyde informed them was in a "pretty expensive" part of Atlanta, especially for widows and orphans.

"Kay's not a widow, she's divorced," Jared's mother said, looking perplexed. "And how is Linda an orphan?"

For the second time that day his mother seemed irritated. Jared had noticed before how she swung between moods of romantic infatuation with Clyde and then of halfway disliking him, almost as though she could not make up her mind. Jared understood this. His own ambivalence about his uncle kept him on edge and watchful, uncertain. What would the man do or say next? Could either Jared or his mother trust him?

Jared's father had indulged in bouts of drinking, and occasional violence, but at least they knew him, Jared thought. It was just a matter of his "getting well" from his addiction to alcohol, or so the state hospital doctors had said, and he would be the husband and father they'd once known. But Clyde was so different. Unpredictable. Moody. Apt to follow whimsical notions, like taking them all on this trip out west, despite the fact that he hadn't planned the trip in advance and didn't seem to have a clear idea of their destination. Once he'd mentioned Santa Fe. Another time, San Diego. These and other cities had qualities he'd "heard good things about" and such rumors were the lure, it seemed, that would pull them out west despite Nina's and Jared's puzzlement, their uncertainty.

Now Clyde said, "I was just funning you." That was a folksy expression he sometimes used. Another was, "Ya'll come back now, y'hear?" And, "Don't let the door hit you in the butt on your way out."

Nina and Jared laughed dutifully at such "jokes" but Clyde was just as likely to say something offbeat or even off-color. Despite his apparent love for Rooney, he'd given various conflicting reasons for not bringing her along, from the benign ("She'll be better off at Billie's place") to the callous ("To tell you the truth, she bleeds too damn much. That's the last thing we need, cooped up in a small car like this. It's a smell I can't tolerate"). Sometimes neither Jared nor his mother knew how to react to Clyde's talk, and he did talk a great deal as they drove, so they simply kept silent, now and then exchanging troubled glances.

"Very funny," Nina said, not glancing aside. For some reason she added, "Linda's such a sweet girl."

Clyde glanced at Jared in the rearview mirror. "A looker too," he said. "A cute girl."

"She *is* cute," Nina murmured, but Jared said nothing.

"I think I hear wedding bells," Clyde said facetiously, grinning. "I think I hear the pitter-patter of little—"

"Knock it off," Jared said, grumpily. Then he drew a quick breath; he had old-fashioned ideas about respecting his elders, which his mother and his youthful father had drilled into him.

Nina said, "Exactly."

Clyde laughed aloud. "Well, you two are a barrel of laughs, aren't you?"

Jared saw that his mother was frowning. "Didn't you miss the turn?" she asked. "Kay lives off Highland Avenue, and I think we passed it already."

Abruptly Clyde looked around him, as if embarrassed. Then he said, "Just let me do the navigating."

"I will, if you know where the hell you're going."

A slow smile spread across Jared's face. He'd never heard his mother say "hell" before. Then he said, "We did miss the turn. We passed Highland about half a mile back."

So Clyde pulled into a church parking lot and turned around. It was about five-thirty and the street they were on, Ponce de Leon Avenue, was clogged with rush-hour traffic. Clyde, under his breath, cursed when a traffic light changed to green and then to red again after they'd moved only a few car lengths. He hated traffic, which was one reason he wanted to drive out west, where there were fewer people and fewer cars; where you could breathe clean air and cleanse your soul. Clyde had really said that—"cleanse your soul." Neither Jared nor his mother had contradicted him.

Finally they arrived at Kay's, and the house looked just like the photograph Kay had recently sent Nina, though the yellow brick could use a pressure-wash, Jared thought, and the covered porch was messy—a single wicker love-seat with leaves and dirt all over the cushion (you wouldn't want to sit there) and a small matching table stacked with dog-eared magazines, old catalogues, newspaper inserts. This would be a pleasant place to sit and watch people go by, Jared thought, if it were cleaned up a little; though brought up in a small town, he felt an attraction to big cities, the ceaseless pedestrians (joggers, dog-walkers) and traffic drifting by. Kay's house, with other houses close on both sides, seemed a little oasis amid the chaos of midtown Atlanta. He understood why she liked living here.

Kay answered the door with a surprised look, as if Nina hadn't just phoned her and she wasn't expecting company. But then Jared remembered—the haircuts.

"Jared? Clyde? What on earth—"

Clyde made the obvious remark, "We shaved our heads."

Kay opened the screen door and motioned them inside, where the house smelled of furniture polish, air freshener. Evidently Kay had tidied up for them in here, at least. Once they were all in the cozy living room with its small fireplace and built-in bookcases flanking each side, Kay looked at them again, one hand on her hip.

"My God, you look like army recruits! Or the Manson family!" She laughed.

"Manson family?" Jared said.

Kay reached out and hugged him. "Oh, they were just these criminals back in the sixties, they shaved their heads for court... And, Nina, there's something different about you—but you look gorgeous, as always."

The two women hugged, too, and then Kay in her ebullience even hugged Clyde, who had been standing off to the side looking glum, a mere bystander.

Nina pointed to the back of her head. "Ponytail," she said.

"Of course!" Kay cried. "Very cute. Now come on back, you three."

She sat them at the oval-shaped kitchen table, which was pleasantly scratched and worn, and where Kay had set out bowls of chips and some kind of yellow-orange cheese dip.

"Something to drink? Coke? Sweet tea?"

Once they were all settled, Jared's mother said, "You look terrific, Kay. City life must agree with you."

Kay seemed flattered by the remark, unconsciously touching her hair, her cheek. "I try, I try...the city is great, but it's difficult to meet anyone here. I mean, the neighbors are nice, but they're all couples and families, and I haven't yet resorted to the personal ads." She laughed brightly. "I mean, sometimes it gets—"

Clyde said, "Where's Linda?"

Kay seemed taken aback, as if this were a personal question; or perhaps she'd realized how blatantly she had confessed her loneliness, in the first minutes of her guests' visit. She laughed again. It was her common response to any remark or question—that bright, ribald laugh. Jared, watching her closely, thought that Kay really was a pretty woman, and it was surprising she would be lonesome. Her dramatic red hair was done in a permanent, and her features were sharp but regular; she had large eyes that usually wore an expression of bemusement or mischief, and a wide mouth gleaming with dark-orange lipstick. Jared could sense Clyde's slight discomfort in her presence, as though he were attracted to her and didn't enjoy the fact. Kay kept running a hand through her hair, as if with one more adjustment she would finally get it right.

"Linda? Oh, she has a little job now, didn't I tell you? A neighbor across the street owns this ladies' clothing store, Fishburne's, and she lets Linda work there a few days a week, doing giftwrapping, unpacking shipments, just minor things. I mean, she's only fourteen and isn't really supposed to be working"— Kay lowered her husky, intimate voice—"but Rhonda said she could use a little help around the place, and Linda needed something to do besides keeping her head stuck in a book all day!" Again that raucous laugh.

"When will she be home?" Jared asked.

"Listen to him," Clyde said, a bit snidely as though Jared had expressed some sinister curiosity.

"Oh, anytime now. She gets off at six, and Rhonda gives her a ride."

There was a brief silence. It occurred to Jared that neither he nor Clyde knew Kay very well, and there seemed to be an awkwardness even between Kay and Nina. The two women had been close friends but now they were in a new place, and they even looked different, so he supposed he understood. Still, it seemed odd. Like Nina, Kay had dressed up for the occasion, in a bright-yellow dress that showed her ample cleavage. He'd seen Clyde's eyes stray to Kay's breasts more than once. The Linda in his mind's eye, by contrast, was "cute," as Clyde and Nina had said, and must have taken after her father, with her dark straight hair and rather pale, haunted face. He recalled thinking, back home, that she and Kay hardly looked like mother and daughter.

As though reading his thoughts, Linda turned her key in the front door and came back to where they were sitting in the kitchen. There were hugs and exclamations of delight all around. Circling his arms around Linda, Jared marveled at how thin she was; it felt as if he were hugging someone not physical at all, a phantom. Yet her face attracted him, with her deep, wide-set dark eyes, that pale unblemished skin, the tucked-in smile as she lifted her gaze to him.

"How have you been, Jared?" she said, shyly. "Why are you bald?"

"I've been fine," he said. "Got a haircut."

The adults were laughing. Clyde said, "Come on, kids, you can do better than that. What kind of romantic reunion is this?"

Jared saw that Linda's face had flushed, just perceptibly; she cast her eyes down.

Kay said, "Hey, you two want to sit on the front porch? You can get reacquainted."

Jared said, "Sure," wondering what Linda was thinking. But she followed him willingly as he went back through the living room to the porch. Quickly they brushed the leaves and other debris off the wicker loveseat; they sat. Linda rested with her hands carefully folded on her lap.

She said, "I meant that question, Jared, it wasn't just small talk. How have you been?"

He smiled, gently. He felt the need to console her, somehow, for there was a sorrowful look to her sloping shoulders, to the demure way she'd folded her hands in her lap. She wore an ordinary navy-blue dress and plain, rather clunky dark-blue shoes. The dress had a white, frilly collar, and she wore a gold chain with a tiny, delicate gold cross. Was Linda religious? he wondered. In all their past conversations, sometimes about philosophy or literature, she'd never ventured onto that topic. Maybe in her mind a set of religious beliefs was settled, known, but when he'd expressed his own impatience with organized religion, feeling his way toward a position he'd never before articulated to another person, she'd simply nodded and looked down, as though he made sense. Or so he'd thought at the time. Maybe she'd just been indulging him, waiting until his absurd doubts were expressed and they could move on to something else.

Jared shook his head, grinning. "We're quite a family now, Mom and Clyde and me. Like this sudden vacation of ours…"

Linda's eyes widened in interest. "Where are you going?"

Jared shrugged. "Out west. We haven't picked our final destination. We have ten days, I think, before Clyde's vacation is over."

"He works—in a mortuary, doesn't he?"

"Yeah, but his boss is there, and a couple of other workers. They can do without Clyde for a while. It's weird, but he does like his job." He grinned again, caught at using a word kids no longer said in his grade. So he repeated it, with comical emphasis, "*Weird*…"

Linda laughed. It was the first time she'd smiled since arriving home from work, and Jared felt gratified. But only for a moment. She still seemed sorrowful, somehow, as though harboring a personal burden.

Jared reached across and touched her cheek. "You're sweet."

Again she flushed, but the look in her eyes suggested he had pleased her. So he reached over again and touched her again.

Finally, out of nowhere, they were kissing. Tenderly, gently at first, then with more passion. Jared felt her body relax against his, and he felt a brief stirring at his crotch even though this was an innocent embrace and these were rather pure, teenage kisses that wouldn't turn into anything dark or transgressive. After all, they could hear the adults' voices and laughter from two rooms over. Jared was a virgin, and of course Linda was, and there was little impulse to go any further, and finally he kissed each of her cheeks, then her forehead, and he pulled back.

"Sweet," he said again.

She smiled, and he saw how her face had flushed a deep-crimson this time. Had he done that? Had he roused her to something like passion? She seemed to be breathing heavily, her thin chest heaving back and forth. He saw her gold cross glinting in the light from outside the screened porch. He probably shouldn't have touched her, he thought miserably. This time tomorrow Jared and his family would be gone, leaving her here with whatever burden she had, and whatever that was, he would probably never know. He would leave her with a new, slight, but definite burden of sadness, loneliness. Was that the trouble he sensed in her?—a simple loneliness?

"I wish you could come with us. It's just for a week or so," he repeated. "I mean, it'll be nothing fancy, just roadside motels and seeing the sights along the way, but I could ask my—"

She put two fingers to his lips. "No, Jared. It's all right." She smiled, but this time her smile was thin and unconvincing. "I have to work, and take care of Mom. I don't know if she told you, but she lost her job last week—for 'inappropriate behavior,' they told her. She was working at Fishburne's before me, and evidently she was laughing and flirting with the male customers, and one day they claimed they smelled liquor on her breath."

Linda kept her large eyelids lowered as she recited this tale of woe. "So she got fired," she repeated, "and her friend was nice enough to hire me, part-time. But I don't bring in nearly enough money—I mean, Grandma gives us money, but she's getting older and sometimes she forgets, and so—"

Quickly Jared reached back for his wallet and pulled out his money; there wasn't much. A few twenties, the rest fives and ones. Money he'd saved from his grocery store job and brought along on this trip to buy food, incidentals. Clyde would take care of him, he thought.

"Here, take this," and Jared stuffed the cash into one of her limp hands. "I don't need it."

She held it out to him. "No, you keep it, please. You'll need it for your trip."

"It's yours," Jared said simply, and he stood, as though ending the transaction. He towered over her saddened, slump-shouldered form; she was staring down at her hands as though she'd never seen money before.

"You're too kind," she whispered. "Better be careful..."

"Careful?"

"You shouldn't be this kind, to me or to anyone. You need

to keep something for yourself," and he knew she wasn't talking about money.

His voice lowered. "I will."

She said, "Good," and stood to join him, folding the cash into the pocket of her dress. "C'mon, let's visit with your mom and uncle."

He took hold of her thin arms. "Please take care of yourself," he said, "and of your mom. I'll keep in touch while we're gone, so you can let me know if you need anything."

He bent down and kissed her, this time in an adult way. Again he felt her responding, surprised and pleased.

As they turned to pass back through the living room and into the breakfast area where Clyde, Nina, and Kay were chatting, Jared knew that something had just happened to him out on the porch, though he wasn't quite sure of what it was. He felt longer-limbed and certain within himself, less gangly, less tentative. This awareness had sneaked up on him somehow. His life, he thought, was shuttling forward quickly, perhaps too quickly, and in any case he felt certain that he would never be the same. Was this a good thing? he wondered. The answer did not come.

They reentered the room, timidly, and took the extra chairs Kay had pulled from the kitchen, placing them on either side of her. She was telling an elaborate anecdote about a man she had dated briefly after she and Linda moved back to Atlanta: about the way he would call before most of their dates and rearrange their plans, or sometimes even stand her up entirely. Of course, it had turned out that he was married.

And he wasn't the only one.

"It's happened three times since I've been here," Kay said, laughing.

"Three times?" Nina said. "But that's..." She trailed off, not wanting to say what everyone was thinking.

"Are you bringing this on yourself?" Clyde asked. "Are you deliberately picking unavailable men?"

"Clyde," Nina murmured.

Clyde looked awkward, as though he'd ventured into women's territory where he didn't belong. "Sorry," he said.

Kay had seemed taken aback at first, but now she was nodding vigorously. "I'm sure you're right, Clyde. I do know how to pick them, don't I? For one thing, Martin was never faithful, right from the get-go..." This reference to Linda's father echoed in the air, and Jared could tell Kay wished she hadn't spoken the man's name, for Linda's sake. Linda's response to anything untoward was to lower her eyes, showing her large, pale eyelids, and she did this now, making Jared want to cross over and embrace her.

"Anyway, don't be sorry," Kay said. She shook her head. She reached for her cigarettes (Jared had noticed that the faint smell of cigarette smoke filled the house) but discovered the pack was empty. "No, no, don't be sorry," she said again, as though speaking to herself.

As if on cue, Clyde and Nina both glanced at their watches, prompting Jared to glance at his own. It was 6:15, time for somebody to suggest having dinner, if they were going to have dinner together. But this clearly wasn't going to happen. There was too much awkwardness and tension in the room. Jared didn't like the way Clyde was staring at Kay, his eyes dark and fierce with something that must have been lust. Why was Kay overdressed, Jared thought, on this ordinary day? Why the exposed cleavage at which Jared, too, kept glancing, unable to help himself?

Nina said, "Well, we don't want to overstay our welcome. We should get back to the motel, get some rest..."

"Yeah," Clyde said. "We drove all night."

"All night! Really?" Kay said. "But what's this about a motel? You guys need to stay here tonight. I've got a guest room, and if Jared doesn't mind sleeping on the couch..."

Clyde and Nina glanced at each other. They had all three packed an overnight bag in case Kay invited them.

Unexpectedly, Linda chimed in. "Yes," she said. "Please stay."

Nina came up with the usual false protestations, not wanting to inconvenience Kay and Linda, not wanting to impose, but

Kay waved her orange-tipped hand, dramatically. "No, I won't have it! You've *got* to stay here! All I've done today is work on my stupid resume; maybe you could look it over for me, Nina? I can't read it again. And maybe one of these handsome men"— she glanced at Clyde, then Jared—"would escort us to dinner? I have plenty of stuff for breakfast tomorrow. Eggs, bread..."

"That's a lot of trouble for you," Nina said, under her breath.

"Yeah, it would be a pain," Clyde said.

"I can make French toast in the morning! Or I've got cereal, if Jared prefers that. It's just corn flakes, but—Jared, are corn flakes all right? I'm afraid it's all I have." She spoke in a pleading voice.

"Sure, that's fine," Jared said quickly.

Again Clyde and Nina exchanged glances, and Jared saw Clyde's near-imperceptible nod. So Nina said, "Well, if you're sure we're not in the way..."

"Oh God, no!" Kay exclaimed. "God knows I need the company."

Linda looked up at this, and Kay went on: "Of course, I have my sweetie here, but we need some boys around, too, don't we, Linda?" Kay laughed. She reached again for the empty cigarette pack and then remembered and this time crumpled it up.

"I know a perfect place we can have dinner—it's this Italian place in midtown, just a block off Peachtree. Nothing fancy, but the real thing, you know? Authentic? But Clyde—would you mind if we stopped at Kroger on the way? I'm totally out of cigarettes."

"Sure," Clyde said doubtfully.

"I thought you were"—Nina hesitated—"I thought you were going to quit. Remember, we talked a couple of weeks ago and you said—"

"Oh, I say a lot of things," Kay said, whimsically, "but I don't necessarily *do* them." She laughed, spreading her fingers for some reason as if checking her nails, but this time no one laughed with her; in fact, no one even smiled.

21

J ared woke and rose from the sofa quickly, as if caught doing something shameful even though he was alone in the room. Dressed only in his boxer shorts, he hurried into the kitchen and poured himself a glass of orange juice and hardly had he taken a sip before his mother and Clyde were behind him.

"Thirsty?" his mother said fondly, touching his bare chilled shoulder with her warm fingertips. As they'd come in from the screened porch yesterday his and Linda's hands had clasped briefly but his mother's hand was warmer than Linda's had been. This meant nothing, he told himself sternly. A girl's hand, a mother's hand: the difference meant nothing and he should think of something else.

"Sure," he said. "All that salty Italian food from last night."

"It was good, wasn't it?" his mother asked.

He shrugged. "Guess so."

Clyde laughed, gently. "Listen to that. 'Guess so.' You can't please the kids these days."

Jared wanted to end this trivial conversation and he was self-conscious standing there in nothing but his underwear, fearful that Kay or Linda might come into the kitchen, so he mumbled something and went back into the living room and found his cutoffs, then his T-shirt that he pulled over his bald head. Clyde and Nina followed him.

"So what're we doing today?" Jared said idly.

Clyde hesitated, then said, "Your mom wants to get her hair done."

Nina said quickly, grabbing hold of her ponytail then letting it drop, "Yeah, I guess I'm tired of this. Tired of being a plain Jane. It was your uncle's idea, Jared. What do you think?"

Clyde moved closer to Nina. "You're anything but plain," he

said. And he added, "Then we're going to some places around town… Don't you remember I told you about the Cyclorama, that show where they reenact the Civil War?"

Nina laughed. "I don't think they reenact it. They just—"

Clyde grasped her wrist and squeezed, so that Nina couldn't help wincing. Her laughter died in her throat. "Stop. That hurts," she said.

"*We're* going to reenact the Civil War," Clyde said, "if you contradict me again."

Nina seemed not to hear the tone in his voice, harsh and almost threatening, but Jared heard. He locked eyes with his uncle. Nina, rubbing her wrist, continued blithely, "It's just a huge old painting, it's circular and the audience is turned in one big revolution until they've seen the whole thing. And there's this insipid short film that goes along with it." She paused, now aware that Clyde and Jared were staring at each other. "It's just a tourist trap, really, but if you want to go…"

"I'm sure he's dying to go *now*," Clyde said evenly. "You've made it sound so appealing. Besides, I thought you'd never been…"

"The Cyclorama? Everybody goes once, before they know better," Nina said. "When I first moved here, I only worked three days a week at the hospital, so I had plenty of time off. One day, a girlfriend and I—"

"We get the picture," Clyde said.

Nina turned—she'd been staring at Jared's glum face—and poked Clyde. "What's with you?"

"What's with me?" Then he repeated mockingly, in a high-pitched voice, "What's with me?" He added, "I'll tell you what's with me," and this time he grabbed her waist and began tickling her mercilessly, and Nina begged him to stop, stop, and finally she wrested herself away from him. Again she looked at Jared, who still wore his glum face, standing slump-shouldered with his hands in his pockets. He looked like any teenage boy in his white T-shirt and cutoffs. His mother had put on the same dress she'd worn yesterday, and Clyde wore a gray T-shirt and some black jeans, and for a moment they all stood there as if frozen, a tableau.

Then Kay appeared in the living room, still in her bathrobe. She looked puzzled and amused.

"Hey, you guys," she said. "Good morning. What would you like for breakfast?"

The moment of tension had lingered, and even Kay appeared to feel it. But she soldiered on with her pleasantries. "I can make us some French toast, or fry up some eggs. How does that sound?"

One of them had to speak, Jared thought, so he said, impersonating that boy of exactly his age, "How about some cornflakes?"

After breakfast, Kay suggested that instead of the Cyclorama— it truly was "tiresome," she said—they all visit Lenox mall and do some shopping.

"I need some new shoes, and you'll want something," she told Nina, "to go with your new hairstyle." She gave a little smirk. Kay had her own hair done by an elderly lady who worked out of her home, and though today was Sunday, she was happy to work Nina into her afternoon schedule. "Then we'll go to Mrs. Carpenter's, and you boys can do—something or other."

"Oh, we can't leave them alone," Nina objected. "They'd have nothing to do."

"We'll have plenty to do," Clyde said. "I'll take Jared here to lunch, and there's movies galore in this city." He looked at Jared. "How long since you've seen a movie, kid? In a real theater?"

Jared shrugged. "A long time," he said. "Linda could come with us."

"Oh no," Kay cried, "she's coming with *us*. Mrs. Carpenter's going to trim our hair, too, as long as she's doing Nina's."

So it was settled, and after some time over coffee and the

Sunday paper, Kay herded Nina and Linda out the front door. "You boys don't get into any trouble!" she cried over her shoulder.

Nina paused, giving Jared a considerate look. "You'll be all right?" she said.

Jared felt patronized and made the appropriate dour face. "We're just going to a movie, Mom. For Christ's sake."

Clyde laughed. "Yeah, quit treating him like a five-year-old."

Jared squirmed with embarrassment, especially since Linda was there. He could feel his face reddening.

"All right, we're off!" Kay said. She was wearing a caramel-colored dress this morning, with a white leather belt, purse, shoes; with her full makeup and her hair freshly brushed, Jared thought she looked quite glamorous. His mother, wearing a plain navy blue skirt and white blouse, seemed dowdy by comparison, like an unpopular high-school girl. Again he felt slightly embarrassed in front of Linda, though knowing that Linda probably hadn't even noticed what Nina was wearing. Her mind was loftier than that, he thought, which was one of the reasons he liked her so well.

Now she touched his arm. "Bye, Jared."

He responded, surprised. "Bye."

Clyde said, "Don't worry, you lovebirds, it's only for a few hours. Absence makes the heart grow fonder, you know."

Linda smiled faintly.

Clyde and Jared stood on the front porch and watched as Kay's silver Mercedes backed out the driveway. All five of them waved, Kay putting her hand out the window and giving the "royal wave," her hand cupped, to Clyde and Jared as they drove off.

"That woman's crazy as a bed-bug," Clyde said.

"Maybe," Jared said. "But Linda isn't."

"No, you've got yourself quite a catch. Don't screw it up, kid."

"I won't."

Back in the house, Clyde said, "We both stink. Go ahead and

get your shower, and then I will. I don't want to sit next to you in the movies with you smelling like this."

"Gee thanks," Jared said. "You're no spring lily, yourself."

Playfully Clyde poked him in the stomach, and Jared poked him back. Jared crossed to his duffel bag that was sitting on one end of the sofa, got some fresh clothes, and went into the guest bathroom Kay had shown him before she left. She'd given them a tour of the house, and Jared knew Clyde and Nina were wondering, as he was, how she could afford this—the rooms were spacious and newly renovated, the bathrooms overlarge and sparkling. As Clyde had said, this was an expensive part of Atlanta, newly "gentrified," yet Nina was unemployed. Her car and clothes were expensive too. He stepped back out of the bathroom and found Clyde in the guest bedroom. He'd just picked up the phone.

"Hey, I wonder how Kay affords all this," Jared said. "This house, the car and clothes…"

"I've got to call Billie," Clyde said, pointing to the phone. But Jared didn't walk away, so Clyde said before dialing, "I think Nina said she inherited some money."

"But they're poor now. Linda said as much."

Clyde grinned. "Women don't know how to handle money," he said. "Just remember that."

Jared thought a moment and said, "Okay."

"She's probably sunk everything into her house and possessions, and now she's 'land-poor.' She can always sell if she gets desperate."

"I hope Linda gets to go to college," Jared said, the thought coming out of nowhere. "She's too smart not to go."

"Me too, kid, me too. Now let me call—"

"You're calling Aunt Billie? Checking on Rooney?"

"Of course," Clyde said. "And the family of that old lady we left behind, unburied. That place can't run without me, you know, though Luther's smarter than he acts. I reckon he can keep things going."

Jared turned and went back to the bathroom. It had an enormous walk-in shower of the kind he'd seen on TV shows but had never used before. The walls of the shower were a swirled beige-and-white tile, and there was a brown pebbly flooring that soothed the feet. Jared had never experienced "luxury" before: the small wood-frame house where he'd lived all his life probably wasn't up to code, and more than once he'd heard his father, who had a penchant for worrying, express concern that the place would "go up in flames" one day. He'd driven an old rusted pickup that had simply gone to the junkyard after he died, and Jared believed the old Toyota his mother still drove had been purchased for $700 and was on its second hundred thousand miles. He'd never even been inside a house like this, and he thought ruefully that his mother had never worn the kind of pretty clothes and perfumes that Kay Hanratty evidently took for granted. Still, he did not have any unfulfilled longing for nice things and didn't believe his mother did, either. They were plain, regular people, he thought, and they were happy that way. As he turned on the shower and began soaping up, he even told himself that he would not enjoy such luxury on a routine basis; it would feel strange, unfamiliar, not meant for him.

His shower would be quick, he thought; he'd dry himself on one of Kay's plush beige towels, put on his fresh clothes, and go with his uncle to the movies.

But something happened—the bathroom door, which he hadn't locked, suddenly came open, and there was Clyde, staring at him. "Hey, kid," he said. "Starting to feel better?"

The door to the shower was clear glass, not frosted, and Jared turned slightly so Clyde could see only the curve of his buttocks, not the front of him. Thankfully, the door was beginning to coat with steam.

"Did you need something?" Jared said.

"Yeah, a shower," Clyde said, and to Jared's dismay his uncle tugged off his shirt and jeans and briefs, opened the shower door, and came inside with Jared. Instinctively polite, Jared moved aside so Clyde could share in the stream of water, even though he was shocked to his core and felt his blood running cold (despite all the hot water that enveloped him) in his head, chest, and groin. Clyde had taken the soap from Jared and begun soaping himself, too, and after a moment he said to his nephew, "This is the life, ain't it?"

"Yeah," Jared said. "Guess so."

Now Clyde turned to face him directly; the soap had already washed down off both their bodies. Clyde had said this before, but he said again, "You're a good-looking kid," and now to Jared's further shock Clyde looked down frankly at Jared's crotch. Jared was trembling, though he knew this wasn't visible in the steam and blur of the hot water. He had never felt so exposed and embarrassed in his life.

In recent years, the only adult male who'd seen him naked was his doctor, whom he'd visited a couple of times for physical exams; and the PE coach at school, who sometimes ventured into the boys' shower room in the gym, pointedly keeping his gaze level with the boys' faces. But now Clyde lowered himself on his haunches until he was at eye-level with Jared's genitals. Jared was not breathing. He willed himself not to get hard, but nonetheless he could feel himself getting bigger, his penis filling involuntarily with blood. By the time he thought he might bolt out of the shower, Clyde rose and said matter-of-factly, "Yeah, good-looking, and you've got a nice dick and set of balls. You'll enjoy all that, one day. So will the girls." He laughed aloud, the sound muffled by the constant hissing of the shower.

Jared said nothing.

"C'mon," Clyde said, "let's get out of here, we're clean enough." He laughed again, this time more gently. Then, as if venting an afterthought: "You ever fucked a girl?"

Jared stared at his uncle, winded. He forced himself to take light, shallow breaths.

"N—no," he said.

"Oh, man, there's nothing like it." Clyde grinned. "A nice, tight pussy like girls your age have, you're going to go out of your mind."

Jared said nothing. Clyde had turned off the shower and stepped out of the stall, grabbed a towel, and begun drying off. Jared watched him, slack-mouthed. Inadvertently he looked at Clyde's penis, which was much larger than his own, flopping to each side as the towel caressed it, the shaft thick and hairy, the reddish-purple head protruding as Clyde patted it gently, then finished up by drying his legs and feet. The shower door was open and Jared stood there naked, exposed. Clyde tossed the towel at him. "There you go, kid. Let's speed it up, okay? We've got a lot of stuff to get done. I need to stop by that motel and get some of our money back, and then we'll go buy some new stuff—some clothes, maybe—if the women can, we can—and then we'll take in that movie if you want." By now he was out the door, but he called back, "Anything playing that you want to see?"

Jared had quickly wrapped the towel around his waist, and stepping out of the stall he tried to see his features in the fogged-up mirror above the sink. With both hands he wiped the fog off the mirror but, seeing how scared he looked, he withdrew his hands and began drying off as if this were some ordinary shower, some ordinary day.

22

J ared and Linda were sitting alone at the dining room table, chatting. Clyde had gone with Nina and Kay to buy some groceries—"and some other supplies," he'd said mysteriously—and had grinned at the idea of leaving two teenagers alone in the house. He'd said to Kay, "He can't be trusted, believe me," and Kay had laughed airily and said, "Maybe not, but *she* can," which Jared thought was true enough. What Clyde didn't know was that Jared could be trusted too. He and Linda were still callow teenagers, he thought. Probably he would stay a virgin for a long, long time. This thought had come to him this morning even as he had blotted away what had happened in the shower yesterday with Clyde. No need to think about that. No need to dwell on that. Today was May 18, 1992, so yesterday was the seventeenth. Despite himself he knew he'd remember that date for the rest of his life.

He and Linda had been talking about nothing in particular, but now she pointed to his wrist and asked, "How'd you get that scar?" Jared looked down and saw the thin but pronounced one-inch scar across the inside of his wrist; one day last summer, at his grocery store job, he'd been opening some cardboard cartons of toilet paper in the back room and he'd pulled his box-cutter a bit too hard and slashed a deep cut into his flesh. Another boy in the back room had heard Jared cry out and, seeing the bright spurt of blood, had laughed and shouted, "Nice job, McCune! Way to go!" but he'd run out and gotten the store's assistant manager, a lanky, good-natured man in his thirties named Jim Casey, who quickly found a first-aid kit, wrapped the cut tightly in gauze, and took Jared to the emergency room. A young Asian doctor had cleaned the wound, stitched him up, given him a tetanus shot and, smiling merrily, pronounced him "good as new."

On the way back to the store, Jared did not feel good as new. He felt like an idiot, and knew that the other guys, and even Jim Casey—who smoked a cigarette as he drove, with the window halfway down—would kid him for days, which they did. Jared didn't care too much about that. But until then he'd felt the grocery store job was the one thing he was good at, outside of school: that's what bothered him. Except for basketball he wasn't that proficient at sports, he was shy around girls, but at the store he could sack items faster than the other, older guys and, if he were old enough to be a cashier, he knew he'd be faster than any of the middle-aged women cashiers who'd worked there for years. But now this. Jim Casey had told him to take the rest of the afternoon off, and when he'd gotten home his father, sitting on the front porch holding a shot glass of bourbon—it was Saturday, soon after he'd been fired from his job—had sized up the situation and said, not smiling, "Yep, you're a McCune, after all. Always screwing up." He laughed, exhaling smoke from his cigarette.

"Gee thanks," Jared said. Inside the house, Nina had made the expected motherly exclamations of dismay and sent him up to bed.

"You rest for a while, read a book," she told him. "I'll bring you a Coke in a few minutes."

"I don't need to rest up," he said.

"You might have lost some blood, so you never know. I just bought some sugar cookies yesterday. I'll bring a few of those up too."

He hadn't lost any blood to speak of, but he decided not to argue. It was a hot July day, and there were worse things to do than to lie on his bed, reading a book. He remembered thinking that he might call Linda and tell her what had happened, but he hadn't placed the call.

So now he told her. She made commiserating noises and touched his wrist with her fingertips several times, which felt more soothing than he'd have expected. There was little that could soothe him, these days.

"That must have hurt," she said quietly.

He paused. "It didn't feel good." Then he rose and went into the living room and brought back the satchel where he kept his Rubik's cube, a few favorite books, various mementoes. He lifted something out of the satchel and held it out for her inspection.

It was the box-cutter, still stained with his blood. On the day of the accident, he'd slipped it into the pocket of his blue jeans, not exactly knowing why, and found it there a few days later, the blade reddened and mean-looking. For some reason he didn't want to throw the box cutter away, so he'd tossed it into the satchel with his other things.

Linda said, "A girl I know at school, Melanie Ritter—you know her, I'm sure—well, she has something like this."

"A box-cutter?" Jared said, surprised.

"No, a box where she keeps mementoes, things that mean something to her—a memory box, she calls it. It's a pretty box covered in red velvet, not just a satchel like yours. She told me she had a puppy once, but it got run over, so she saved the little collar and put it inside the box. And her five-year diary is in there. And some dried flowers from a bouquet one of the boys gave her."

"Well, mine isn't like that," Jared said.

"No?"

"It's not a memory box," and he couldn't help thinking that such a box was something only a girl would keep. "It's just a bunch of junk, really." He laughed.

"But you wouldn't throw it away, would you?"

He thought for a moment. "I guess not…"

"They're associated with memories, those things, like the box-cutter for the day you hurt yourself. And the Rubik's cube because you discovered you're so good at solving it. And those three or four books—they must be books you especially liked, right? And…" She peered into the satchel. "What are those?" she asked. "Little pellets, or…?"

Jared laughed, embarrassed. "No, they're just a few BBs,"

he said. "From a BB gun I used to have. My daddy gave me the gun one Christmas when I was about ten, and soon after I went out and shot a blue bird out of one of the pine trees out back. The bird fell almost at my feet, all bloodied and twitching. For some reason"—here he hesitated—"I didn't like it that I'd done that, you know, randomly killed this little bird that wasn't hurting anything, so—so I took the gun and a shovel, then I dug this little pit out in the woods and buried the gun there. You're the first person I've even told this to… But I had some leftover BBs, of course, so I put them into the satchel."

Jared held the satchel open, and he and Linda watched as the B-B's rolled around from corner to corner.

He laughed briefly, through his nose. "Stupid."

"It's not stupid," Linda said. "It lets you remember—that's all."

He thought how Linda was like his mother, always putting more meaning into something than was really there. But he didn't want to argue.

"I guess so," he said.

They both looked up—the dead-bolt had turned, and Clyde, Nina, and Kay came through the door, laughing. Jared wondered idly why they were laughing but mostly his thoughts were about his mother and how she looked, for the day before she'd not only gotten a haircut into what Kay called "a stylish bob, flapper-style," but she'd decided to dye her hair a platinum-blond.

"You look like a movie star!" Clyde had exclaimed, when he'd first seen the haircut, and Nina, looking abashed, even a bit ashamed, had said, "Yeah, from around 1925."

"Well, what do you think of your mom?" Kay had asked Jared. "Pretty glamorous, huh?"

"Yeah, I guess," Jared had said, and then, inspired, he'd added, "You look like Bonnie."

"Bonnie?" his mother asked. Clyde, Kay, and Linda were all staring at him, too. "Don't you get it? 'Bonnie.' From Bonnie and Clyde."

Kay had laughed, and Jared had noticed that his mother

glanced away; Clyde just smiled, uneasily. "We're nothing like *that* Bonnie and Clyde," he said, more forcefully than the moment required.

"Yeah," Nina said, trying to sound amused. "We haven't robbed any banks. We haven't shot anybody."

"Not yet." Kay laughed. She pointed her index finger at Clyde and made a shooting motion. "Pow."

Clyde clutched his heart. "Got me," he moaned.

But now the uneasiness from that exchange seemed to have vanished; the three adults had just gotten back from the grocery store, as if they shopped together every day of their lives, and they set the lumpy, overfull sacks down on the dining room table.

Kay extended her arm toward the sacks, like a model in a showroom. "Guess who's cooking dinner tonight?"

"I wish you'd let us take you out," Nina said, uncertainly. Since her haircut she'd developed a gesture of pulling at the back of her hair, seeming newly astonished each time that her hair was so short.

"No way," Kay said, shaking her finger. "You guys took us to that nice Italian place. Tonight it's my turn."

Clyde stretched his arms. "I feel like staying in, anyway," he said. He glanced from Jared, who sat glaring at him, to Linda. "That okay with you guys?"

"Oh, sure," Linda said, smiling. "We're not hard to please."

"Listen to that," Clyde said. "*We*. She's already speaking for you, kid."

Linda said, "Oh, I didn't mean..."

Jared said nothing.

"Salmon steaks? How does that sound?" Kay asked.

The adults had all focused on Jared, who was being so pointedly silent. He struggled to be polite. "Good," he said, with a small twitch of a smile.

It was best if he didn't even look at Clyde, he told himself. So he let his gaze shift from his mother, who wore a simple black dress that contrasted dramatically with her whitish-blond hair, to Linda's glamorous mother, and finally to Linda herself. She was wearing a pink angora sweater with that delicate gold chain around her neck, its tiny gold cross. The cross winked in the light from the dining-room chandelier.

Now everyone but Jared rose and began helping carry the grocery sacks into the rectangular, white-tiled kitchen. Even from where he sat, Jared noticed that the kitchen was sparkling, even over-bright, and he'd noticed before how clean the house was, as though Kay and Linda had made a special effort before their company arrived. During their ride over here, Nina had said something again about Kay being "lonely, I think," and Clyde had said quickly, out the side of his mouth, "All women without a man are lonely." Nina had said nothing, and neither had Jared, who arranged his face into the semblance of a smile and went into the brightly lit kitchen to join the others.

At dinner they talked of various things, including the upcoming election. This was the last topic that would have engaged Jared, but he listened with some interest because it showed what the adults were thinking, and what was going on in that inaccessible great world outside the dark car windows as they drove through the countryside at night. He had already gathered from newspapers he saw at the grocery store and from TV "news bulletins" interrupting his favorite shows that the young silver-haired governor from Arkansas, named Clinton, was doing well, and that his opponents would likely be President Bush and a third candidate, the upstart billionaire Ross Perot about whom Jared knew little except that, as Clyde had put it one night, the guy was "half-crazy." As Nina and Kay, helped by Linda, worked busily in the kitchen, Kay kept throwing her opinions cheerfully over one shoulder. She was sautéing the salmon steaks, and kept bending to check the burner.

"I really *love* Bill Clinton," she said. "He's some fresh blood, y'know? Just what we need." She hunched her shoulders with a kind of girlish glee. "He's easy on the eyes, too, isn't he?"

Nina said, uncertainly, "You don't like President Bush…?" It was clear she had no opinion on the matter but felt obliged to answer Kay. "He's…"

"He's an old gray-faced patrician who won't get anything done, except on behalf of other gray-faced patricians," Kay said firmly. "Clinton is a *Democrat*. He's for everybody, Black and white, rich and poor—"

Clyde said, "Don't be too sure." He was rifling through the Atlanta paper, as though reading about these very matters. "Clinton's got something in his eyes, a lean and hungry look underneath that Southern charm. I don't know, there's just something about him…"

Kay was turning the fish steaks in the pan. "You think so? I don't know, I think he's got some empathy…" She added, "Hey, what do you kids think? If you kids could vote, who would you vote for?"

Linda gave her mother a nettled look, for some reason not liking the question, but Jared, who sat across the table from Clyde, and glanced at him even though he was answering Kay, said more loudly than he intended, "Perot!"

The others seemed taken aback.

"Jared, you've gotta be kidding, hon," Kay said. "The one with the charts, and the redneck accent? I don't think so…"

Jared said, "I like him," even though this wasn't true. He supposed that if he voted, he would vote for Clinton, but for some reason, tonight, he wanted to be contrary. He did not like Perot, who looked and sounded like somebody's daft Southern uncle.

Clyde gave a half-smile, a crease lifting one side of his mouth. "You're just trying to stir things up, aren't you?" he said to Jared. "You don't give a shit about politics."

"Clyde…" Nina murmured, gesturing her head toward Linda.

Clyde gave a little bow. "Sorry, young lady. Sometimes my mouth gets ahead of my brain."

The phone rang in the other room and Kay told Linda,

"Honey, would you get that? The fish here is just about done."

Nina was working slowly on their salad, dicing radishes and onions.

Linda came back from the living room and held the cordless phone out to Clyde. "It's for you," she said politely.

"For Clyde?" Kay said, surprised.

Clyde said quickly, "I'd given Billie your number, just in case…" but he didn't finish this thought, turning his attention to the phone.

"Yeah? Really? But what did they—?" Pause. Jared's heart was beating erratically. He didn't like what he heard in Clyde's voice—something like panic. "When was all this? What did you tell them, Billie? Remember, I instructed you—"

Now everyone in the kitchen was watching Clyde, listening frankly to his words.

"Okay, okay, that's good. At least you didn't— Listen, how's Rooney doing?" Pause. "Yeah, well, kiss her for me… Okay. I'll talk to you soon. I will, Billie. Okay. G'bye."

Clyde sat holding the phone and looking disconsolate.

"What is it?" Nina asked. "What did she—"

Clyde looked up, startled, as though unaware anyone had been listening to him. "Oh, nothing much," he said. "Someone was just nosing around the house, asking about me…"

"Someone?" Nina said.

"A client," Clyde said firmly, and Jared knew at once that he was lying. But Jared said nothing.

"Yeah, something about the place being closed this weekend. Luther was supposed to work, but you know how these—" Clyde stopped himself. Jared closed his eyes in relief.

"Anyway," Clyde said suddenly, "I'm afraid we've got to be going."

"Going!" Kay screeched. "But dinner is just now ready!"

"I know—I'm sorry, but something has come up. It's my sister, Rooney, she's sick with some kind of fever"—he was blatantly lying now, and everyone knew it—"and we need to get back down there. Nina, Jared, get your stuff together."

"Oh, all this beautiful salmon!" Kay said, on the verge of tears. "What will I—"

"You'll have some delicious leftovers tomorrow," Clyde said, crossing to where Kay stood at the stove and kissing her cheek. "I'm sorry, Kay. I really am."

Kay wiped her eyes with both hands. "Well, if your sister is really sick..."

"She is," Clyde said quickly. "Nina, Jared...?" And with that the two of them began rushing around, made their apologies to Kay and Linda, and hurried out of the room to pack. Ten minutes later they were ready.

Kay had stayed in the kitchen, wrapping the salmon in tinfoil, and Linda had drifted over to her mother, putting one arm around her waist. They made a pathetic tableau as Clyde, rushing Nina and Jared along, came back to the kitchen for a quick goodbye.

"I wish you wouldn't leave," Kay said, simply. Her eyes shone.

"Aah, don't worry, we'll be back sometime," Clyde said. "In the meantime, keep looking; Mr. Right will come along."

"Sure he will," Kay said dourly.

Nina said, "Clyde, if we're in such a hurry, we ought to get going."

"Yeah, yeah," Clyde said, glancing at his watch. "We ought to be there by two or three o'clock. It's a good thing, as Billie sounded pretty upset."

"All right, go. Go," Kay said, resigned. "Linda, turn on the porch light, will you?"

That easily, that quickly, their leave-taking was accomplished. Jared shoved his satchel into the back seat. Clyde and Nina were already in the front seats, like his counterfeit parents. Nina sat quietly, her shoulders sagging a little. Yes, Jared thought, counterfeit. The both of them.

Kay and Linda stood in the light of the front porch, which surrounded them like a halo. They were waving. They were half-waving.

Clyde tooted the horn in a friendly way and called out to them, "See you in the funny papers!"

Kay and Linda both smiled, but nobody in the car was smiling. They were swathed in darkness, the scant light from the dashboard and the streetlights making sinister shadows that wafted through the car as they backed out the driveway and onto Highland Avenue. By the time they reached I-20, Clyde did exactly as Jared had predicted, and instead of turning east, back toward home, took the exit heading west. Uncharacteristically, Clyde said nothing. And Nina said nothing. They were going west, just as Clyde had promised all along.

Then what had the phone call from Billie been about? Jared didn't know. Jared didn't dare to ask.

They drove. They drove all night.

PART FIVE

NINA

23

They'd crossed the state line into Mississippi before Nina remembered it was her birthday.

This wasn't the first time she'd forgotten. Through the doleful years of her husband's illness she did not experience time, as had been her way during her schoolgirl years, as a gaily mottled patchwork of holidays and birthdays and "special occasions" bearing her along through her life, year by year, in the lightsome manner of a young person who did not indulge in much serious thinking. Her marriage had changed all that. After Travis died, she'd wondered fitfully if she might return to that early insouciance, that ignorance of serious cares, or if her life simply lay blasted beyond all repair or rejuvenation. She didn't know. Still she didn't know. In Clyde she had found some odd new surge of energy she knew enough, at least, not to trust, though here she was, traveling with him and her son on a night journey to nowhere.

Their route had become erratic, for after Birmingham, Clyde had veered north on Highway 78 toward Tupelo and Memphis. They had passed a sign marking the exit to "Greater Tupelo" when she recalled that as a teenager she'd faithfully written an entry in her diary on each of her birthdays, a habit encouraged by Nana, who'd given her a pink five-year diary complete with a tiny lock. Nina didn't remember which birthday this was, only that the weather was unusually cold for May. It must have been her thirteenth, maybe her fourteenth. After Nina had her bath and washed her hair, her grandmother made a fire in the living room, surely the last one of the season, and the two of them had sat together on Nana's loveseat in front of the flickering amber firelight. Nana had run a brush through her hair, slowly, dreamily, as gradually it dried in the blessed and comforting heat, and Nina remembered that her eyes had closed in the luxuriant sense of being cared for, cherished, loved—something she'd never quite felt before or since. How intensely she'd loved her grandmother! That night, in her room, her hair styled by Nana in an old-fashioned pageboy, Nina had taken out her diary and written her random thoughts for more than an hour.

Some of it was about her grandmother, though much, she supposed, was about some boy she liked at school, or a popular girl who'd thrown a party but had not invited Nina, hurting her feelings, or about school itself, the nuns and lay teachers, all of whom she liked well enough though she was close to none of them. Nana, who did attend mass occasionally but not every Sunday as the church commanded, told her granddaughter smilingly not to let the priests and nuns get her in their snares, that all religions were basically the same and none superior to the other, and maybe they even did more harm than good, she didn't know, such matters were way over her head, but it was all something Nina shouldn't worry about… "Just try to be kind to other people and enjoy your life," the old woman had told her, "that's really all you need to know," and Nina had tried to heed this advice throughout her teenage years, and even into her twenties and beyond… *Try to be kind to other people. Enjoy your life.* Had she failed at even these simple grandmotherly admonitions?

Probably, Nina thought. She longed for the diary, that token of her lost youth, but where the hell was it? Her boy had the presence of mind to gather his essential possessions, which did not include a diary, inside an old school satchel he hauled around with him wherever they went, but Nina tended to lose things—books, jewelry, husbands—and had no idea where the diary was. For some reason she looked over to Clyde, as though he might provide the answer. She wondered if the diary were somewhere in her messy bedroom desk, where possibly Clyde could have found and read it; one time, she'd caught him shuffling through the top drawer, and when she'd entered the room, he looked guilty and said, "Just trying to find some stamps." But how often had he rifled through her things, when she was gone? What value, if any, did he give to her privacy?

She said, in what she considered a bold, even accusatory way, "Did you ever see my old diary?"

Startled out of his driver's daze, Clyde said, "What?"

"I had this little diary, covered with pink cloth, that my grandmother gave me. Have you ever come across it?"

"Of course not," he said, sounding offended. "If I had, I would have told you."

Nina looked back to the dark road, feebly illuminated by their headlights. "Okay," she said.

Abruptly, Jared said, "I've seen it. Up in the attic."

Nina felt a wave of relief. Jared would never have looked into the diary, and she didn't think Clyde had ever been up in the attic. Her teenage secrets were safe. She smiled, thinly.

"Okay, good," she said. "I was afraid I lost it. I don't have very many of Nana's gifts. Not anymore."

Now it was Clyde's turn to smile. "Nana?"

"Nana," she said firmly. It was the first time she'd shared that name with Clyde.

Clyde gave a shouted laugh. "Nana and Nina. Quite a pair."

Nina said, "I've heard that joke before."

"Me too," Jared said, censoriously.

"Well, gang," Clyde said, "it's a new one on me." He laughed again. "What other gifts did you get from Nana, Nina?"

"Stop it," she said.

The rebuke sounded forceful, and he did stop, though the smile didn't quite leave his face. Jared, as if wanting to break the tension, leaned forward from the backseat and said, "When are we stopping? I'm getting sick of this drive."

"Are you?" said Clyde with his familiar, thinly veiled sarcasm. "Are you getting sick of it?"

"Yes," Jared said.

"Me too," Nina said.

"Did Nana ever give Nina a noogie?" Clyde asked as he reached across and gave her one.

She slapped his hand away. "Stop it, I said!"

"There's an exit coming up, for Oxford," Jared said. "Maybe we could stop there."

Clyde asked, in a tone impossible to interpret, "You want to do that?"

"Yes," Nina said, rubbing the side of her head.

"Me too," Jared said. "Whatever town comes next, let's stop."

So, in a mile or two, Clyde turned off the interstate. "Pretty soon," he said, "we're gonna need to get rid of this car. I reckon Oxford, Mississippi, is as good a place as any."

"What?" Nina said. "Get rid of it?"

Jared said, "But why?"

"You two sure ask a lot of questions."

"Why are we getting rid of the car?" Jared repeated.

Clyde nodded, holding the wheel fiercely at ten and two. "Yessir, an awful lot of questions. I wish you'd just stick to the plan, and hush."

"What plan?" Jared asked.

"What plan?" Clyde repeated, mockingly.

Nina, disgusted, did not even bother to speak.

Although she knew well, of course, that if she were another person, looking on, she might find Clyde's antics and wordplay funny, at the moment she could not help but take his behavior personally. Yet her displeasure did not last very long. Watching him out the sides of her eyes she was impressed, as always, by his sheer manly confidence, his strong-boned face and hands, his handling of the car as though he were a professional driver and knew exactly where they were going. Despite the setbacks in his life, the outright failures, Clyde maintained that eerie composure and self-confidence that Travis had lacked utterly toward the end of his life and that Nina could not help but find strangely admirable in his younger brother. She did not stay angry, no. She had made a commitment, of sorts, though she and Clyde did not speak in such terms, and if Clyde were the one to back out, she would feel a sharp sense of loss and the pain of her riven heart would surely be more than she could bear. She tried not to think about Clyde's motives or her own. She had no idea, really, why Clyde wanted them to take this trip out west, and at times it seemed pointless. At other times she grew quiescent and their journey had in her mind all the indelible hallmarks of fate itself.

By the time they reached the motel in this place called Oxford, near a university whose nestled darkened buildings she could glimpse in the moonlight, she had lulled herself into a state of calm, her feverish thinking gradually abated not unlike the way a temperamental small child cries itself to sleep. As they had done two nights before, they hauled their belongings into the room—just one room this time, Clyde said they needed to conserve their money—but with two beds that looked so welcoming to Nina. She dared not say that she would rather lie down peacefully next to Jared than with her lover, but it was true she didn't want to sleep in his bed, not until her head cleared and she understood with a single mind what the hell they were doing.

Clyde, of course, did not seem assailed by any such wondering thoughts or creeping self-doubts. Once they'd settled in, he'd gone immediately to the telephone. She listened, or half-listened, to his side of the calls while unpacking her suitcases. Clyde spoke first and perfunctorily to Billie—asking after Rooney, mainly—and then he called one of the men who worked at the funeral home, she supposed it was Luther, for she'd noticed in Clyde a particular kind of condescension whenever he spoke to a Black person. (Travis had used this same tone: almost as if the McCune brothers had learned to speak to Blacks as one would lecture gently to small children.) That's when Nina stopped listening altogether. She glanced over to Jared, who sat at the end of his bed watching the TV set that was playing a rerun of a situation comedy featuring raised, near-hysterical voices and, every few seconds, canned laughter that did not sound convincing.

"What're you watching?" Nina asked.

"Nothing," Jared said.

Clyde waved an arm to silence them, and they did fall silent. Clyde pointed to the phone and then returned to his call. And anyway, Nina thought wildly, what could she say to her son? *Let's get out of here, just you and me, grab the keys and get in the car the next time Clyde visits the bathroom, we'll leave all our stuff behind, most important leave Clyde behind, let's drive back to Georgia and resume our old life and pretend none of this ever happened. And then*...But here her thinking faltered. What would they do for money? she asked herself. It would require a year of new courses before she could go back to nursing, if she could go back at all. She no longer felt like a nurse, in any case; she did not know who or what she would become if she left Clyde. People back in that town were gossiping, whispering about them, and if she returned not only she but Jared would suffer as well. And when the thought "leave Clyde behind" had come to her, she blanched, for she did not want to leave him. Not really. No. Despite everything she cared for him, still—far more, she knew, than she had ever cared for Travis—and this simple fact kept her in place.

She said nothing further to Jared and went back to unpacking her bags.

Finally Clyde was off the phone. That's when she stopped unpacking.

She turned and gave him a look that he must have found alarming, for his eyebrows were raised slightly above his questioning blue eyes. Even Jared, a moment ago preoccupied with his TV show, looked over as if feeling the sudden tension between Clyde and his mother. Now he grabbed the remote and snapped off the TV, leaving an ominous silence in the room.

"What?" Clyde said to Nina. "Is something—"

"Clyde, let's go back. Back to Georgia. I mean it." But she did not really mean it.

"Back? Are you—"

She glanced at Jared. "He needs to be in school, and I need to go back to nursing, to the job I was trained for, I can't just—"

"—*just?*" He spoke the word with infinite contempt. He spoke the word as if it were a curse.

"I don't mean it that way, I still want us to—I mean"—again she glanced at Jared—"it's just that everything's moving too fast; I've never even been out west and I really don't see the point. What's out there, anyway—deserts, hot weather?... I want to go back and think all this out. It's like we're running from something instead of moving *toward* something, we need to talk more, we need to decide what we want to do, and why."

She didn't know if her words made sense—in fact, she was certain they did not—but she stuck to them, her fists clenched at her sides.

Clyde ran his tongue along his upper lip. "You've gone bat-shit crazy," he said.

"Maybe," Nina said.

"Jared, go down to that ice machine we saw in the stairwell, get us some ice." Clyde pointed to the empty, upside-down ice bucket on the room's one little desk.

"Mom?" Jared said.

She could not turn to face her son. "Yes, some ice," she said, her voice croaking slightly. "I'm thirsty."

"I'm thirsty too," Clyde said. "Would you mind, Jared?"

Jared wasn't stupid and had to know they were just getting rid of him, but his gangly limbs moved obediently to the door; the bucket swung at his side as he went.

"I'll get us some Cokes," he said at the doorway.

"Yeah, do that," Clyde said gratefully.

The minute the door closed behind the boy, Clyde came forward and grabbed both her arms. "What the fuck you think you're doing?"

She turned her head, as though he'd slapped her, then she turned it the other way.

"I want to go home," she said unconvincingly.

"We *are* home," Clyde said. "Wherever we are—that's home."

"We live in Georgia," Nina said as if reading the words off a card. "That's our home."

Now he did slap her, hard. Nina raised one hand to her cheek and tears filled her eyes. She hadn't thought he'd do that, ever. She didn't want him to do that, ever again. So she did not slap him back but let her head mimic a hangdog posture and expression, noticing the carpet was muddy-colored, like their car, and not very clean. She could see little threads and stains in the carpet and for a moment she thought her knees might buckle but she managed to stay upright and allow herself to think, clearly, *Yes, I'm bat-shit crazy, beyond all redemption,* and then she took a step sideways and sat on the bed nearest to her, hoping Clyde wouldn't take this as an invitation. You never knew with Clyde. You never knew. He stood staring down at her like you would stare at a small dog you had kicked, and he said, "I'm sorry."

"Sure you are."

"Really. I am."

"Is that right," she said.

"We need to talk, all of us—you're right about that. There's something I need to tell you." But the moment she looked up to see that his face had paled dramatically, the room door opened and there was Jared with the ice bucket, and three Cokes held precariously in his other hand.

That was the beginning of the end, I suppose.

This motel room did not smell particularly good, and it looked worse. I tried to distract myself by pouring the Coke over the cluster of ice in the glass my son handed me. Then, from where I sat on the edge of the bed, I glanced across to the mirror above the chipped little desk and saw to my dismay that I belonged in this room, sitting on the side of this lumpy bed. My short dyed-blond hair was windblown from riding in the car and my lipstick, the only makeup I'd bothered with, had been mostly chewed off, and I was pale, paler even than Clyde who I suppose had reason to be pale. I wore an untucked black blouse and blue jeans, the only sign of my old life being the little crucifix I wore at my neck. Nana, you had given me that. On my wedding day. You'd smiled an ambivalent smile and said, "It can't hurt, and maybe it'll do some good. Have a happy life, darling."

This was a blessing, not a curse, I told myself.

So I clung to that. I clung to that.

24

Of course, he finally told them. He told them everything and they had no choice but to believe him. He spoke so earnestly, and ruefully, his forearms against the table with his cuffs folded back just so, one fold, two folds, just as Travis had done. Exactly as Travis had done. She wished she didn't remember such details because in the past they'd brought her closer to Clyde, made her want to put her arms around him and bring him near but that impulse had fled—at least for the moment—as he sat there calmly telling her, and a rapt Jared, how he had killed a man.

He hadn't meant to kill him—he kept stressing that. It was an accident. It was self-defense. Still, the man was dead and Clyde, a younger and stronger man, was alive. So they were after him. Surely they were after him. Seeing Clyde's morose expression, Nina thought: *I was right, we're running away, not toward,* but she pushed the idea back into the roiling chaos of her mind. *What does this make me and poor Jared, accomplices, accessories?* She let all the legalese surface from the cop shows she'd watched over the years, and probably the same phrases were running through Jared's mind too.

She glanced at her son. His face had turned pale and clammy in the candlelight.

They were seated in a restaurant near the courthouse square of Oxford, Mississippi, on a balmy May evening of 1992—her birthday. It was the strangest birthday she'd ever known. Once Clyde had gotten out the gist of his tale and begun repeating himself, stressing this fact, stressing that assertion, she let her mind drift from his urgent telling into her own wonderment and despair. For what would happen to them? What would happen when the authorities found the old man's body and saw the evidence of strangulation? Clyde said he had simply been trying to subdue Tolliver, who'd become irrational when Clyde told him he was quitting, moving out west, out to New Mexico; it seemed Clyde had come to represent something of a child-figure to the old man, the son he'd never had—something as ridiculous as that, plus he'd worked hard at training him, teaching him the business—and Tolliver had begun flailing at him, beating at his shoulders, his arms, so that Clyde had to grab the man's hands and had somehow turned him around—it had happened so fast, that cliché was true!—and pull his own strong arm across his throat, just to subdue him, just to calm him down. And pulling his arm against the old man's throat *had* calmed him, for he grew quiet, and slowly Clyde released the pressure of his arm against the old man's throat, and that's when he knew. For instead of coughing, sputtering, the old man simply slid down Clyde's body toward the floor in a kind of macabre swoon, and though Clyde tried to hold him up, there was no stopping that slow downward drift of mortality, old Tolliver was surely dead with his face pale as one of the corpse's out in the viewing rooms but without makeup, without amelioration of any kind. Clyde saw that face every day, male, female, it didn't matter, he saw it and recognized it at once, the face of blank mortality, utter deadness, implacable.

As if sensing that Nina's thoughts had wandered, Clyde grabbed her soft white forearm and said, "You believe me, don't you? Honey?"

She said, in a doubtful monotone, "I believe you."

"I mean, you know I wouldn't— I wouldn't ever— Jared? You believe me too?"

"Sure I do," Jared said. His face still held that rapt look and he was almost smiling. "Sure."

Clyde touched Jared's forearm too. "The pair of you is all I've got, though I'm sorry I involved you in this, I really am, but I figured we could get away and maybe they'd think it was just an intruder come into the place to rob Tolliver, you know? And things got out of hand, so they took the money and ran? I did take the cash out of the safe and left the door hanging open, to make it look like a robbery and also because I knew we'd need it, even though running off like I did makes me look guilty as hell." He withdrew his hands and cupped his face in them, allowing himself this self-pitying gesture only a moment—it really wasn't his style—and then he checked their faces as if to see how his own must look to them. Nina could not feel her own face. She kept staring at Clyde, though she would look at Jared briefly, checking on *him*, and return to gazing at Clyde as if responding to some force-field of energy that would not let her glance away.

The restaurant they'd found, she couldn't remember its name, was about half full on this weekday night. It was, she supposed, for a town this small, one of the few "nice" restaurants, with a brick wall along one side (the space had once been a tobacco barn, their waiter had told them, with the smiling glibness of one who must repeat this fact many times each evening) and with white tablecloths and candles all flickering in the crepuscular light cast down from antique-looking chandeliers. On another night, in another circumstance, she might enjoy being here. The large room buzzed with conversation from the fifteen or twenty tables, she could smell the vanilla wax from the two tall candles at their table; yes, she felt it was a pleasant place, a pleasant atmosphere, but no she did not feel it, only observed it. She did not know what she really felt. This man across from her, he was a murderer? He was confessing this not only to her but to her innocent (yes, fourteen is innocent, even for a boy) and handsome young son who sat with his face clammy and rapt in the candlelight, staring at his uncle? Out of nowhere, Jared spoke.

"What did it feel like?" he asked.

Clyde frowned. "Feel like?"

"Killing somebody. Killing another person."

"Honey, what a question," Nina whispered.

"But what exactly did it—"

At that moment the smiling, rather unctuous waiter with his

curly dark hair and white apron approached the table to ask if they'd decided on their order.

Clyde waved a hand in the air, dismissively. "No, come back," he said.

"Certainly, sir," the waiter said, retreating into the buzzing noise of the restaurant.

Clyde squared his shoulders, took a sip of wine, and glanced uneasily at his entranced nephew. "What did it feel like? You mean—?"

"Killing another guy," Jared said, in a queer humming monotone. "How did that feel?"

Nina felt the need to laugh. She did laugh. "Sweetie, what a question!" she repeated. "I'm sure it felt terrible, once your uncle realized—"

Clyde nodded, grateful to be fed his lines. "Yeah, it felt terrible."

The words sounded hollow and Jared wasn't satisfied.

"No, really, I mean the moment he stopped struggling, stopped breathing, how did *you* feel? Was there something—you know, enjoyable about it?" Now it was Jared who seemed to be suggesting what Clyde should say. "Was it...I mean, this isn't the word...but was it fun?"

"Jared!" Nina cried.

Clyde looked at his nephew, levelly. "I suppose so," he said flatly. "I suppose it was fun."

"Clyde, don't encourage his nonsense!" Nina said, giving that uneasy laugh. "I mean, the two of you, you're impossible," she said, using a word she would never use—*impossible* was a word out of some old movie melodrama—so she went quiet before she said anything else incriminating or absurd.

Clyde nodded, taking another sip of wine. He said, "Yeah, we're impossible, all right."

By the time they got back to the motel, a cloak of silence had enveloped her. Nina felt she could not breathe. She took a shallow breath, then another, and briefly she imagined she might grab Jared by the hand and get out of there, take a taxi somewhere, get away from this man, this murderer. She kept eyeing Jared, hoping he was all right, but actually he seemed fine; he'd chatted with Clyde during their stroll back from the restaurant, talking of random things, never once mentioning old man Tolliver or the killing or any of that. Nina must train herself to use that word, *killing*, not *murder*, for clearly it had been self-defense, but why hadn't Clyde stayed in town and just explained everything to the police? They'd have understood, surely. They'd have believed him. For why would Clyde murder a frail old man more than twice his age, and at that the old man who'd employed him, who'd in a way rescued him by giving him a job and a future? Nina didn't know why Clyde was driving them to Santa Fe, or wherever—was he lying? Maybe he had indeed murdered the old man for some reason of his own! And it was then, standing by the little prefab faux-mahogany desk in the motel room, Nina put her hands over her face as though about to give way to an upsurge of tears, but no tears came, floods of tears weren't her style, and besides if she wept it would upset Jared, who sat on the bed doing, of all things, his Rubik's cube, as if working the puzzle one more time would solve their problems once and for all.

Nina felt the need to break their silence—Clyde had lain down on the bed, his shoes and socks off, and was staring up at the ceiling—so she said, "But, Clyde, I don't understand. I don't understand why you pulled your arm so hard against his throat, a feeble old man like that, and you're so strong—"

Clyde raised himself on one elbow. "Didn't know my own strength, I guess. Obviously, I'd take it back if I could. We wouldn't have had the argument, I wouldn't have gotten so mad—"

Nina blanched. "You didn't say that, back in the restaurant. That you were mad."

"Sure I did."

Jared looked up from his puzzle. "Mom's right. You didn't."

Clyde clenched his eyes tight, in a jokey way. "Oh no, they're ganging up on me," he said.

"What made you mad?" Nina asked. She could hear her persistent whine, which she didn't like the sound of, but she had to uncover what she could.

"What 'made' me mad...?"

Nina said nothing.

Clyde raised himself into a sitting position, letting his legs fall over the edge of the bed. His bare toes were wriggling. "I don't know, something about his attitude. I mean, I was just telling him I wanted to move, to get out of that muggy Southern town and travel out west into the dry air, where I could breathe again, you know? But instead he just thought of himself, his lousy business and how I'd be 'skipping out' on him." Clyde nodded, as if he'd hit upon something. "Yeah, those were the words he used..."

Nina said, "Well, you can sort of understand, can't you? After he'd taken you in, during that time when you couldn't find anything, and given you a job, and trained you to take over one day? Like you said, you were almost a son to him."

Clyde laughed derisively. "Right," he said.

Jared kept working at his Rubik's cube, with its clicking noises. Then he said, "Done," and tossed the completed puzzle onto his bed.

Clyde laughed again.

They were silent a moment, Clyde sitting tensely on the edge of his bed, Jared sitting cross-legged on the other bed, Nina standing between them, looking from one to the other.

"But what will we do, Clyde?" she asked. "I mean, we've got to go back, you've got to contact the police and explain to them, just let them know what happened the way you just told us, and surely they'll—"

"Surely they'll put the cuffs on me and throw me in the slammer for life," Clyde said, snidely. "Brilliant idea, hon."

She kept hearing the pathetic words in her head, *But what will we do, Clyde?* How she hated herself sometimes! She should make her own decision about what to do! Yes, after insisting she wanted to sleep in Jared's bed, make some excuse about Clyde's snoring or something like that, she'd sleep close to Jared and when Clyde began to snore (just like Travis!) she'd nudge Jared awake and put one finger over her lips. *Ssh. Don't make any noise.* Then she'd tiptoe into the bathroom and take the bag she'd packed swiftly and silently after Clyde got into bed and they'd go down to the motel desk, ask the manager to call a taxi, and then take the cab to the police station. She wasn't getting into that smelly Toyota, not for another minute... They would explain everything to the police, give Clyde up, beg for mercy, talk to the officer—surely there would be one kindly officer, in a small town like this!—one who would listen to a pale pregnant woman with her son in tow! She would, she thought frantically, feverishly, try to impersonate a rational, normal woman who'd simply gotten herself into a mess and needed some help.

Or maybe she wouldn't go to the police. Instead she'd take some money out of Clyde's wallet, enough to pay for a bus trip to Memphis—she knew that was the nearest big city, she'd heard Clyde mention that—and then from Memphis she and Jared would find their way back home. She would call Kay and have her wire the money for a plane ticket back to Atlanta, and there they'd rent a car for the trip. Yes, she could accomplish all this. She looked at Jared and saw that his hair already had begun to fill back in, just a little; before long he'd be back to normal, and she would go to a hair stylist the day she got back to town and get her hair dyed back to its natural auburn shade... Then Jared would go back to school—there were only a few days left in the spring term, and he wasn't going to miss them!—and to his work at the grocery store, and she'd start applying for jobs. She didn't care if people talked, she instructed herself. She didn't care what they thought. Maybe they'd even talk about moving to Atlanta, at least for the summer, living with Kay for a while if Kay didn't mind. She knew she could accomplish all this! And she would not miss Clyde, she instructed herself. Not even slightly.

❧

She never did tell them it was her birthday.

❧

Just before midnight, lying in bed, she felt something—a languid kick in her abdomen. One kick, and then stillness. She knew, she seemed to know...but don't be ridiculous, she told herself, you don't know anything. She was whimpering, softly. She did not know what to feel.

It was two o'clock, then three o'clock, and of course she could not sleep, the stillness and uncertainty in her abdomen distracted her, so she lay there struggling to think about her birthday (of all meaningless things!) and not about the—the other. For the first time in her life, her birthday had gone unnoticed by anyone. She had dreaded a call from Billie earlier in the day, for she tended to remember such things, but even dependable old Billie had forgotten.

So here she lay, like one of those stilled figures Clyde arranged in caskets back at the funeral home, unable to move, feeling an utter deadness at the pit of her stomach.

She was surprised, a little, that Jared had not remembered what day this was, but their lives were in such upheaval, and he seemed so preoccupied, she supposed it was understandable. Teenaged boys need to be reminded of their mother's birthdays, don't they?—even a boy as sensitive and sweet as Jared. As for Clyde, he'd never even asked when her birthday was, nor had she asked after his...

Her grandmother used to say that if you pushed all the thoughts out of your mind, you would go to sleep. But after only a few seconds, her eyes opened again. How could she clear all the clamorous notions from her head? Her grandmother, though very shrewd about life, was a rather simple older woman who never had trouble sleeping—but the granddaughter was another story. She could not stop the incessant rampage of her thoughts. She could not stop trying to understand herself. She could not—

A memory came to her, one she accepted grudgingly: as they'd exited the restaurant this evening, a young man had been entering. He had a pockmarked face and dirty-blond, slicked-back hair. His expression was severe, even menacing. He appeared to be by himself, though he was "dressed up" in a dark-blue suit of some shiny material, a starched white shirt, a blue tie with tiny red marks decorating it, like splashes. There was a moment of awkwardness—Clyde trying in his polite Southern way to hold open the door, the other man shrinking back, insisting that Clyde and his family come out first—and finally the pockmarked man yielded, and came alone into the restaurant. He glanced at Clyde, at Jared, and then fixed his gaze on Nina. His eyes were a light hazel, yet they glared at her as though she'd done something to offend him. Nina shivered. All this had happened in only a few seconds but she would never forget the encounter with the pockmarked man through the rest of her life.

No, she would not forget: for he reminded her of someone. When she was a young girl, there was a man, a drifter, very much resembling the man they'd encountered at the restaurant, who had entered a boarding house in Chicago and had slaughtered eight student nurses. (There had been a ninth nurse present that night, but she had escaped the man's attention by hiding under a bed.) This had happened on the night of July 13, 1966, and Nina had been thirteen years old. She saw the blaring headlines of the newspaper story (knowing better than to mention the story to Nana) and when her grandmother's copy of *Life* magazine came a week or two later she saw the cover story about the crime, entitled simply, "The Nine Nurses." One of the most vivid memories of her childhood was her perusing of that article. By the time Nana came into where her granddaughter sat on the crushed blue velvet sofa in the living room, paging through the oversized magazine, it was too late. Nina had already read the article, she had already gone through the photographs of the nurses and the killer several times, staring, aghast, by the time her grandmother said, "What're you reading, honey?" When the old woman saw the cover of the magazine, she pulled it gently out of Nina's perspiring hands. "Oh, you shouldn't read things like *this*," Nana had said, "that's for grown-ups," and as she hurried toward the kitchen, where she would toss that copy of *Life* magazine unceremoniously into the trash, Nina could hear her say, "It's not for anyone, really. Don't know why they print this kind of thing."

But, yes, it was too late. Little Nina Sellers no longer needed the magazine, anyway, for its images and phrases had seared themselves into her memory.

Richard Speck—that was the murderer's name.

Later, in her teenage years, she would think that "Speck" was an appropriate name, for he'd been a mere speck of a man—a drunkard, a drifter, a killer. Nina pondered his face: so badly scarred by teenage acne and yet, if it weren't for the scars, he might even be an attractive man with his muscled, tattooed arms and shoulders, his abundant dark-blond hair, his prominent nose. But no. *A speck. The dregs of humanity.* For no reason anyone ever determined Richard had broken into the back door of the young student nurses' boarding house late on that night of July 13 and he had somehow managed to gather the women into a single room, where he tied them up, insisted he would not hurt them if they stayed quiet, and then, one by one, took them into other rooms to slaughter them. Some by stabbing. Some by strangulation. Little Nina had turned the newspaper pages and, later, the big glossy pages of *Life* with her lips parted, her eyes opened wide; she could not believe what she was seeing and reading. Some of the nurses were from the Philippines, others were Americans; some were pictured in their nurses' uniforms, including their perky white caps, and others wore ordinary street clothes, smiling for the camera. Smiling hopefully. Smiling toward the future. Nina had stared particularly hard at the snapshot of Corazon Amurao, the Filipino nurse who had escaped Richard Speck's murder spree and who would later testify at the trial, identifying him and thus helping convict the killer and send him to prison for life. *Richard Speck.*

She would never forget that name. She would never forget that face.

Through the years she would occasionally see follow-up stories in newspapers or on the TV news, which always showed Speck's cold, pockmarked features, and which sometimes "updated" the public about the life of Corazon Amurao. Nina had been pleased to read, shortly before this past Christmas, that Speck had died in prison, of a heart attack; she'd always had the vague discomfiting fantasy that he might one day get out, and go on another rampage against nurses. The mass murder in Chicago had nothing to do with Nina herself becoming a nurse, for she'd had her heart set on nursing from the age of five or six, and through Nina's childhood her grandmother had given her several nurse dolls, complete with pristine white uniforms, white shoes, and those pert white caps. She had loved these dolls. She had loved the idea of helping people, and even the very word "nurse" sent a pleasurable shiver down her back.

What had happened to all that? she wondered. Several times she had mentioned pursuing nursing again when they got to Santa Fe, but she wasn't really serious, and in any case Clyde always made some dismissive comment or other. "Wouldn't you have to go back to school, get another license?" he'd asked, frowning.

"I could do that," Nina had said.

One time Clyde had patted her stomach. "You'll have a baby to nurse," he said, "that's more important than tending to strangers. I'll make plenty of money to support us, you'll see."

"It's not the money—" Nina began.

"And besides," Clyde interrupted, "the system cheats nurses. Doesn't pay them enough. They know almost as much as the doctors, more sometimes, but they get paid a fraction of what those guys get. It's not fair. I won't let them cheat you, Nina."

"But, Clyde, I *want* to work."

Clyde looked over as if she'd uttered an obscenity.

So she'd let the matter drop, that time. In fact, she let the matter drop every time. She had learned to let Clyde win this or that argument and in the long run she would pick her battles, and she would lose the ones that didn't hurt too much, even if that meant never working as a nurse again, even if there were men like Richard Speck and Clyde McCune and others like them roaming around.

Have a happy life! her grandmother had said, on Nina's graduation day. She would never forget.

They drove. They drove only a few hours each night, slowly and aimlessly, though always west, or northwest, or southwest. Sometimes they stuck to Interstate 20, as they'd done in Alabama, but then for no reason Nina could discern, Clyde would have a sort of panic attack, certain they were being followed, worrying about their car and license plate being recognized. Once, at a rest stop, he took a screwdriver out of the glove compartment and began removing the license plate from a long, pale-blue Oldsmobile, wanting to switch the plates, but just as he'd begun the work he heard the sounds of people coming along, laughing and chattering, so he'd been unable to finish, he left the Oldsmobile's tag hanging by one screw and got back in the Toyota and they drove off. In her side-view mirror Nina could see the people, a couple and two children who were getting into the Oldsmobile, staring after the Toyota, but they hadn't seemed to notice the askew license plate; they simply got in the car as though nothing were wrong. And nothing was wrong, apparently, except Clyde said, "That was a close one."

In such panicked moments Clyde would drive them five or ten miles away from the interstate, prompting Jared to ask, "Where are we going? We're in the middle of nowhere," but no one answered him and soon enough they were on some broken-down old highway, going thirty or thirty-five, and they'd keep turning onto such westward-heading roads until another sign for I-20 would appear, and they'd exit again onto the interstate ramp. Usually there were gas stations near these ramps that sold food, and they'd buy hot dogs and doughnuts (these were Jared's favorites; Nina didn't care what she ate) to devour in the car. Once in a while Nina made Jared clean out the backseat, for there were crumpled food wrappers and empty soda cans everywhere, but each time she looked back there was more of the smelly trash it seemed they could not escape. A couple of times Nina urged Clyde to drive faster, insisting they needed to make more progress, but perversely he seemed in no hurry. "They think we're headed up north, last time I talked to Billie I said we were in Ohio. Ohio!" He repeated the word as if it were a witticism.

Clyde kept assuring Nina and Jared that they'd get to Santa Fe before long, but unusually for him, he did not seem confident. He glanced often into the rearview mirror, he insisted they drive only at night and kept them hidden in motel rooms during the day in rural parts of the Southern states that did indeed seem, to Nina, "the middle of nowhere," and she was surprised by her own and her son's docility as Clyde drove them to a destination that seemed mere words, not a reality where they might soon live and work and behave like normal human beings.

Santa Fe. Nina knew nothing about this city, only that it was supposed to be "pretty," and was light years from the scruffy Southern town where she'd spent much of her adult life. Of course, she hadn't had the time before they left to wonder where they might live, where Jared would enroll in school. As for Clyde, he finally told them he had a contact there, a wealthy, well-connected investor who would help him get a job, but he refused to give much detail about this vaunted opportunity except to say that this "money man" he knew from college had virtually guaranteed Clyde could have a job running a mortuary facility ten times the size of old Tolliver's, and that with his "savings" (Tolliver's money, of course) he'd be a part owner of the funeral home, too, and eventually they'd all be rich and live the good life, the American dream. One night, talking in this vein, he'd reached over and patted her stomach and whispered,

"*He'll* never want for anything, that's for sure," and Nina had felt an emptiness, a coldness there at the pit of her stomach, fearing she might bear some kind of chilled misshapen thing but never a living, squalling creature.

They had just crossed the Louisiana state line into Texas, having spent most of the day in the nondescript city of Shreveport, when Jared said, "Hey, the interstate just got a whole lot smoother. They must have more money in Texas."

Clyde grinned. "They have gobs of money in Texas."

But Nina was thinking of something else. She said, "Clyde, have you ever heard of Richard Speck?"

"Richard what? Speck?"

"Yes." Her heart was beating madly so that the sensation numbed her ears, but she knew Clyde and Jared could not hear the sound, if it were a sound. She was thinking, of course, of the young man at the restaurant, and of the photo she still vividly remembered from those old newspaper and *Life* magazine articles, but she stared straight ahead as if nothing was wrong.

"No, who is he?" Clyde said. He looked over, still grinning, those slantwise dimples like deep scars in his cheeks. "An old boyfriend of yours?"

"No."

"Then who is he? For God's sake, Nina, you brought him up."

"Yeah, who is it, Mom?" Jared said, folding his arms across the top of the backseat.

But Nina refused to look at them. She stared straight ahead. "Nobody, really, I shouldn't have mentioned him. He was somebody…just somebody I used to know."

25

The worst began, of all places, in a drugstore parking lot on the outskirts of Odessa, Texas. Three more days had passed and they were getting restive, especially Jared. He no longer thumbed through the handful of books he'd brought, saying with teenage hyperbole that he'd read each one "a hundred times"; he no longer worked his Rubik's cube ("I'm sick of that thing—it's gotten too easy"); and he would not even look at the moonlit scenery outside the car window, which changed so dramatically as they drove west. Instead he stared straight ahead with his arms folded.

"Simmer down, simmer down," Clyde would say, trying to placate him, but Nina felt much as her son did. This seemed an endless journey. This seemed a pointless journey, and she still couldn't imagine a destination that would please them all.

She did appreciate the landscape, at least, which had gradually lost trees after the "piney woods" of eastern Texas and now seemed barren, craggy, empty of much life at all. Starting about halfway across the state the terrain had become hilly, then mountainous, enchanting Nina's eye with its arid landscape pocked with cactus and, sometimes, if she looked carefully, some desert creature scuttling across the sand. Under the ample moon the nightscape might have been that of another planet. Both Nina and Jared had begged to stop here in Odessa for the night, they'd driven a couple of hundred miles this evening and it was past eight o'clock and they were "bummed out" (Jared's phrase) by all the driving. They needed a break. They couldn't face the prospect, again, of driving until two or three in the morning. Clyde perhaps had made a mistake—from his own perspective, at least—of telling Nina and Jared that they didn't need to arrive in Santa Fe on any particular day, that the job was his and he could start whenever he wanted, and of course Nina reminded him of this, gently. She had developed a cold around the time they were passing through Louisiana, and Jared was clearly so restless—couldn't they "take a break" for a day or even two days? The air out here in west Texas was wonderfully cool, clear, and dry; Nina thought a brief rest would be therapeutic for them all.

But Clyde said no. Had they forgotten they were surely being chased? Maybe Billie had inadvertently fooled the authorities by telling them Clyde had fled north, but why should they take any chances? He tried a joke, asking if Nina thought Bonnie and Clyde "took breaks" whenever one of them had a cold? Neither she nor Jared thought this was funny.

"I'm sick," Nina said, "and Jared is going to come unglued if we can't spend some time outside this damn car. We could go to a movie, go out to dinner... No one knows us here. Please, Clyde? Just a day or two?"

But still he said no.

"Look at the skyline," Jared said, pointing ahead of them. The city of Odessa was surprisingly large, sprung up out here in this desert landscape, and in fact Jared said the population was over 100,000.

"How do you know that?" Clyde asked skeptically.

"I saw a sign," Jared said. "Didn't you see it? Welcoming us to the city?"

"We're not staying here," Clyde said.

"There must be a really nice hotel, in a city this size," Nina said, putting an edge in her voice. "We could splurge a little, call up room service..."

"Yeah," Clyde said, "and by morning the police would be at our door." His profile was severe; he refused even to glance at her. He added, "We'll stay just long enough to get you something for your cold, and hopefully switch cars."

"We're going to *steal* a car?" Jared said. "That's a good way to lay low, isn't it."

Now Clyde did look over. "He used to be such a nice kid," he said to Nina. "Now listen to the mouth he's got on him."

"I'm trying to be logical," Jared said. "Somebody needs to."

He was staring hard at his mother, so she said, "You're right about that."

"Whoo!" Clyde said, laughing snidely. "Listen to them." He had turned off the interstate onto a service road, and from that onto a four-lane highway lined with strip malls and fast-food places. The parking lots were sparsely dotted with cars; it was near closing time.

"There's a Walgreens," Nina said. "I do need to get something."

To her surprise, Clyde activated the turn signal and slowed to pull into the Walgreens lot. The drugstore was brightly lit, all stucco and glass, and looked fairly new. Clyde turned into the second row of cars and seemed to be looking at a woman in her thirties just getting out of a beat-up red Mustang. She slammed her door and hurried toward the store entrance. Without Clyde's saying anything, Nina knew what he was thinking. He was staring at the woman's Texas license plate, his hands clenched on the wheel as he sat pondering in the beams cast across his features by the neon lights.

Nina touched his forearm. "Don't," she said.

Clyde looked over, annoyed. "Why the hell not?"

"What? Don't what?" Jared said.

Clyde said, "While you go in and get your medicine, keep an eye on her, let me know if she's coming out. It won't take me thirty seconds to grab that plate."

"No. I'm not helping you," Nina said.

"Fine, then. Just stay in the goddamned car. I'll be right back. What brand of cold stuff did you want?"

Even as he said this, Nina was sniffling. It was obvious she needed a decongestant. She said nothing.

"Then you'll get pot luck," Clyde said viciously. He opened the glove compartment and grabbed something—was it a gun, had Clyde kept a gun in the car all this time?—then got out and slammed the door and stalked toward the entrance. He'd jammed the gun into his pocket. Nina was surprised that he hadn't simply taken the screwdriver to get the woman's license plate, before going on Nina's errand. Impulsive. Impulsive man. Jared was clearly thinking the same thing.

"Why didn't he—"

"Who knows," Nina said flatly. "Who can read that excuse for a mind."

They were both quiet a moment, and when she finally glanced at her son, his pale face balanced like a balloon on top of the backseat, she saw why he'd grown quiet. For Nina had been staring at the ignition, at the keys Clyde had left in the car. Impulsive man, or cunning man? Was he daring them to leave him?

"Hold on," Nina said. "I have to think for a minute."

"No," Jared said, surprising her. "We can't just leave him."

"We've got to," Nina said sharply. "This is our chance. We'll go into the city and call 911 and this will all be over."

"No," Jared said.

"It's our only chance," Nina insisted. She was thinking back a few minutes earlier, envisioning Clyde's severely handsome profile when he'd refused to agree they might stop for the night. It was such a simple request. He could have agreed. He could have, for once, done something to please them. But there was a granitic hardness in him, a refusal to make concessions, which prevented him from saying, simply, "Okay. Okay." Instead he was teasing them with those car keys. Or had he simply forgotten them?

In the meantime something had happened—she heard a quick intake of Jared's breath.

"Look, Mom," he said. "The backseat of that Mustang."

Her eye followed his, and her breath came more quickly when she saw the two brownish heads in the backseat.

Children! Nina's heart beat fast, as if measuring off the seconds they had left to get away. She feared that her son, who had an impulsive streak like all the McCunes, was about to jump out the back door, run into the Walgreens and tell Clyde about the kids, urge him to leave the mother alone. He would ruin this one chance to get away.

And then, Jared did exactly that.

"Jared, wait!" she called as he slammed his door. He opened the door again, but slightly.

"What?" he said brusquely. "I've got to get inside. I can't let Clyde—"

"He's dangerous, honey, but he wouldn't hurt a couple of children. We've got to think of ourselves, sweetie. We've got to *go*, and get the cops."

"There's no time, Mom." He slammed the door again.

God, there he went. Her baby. She scooted over to the driver's seat, started the car, and drove up alongside Jared. She called out her window, "Get in the car, honey. *Please*."

They were close to the sidewalk alongside the drugstore entrance. Jared said, "Just wait for me here. I've got to warn her, Mom. I'll be back in a minute."

So she pulled into the handicapped spot and sat there, the engine running. She craned her neck, trying to see through the automatic doors of the Walgreens. Every few seconds, the doors opened and someone went in, or someone came out. But none of them was the woman from the Mustang, and none of them was Clyde.

It was true that Clyde wouldn't hurt a child—especially not her own child.

Behind her, she saw a flash of light, and she realized the car passing her slowly was a police cruiser; both officers' heads were just barely visible. There was an impulse to burst out of the car and stop them, tell them everything, but some perverse emotion stopped her. She imagined them reading her license plate and calling it into the computer, understanding she was an accessory to murder…they would haul her away, and then haul Jared and Clyde away to separate detention units, question them all, and none of what they said would make sense for they would tell, of course, three different stories… She felt her heart hammering madly and then, just at the moment she was about to surrender herself and Jared and Clyde with a single phrase—"We're the McCunes, from Georgia"—she understood what the cops wanted. They had pulled up alongside her. "Ma'am, I don't see no handicapped sticker on your car."

Relief flooded her. "Yes, sir, I'm sorry...my husband is in Walgreens, getting me some cold medicine, and I was just waiting..."

"Can't wait here, ma'am." The cop was a young Hispanic man with half a smile curling his lips, as if he thought Nina was pretty, though she knew she must look ghastly under the fluorescent lights. Yet with men, you never knew.

Nina said, "I'll move the car, sir. Thank you."

That was a role Nina played so well. *I'll move the car, sir. Thank you.*

Slowly she pulled out of the handicapped space, and the cop drove off. But she kept looking back, toward the Walgreens lot. Jared was back there, in that store, and it was up to Nina to protect him from whatever scheme Clyde had concocted in his twisted excuse for a brain. She had to get back to Jared. But now she saw the woman from the red Mustang, who was holding a small sack in one hand. She was walking, a bit unsteadily, along the neon-lit sidewalk toward her car. She was in her mid-thirties and had pulled back her light-brown hair in a ponytail; she wore clothes she might have bought at Walmart, or Target. An ordinary young woman, an ordinary night. For a moment Nina studied the woman's face, which was pretty in a mild, nondescript way, and Nina thought with envy how the woman probably had not encountered Clyde while in the drugstore, and how she was going to go home and resume her ordinary life here in Odessa, Texas, without ever knowing of the existence of Clyde, Nina, and Jared McCune.

Lucky her, Nina thought.

Slowly, Nina began circling the lot, glancing around for the police car. For of course she should have stopped them. Perhaps they'd pulled out onto the service road, and she could reach them if she drove fast enough. And she did drive fast. For some reason she pulled down the visor, and stared at her clammy, unwashed face in the blurry little mirror, her hair that had a half-inch or so of auburn coming out from the roots, the rest that fake blond that women had used for decades to lure men and to please them. Yes, she looked horrible, she thought. She looked like a common criminal. That's what she would tell them—*I'm Nina McCune. I'm a criminal*—but using other words she could not now imagine. She kept glancing into the visor mirror. It had been days since she'd worn make up and her features were almost unrecognizable, pinched with anxiety, apprehension. She glanced down at her stomach and saw the slight curvature of the baby that was dead but she could not think of that. She dared not. Quickly she pushed the visor back up and let out a few hacking coughs. She had reached the service road and it was time to make her turn and find those damned cops. Her son was young enough that they would reunite him with his mother in custody, wouldn't they? Wouldn't they?

She sneezed, unable to stifle it. Slowly and silently she rolled down her window, took a breath of the fresh, dry air, and she could hear the night noises of the desert surrounding the car and the sparse traffic going back and forth along the service road. She could hear the sound of wind, of scuttling creatures… Ahead of her, she saw nothing. Just darkness. A darkness without cars, taillights. So the cop had escaped her, she thought ironically.

Did her Jared, her baby, imagine that she'd abandoned him? And as for Clyde, what the hell was he doing inside that Walgreens?

Once Clyde set something into motion, she thought, he did not usually back down. Some new turn of events had started inside that drugstore, and it wasn't a good turn, it wasn't anything good for any of them, not even Clyde. But nothing could stop it. Her only option was to find that cop, or any cop. They would drive immediately to pick up Jared.

Nina pressed hard on her gas pedal and drove into the star-drenched night, turning her back on the life she might have led as the wife of Clyde McCune.

PART SIX

CLYDE

26

Clyde knew he shouldn't have gone up into that attic. He was seven years old and he knew better since his parents had instructed him about it and they had scolded him when he went up there anyway. But he never faced any real consequence because he was so used to doing what he wanted. Once in a while his father would swat him upside the head but it was almost like his father was swatting his own head because a mosquito or a gnat was bothering him. Clyde existed only at the periphery of his old man's consciousness. An annoyance. A puzzlement. Just a small botheration like all his kids for the old man was mainly interested in his drinking and his smoking and sometimes in his wife but that was about all. As a result Clyde was left to do pretty much as he wanted. So were the other kids and what Rooney, in particular, wanted to do was follow Clyde around.

Last night he'd phoned Billie to "check in" and see how Rooney was. He hadn't told Nina or Jared this but Rooney had been sick ever since they'd left her. A high fever. Headaches that Billie was certain were severe because she kept holding her head and crying, "Hurts! Hurts!" And she would say other things. She'd call for Clyde. Where was Clyde? *Where was Clyde?* It was a mantra. A cry of woe.

When *was* Clyde planning on heading back? Billie would say timorously.

Clyde stalked up and down the damn fluorescent-lit antiseptic-smelling drugstore aisle looking for Nina's medicine. He saw a sign for "Analgesics" and thought that aisle might be the one. But why had Rooney insisted on doing everything he did? Right now he could imagine her loping up and down these aisles behind her big brother. And why had she followed him up into that goddamned attic? It was dank and hot and smelly up there. There were cobwebs. Buzzing flies. Wasps. Once Rooney had gotten stung and had cried for hours. "That's what you get," her mother had said. She'd swatted the arm of Rooney's that had not been stung. "Why can't you ever mind your mama? We done told you and told you not to run up in that attic. And Clyde sure should know better."

She'd glared at him. Clyde did know better but he kept his lips closed like a vise and refused to cry. For a wasp had stung him too.

"…Help you, sir?"

The woman in the white coat with her name stitched in blue on the lapel brought him out of his reverie. A tiny cinnamon-skinned woman with friendly eyes and bright purple-painted lips. Her name was *Dolores*.

"No. No thanks. I found it."

He pointed to a display of cold remedies. Dolores nodded knowingly.

"There's something going around," she said. She smiled at him.

"We're not from around here," he said gratuitously. And wished he'd bitten his tongue.

"Oh, from where then?" the woman asked.

He thought quickly and randomly. "Chicago. We've had a cold spring."

"Chicago! I've got two sisters up there!" She laughed and put one palm to her cheek as if to signal they should share information further. Clyde made his grim little smile disappear and said, "Well, 'scuse me." He maneuvered around her toward the cold medicine. Grabbed some tablets and a nasal spray.

"Sure hope you feel better!" Dolores called as she proceeded down the aisle.

"I feel fine," Clyde muttered but not so loud that she could hear. Then he called after her, "Thanks!"

He took hold of his two items and gawked around, looking for the cashier. That's when he sighted her. The woman from the car outside. The red Mustang. Oddly she was sitting on the floor near the center of the aisle so another person could hardly get by. She was examining one bottle and reading the ingredients on the side and then replacing the bottle on the shelf. Then she'd take another bottle and examine the tiny print in the same exacting way. Dolores must not have seen the woman or she'd have surely offered to help find what she needed. Now it was just Clyde and the ponytailed woman on this aisle in the middle of Walgreens at 8:45 of a Tuesday night.

Slowly Clyde approached her. Checking out her hair and clothes. There was a little yellow barrette in her hair that he hadn't noticed before and that her daughter might have put there. He'd seen the kids in the car on his way into the drugstore. One girl and one boy. The girl looked a year or two older. Maybe ten years old. The children glanced at him but then went back to watching their mother as she turned the corner toward the drugstore entrance.

Now he said, "Ma'am? Looking for something special?"

She didn't even glance up at him. He liked that. She must have assumed he was a store employee, though if she'd focused on him she'd know otherwise.

"My kids have colds," she said.

Clyde grinned his halfway grin but obviously it would have no effect if she refused to look at him.

"Yeah," he said. "Same here." And he lifted up the containers he'd selected under the approving eye of Dolores.

Now she did look up. "Sorry," she said. "I thought you were—"

"Nope," and now he tried the halfway grin again. "Just thought you looked a bit flummoxed. Like you could use some help."

"I'm all right," the woman said. Finally she selected the container she wanted and with a grunt she got up from the floor.

Clyde extended one hand. "I'm Frank Edson," he said.

She shook his hand in a meek and tentative way. "Hi, Frank," she said noncommittally.

"Reckon we both need the cash register," he said. And now she gave him another look. It was his damned accent.

"I guess so," the woman said.

They walked awkwardly together down the aisle. A jerrybuilt couple. The almost waif-like woman in her ordinary clothes and the slightly taller and equally slender man in his wrinkled white cotton shirt and blue jeans, his gun invisible in his right pocket. The man's sleeve was rolled up, revealing a smudged dark-blue tattoo on his forearm of the kind you get in the service on some drunken night or other but Clyde had not been in the service. He'd just gotten the tattoo from a "temporary worker" in a tattoo parlor who might himself have been drunk. It had been so long ago that he could barely remember the tattoo said "Lost Soul" in a curlicue script. Now it was unreadable.

When they reached the cashier they waited behind an old man buying some cigars. The automatic door swooshed open and Clyde's heart thudded when he saw Jared standing there. Jared came up and stood next to him, fortunately saying not a word.

"This is my kid," Clyde said to the woman. The woman nodded to Jared. Then Clyde said, "Here, let me get that."

He tried to take her container and put it with the two he was buying.

She looked alarmed. "What? You want to pay for my stuff?"

"Well," Clyde said. He thought a moment. "Since we're waiting here together." He knew this made no sense but he let it stand. *Well. Since we're here together in Walgreens in Odessa in Texas in the United States on planet Earth spinning around in the middle of a soulless universe. Why shouldn't I buy your kid's medicine. What the fuck's difference does it make in the scheme of things?*

Something in the woman had closed off. She hadn't liked his offer.

"Thanks, but I can get it," she said.

"Look," Clyde said. "I wasn't trying to—"

Just at that moment the old man gave a phlegmy cough and took his cigars and began shuffling toward the automatic door.

The woman took a quick step toward the cashier and handed her the children's medicine she was buying.

"This'll be all," she said, as if to hurry things along.

"Yes, ma'am," the cashier said. She was an older-looking witch of a woman with dyed glossy-black hair and painted-on arched eyebrows and a bright red mouth. Clyde wondered if she really thought she was prettier with all that junk on her face. Or pretty at all. He thought: Women!

The young ponytailed woman had finished her transaction and courtesy dictated that she acknowledge Clyde and Jared one more time. She looked over her right shoulder and said to him, "Thanks. Thanks for helping me. Hope your kids feel better."

"Actually I just have the one here," Clyde said as if it made any difference to the woman.

He was afraid Jared would pop off but to Clyde's relief the boy stayed quiet.

"Oh. Okay then." She gave him a little wave that somehow touched his heart.

"Hey, wait a sec," he said. He asked the witchy-looking cashier how much his medicines were and she scanned them and said, "With tax, $14.85." He handed her a twenty and said keep the change and thought to himself she could buy some makeup remover with the tip.

"But, sir—" the cashier began. "We can't accept—"

But Clyde had already ushered the young woman out the door that made that whooshing noise again and drowned out the rest of the cashier's words.

To his surprise the ponytailed woman gave a polite laugh. "I'll bet you made her day," she said.

"Somebody needed to," Clyde said, as if now they were in cahoots against the exceedingly ugly woman with her glossy black hair.

Jared trailed behind Clyde and the woman as if monitoring their conversation. A likable kid but a mysterious kid. Clyde had thought this more than once.

He and the ponytailed woman faced each other. What could

he say to her? *I need you to trade cars with me. Please? I'm not going to hurt you or your kids but I've just got a situation here where I need your car.*

Even Clyde was too wary to say anything like this. So he asked, "What's your name?"

A clouded look came into her face. She whispered, as if not wanting Jared to hear, "Look, I'm still married. My husband and I, we aren't together, but we're married. But my name is Ruth Ann."

Clyde said, "Well. Hello, Ruth Ann."

"Hello," the woman said. "And goodbye."

She turned and walked off. He wanted to say something and in truth could think of a dozen things but they all sounded like the crummy phrases any man would use to try and pick up a woman outside a drugstore in the middle of nowhere. So he stood there. Jared came up to him and for some reason touched Clyde's forearm. "Let's go," he said. "Mom said she'd be right out front." Suddenly Clyde's knees ached. He felt as if he'd been running a race but he knew it was just the stress of the moment. He kicked one leg into the air and shook it and then did the same thing with the other. He knew he should quit fooling around and hurry over to the woman's red Mustang before she started the engine and drove off.

When he turned the corner of the drugstore her car that he wanted so badly was there but of course the old Toyota was gone. There was an empty space where the car had been and Clyde glanced at Jared, who was looking around as if astonished that his mother wasn't there. Clyde thought: So she'd done it. She'd gone off to call the police or else she'd just gone back to Georgia, but in any case soon enough it would all be over if he didn't act quickly.

After understanding he'd lost Nina for good, the first thing he thought about was the money. In the trunk of that smelly old Toyota was a bag with wads of cash totaling close to half a million and with that money he'd planned to set all three of them up in Santa Fe. He had no job waiting there as he'd told

them but of course he would get one. Eventually. Why hadn't
she believed him? He'd planned to buy a computer and gin up
a fake resume and fake references and put just enough truth in
the cover letter to make whatever funeral home he approached
believe in his experience and his skills. He would have gotten
his head shaved again or else he would dye what hair had grown
back that same shrill blond color of Nina's hair. But he supposed he could still do these things, if he could get Jared to believe in him. Clyde would put Jared in school under a fake name
and they would live there peaceably for as long as they could.
Or maybe he'd send him back to Georgia and Clyde would live
alone and happy in Santa Fe. Like everyone else in that city
he would get a tan. He would no longer be recognizable and
somehow he would become "Frank Edson" sure enough. He'd
be just another man. Just another anonymous man with no past
at all. He didn't know if this would happen and he understood
that he was confused, which was a state of mind he hated. His
thoughts were going this way and that.

For what if Nina *did* go to the police? They'd nab him in no
time. Maybe he and Jared should light out for some other place.
Up to the northwest, maybe. He had to think. Once the present
situation was resolved by later tonight, he would be by himself
and he would use his logical mind and he would think.

The ponytailed woman had her body twisted around and
was fiddling with one of her kids in the backseat of her Mustang. As he drew closer he could see she was trying to get her
little boy to take one of the probably foul-tasting tablets she
had bought for him. Evidently the child was already drinking
a canned soft drink and Ruth Ann was holding the can and
urging him to take the pill. This scene was being repeated all
over America. A young mother trying to get her child to take
some medicine. He thought, If only she'd gunned her engine
and wheeled out of the parking lot and done the pill business
once she got back home. Then she would be safe.

Jared the mind-reader said, "No. Don't."

Goddamnit, Clyde liked the woman but nonetheless he approached her car window and to his shock and chagrin saw his own image in the glass. He looked gaunt. Evidently he'd lost some weight during the past week or two. Of course he had. The white wrinkled cotton shirt though slim-fitting seemed to billow around him. And his face looked bad and his hair looked bad. It was still very short. A brown stubble like an evil halo around his head. He couldn't stand looking at himself any longer and so he knocked on the window and Ruth Ann and both her kids whirled around to stare at him.

"Don't, Clyde," Jared said again.

Once she recognized him Ruth Ann rolled down the window. Partway. Grudgingly.

"Mr. Edson…?" she said.

Clyde was bent over and trying to lean into the car to the extent that the half-opened window would let him. He smiled. It was more like a stretched and probably ugly grimace but he smiled. Next to him Jared wasn't smiling.

"Hey there," he said and hoped that didn't sound corny.

"Hey," she said almost apologetically. "We're taking some medicine here." She held up the still-unswallowed pill between two fingers and lifted the soft-drink can in the other. She'd had to balance the opened drink can between her legs so she could roll down the window. He was interfering in her work as a mother. He didn't belong here. Her little boy glared at him from the backseat.

"He doesn't like taking his medicine," Ruth Ann said.

"I reckon none of us do."

"Anyway, it was nice to meet you." Her faint smile was fading.

"Wait," he said. And reluctantly she rolled the window back down. A bit further this time.

"Yes?" she said.

He heard something from behind him. He'd reached into his pocket for the gun and a millisecond after that he heard something behind him. It was Nina's voice saying, *No. No, Clyde no.*

But of course he was hearing things. He whirled around but nothing was there. Nina was long gone.

"Listen," he told Ruth Ann. "My kid here and I are in something of a bind."

"A bind?" Ruth Ann said.

"Yeah," he said. "A real bind. See, our old car's died on us a bit down the road and we wondered if you could give us a ride somewhere. Like to a mechanic shop or somewhere."

Ruth Ann looked stunned as if someone had slammed a two-by-four against the side of her head. "But they wouldn't be open..." She glanced at her watch. "They wouldn't be open this time of night."

Clyde held old man Tolliver's gun in his right pocket and could feel the leather of his belt and the black steel of the gun and his sweating hand all rubbing together.

"No," Clyde agreed. "But if you could just drop us off? So we could wait until morning when they open up?"

"You mean—you want to wait all night?" the woman said.

Clyde grinned. "We've all got to take our medicine," he said. He glanced back at the glaring dark-haired boy and winked at him. The boy's expression did not change.

Something seemed to happen inside Ruth Ann. She'd thought a moment. She'd pondered a moment. And the decision had gone against him.

"I'm sorry...is it Mr. Edson?" She nodded her head as if he'd answered her but she was only affirming some decision she'd made during these past few seconds. "I really can't. You see"—and she gestured behind her—"you see, I've got kids. So I can't just..."

She didn't seem to know how to finish this thought.

Clyde said, "Sure you can. Tell you what. I'll give you a hundred if you'll drive us over there." He had that much in his wallet.

Ruth Ann said, "Just call a taxi. It'll be a whole lot cheaper."

From the backseat Ruth Ann's little boy piped up. "I want my soda pop."

"Me too," the little girl said. "Why don't I get a soda pop?"

But both the children's eyes were on Clyde.

"Tell you what," Clyde said. "I see a McDonald's up the road—see them golden arches, kids?" Both the kids nodded emphatically. "We'll get ice cream and soda pop. My wife is there, waiting for my son and me. You can meet her and see we're for real."

That's when something unexpected and unwanted happened. Clyde had turned his body a bit too far and it sent the little girl into a scream. She started crying at once.

"Mama, he's got a gun!" and Ruth Ann glanced down at his pocket and his hands. She said, "You let us go, Mr. Edson."

Clyde said, "I don't mean you any harm."

"Then let us go home. Please."

"Nothing will happen to your brave little boy and girl. You'll take us to McDonald's, all right? Don't try anything and I promise no harm will come to you or either one of your children."

"Mama, what does harm mean?" the little boy asked.

Clyde knocked on Ruth Ann's car door and with a shaking hand she opened it. The look in her eyes said she was thinking about the gun.

"Don't worry," he said with a kindly look. "I wouldn't hurt a child."

A tear leaked from the corner of her eye. "All right," she said. "I reckon we can take you to McDonald's."

Clyde smiled uneasily. "Good girl. Smart girl."

Ruth Ann said to the little boy, "Don't worry, we're just going up there to the McDonald's."

The boy's dark eyes stayed fixed on Clyde.

"C'mon," Clyde told him. He tried to smile. "I'll let you sit in the front seat, and when we get to McDonald's you can have anything you want."

The boy thought a moment. He looked scared but knew he had to obey the adult man and his mother. He held out his pudgy little arm for Clyde to take and Clyde grasped his hand.

"Mommy, don't listen to the bad man!" squealed the little girl.

Ruth Ann was staring dolefully out the car window at Clyde. She said, "Nothing's wrong with your car, is there?"

"We just need a place to rest for a while. After McDonald's you can invite us over. I promise that no harm will come to you. In fact, I'll give you some money. A thousand dollars."

"Minute ago you said a hundred."

"Now it's a thousand," and, though he knew he didn't have that much on him, Clyde gently led the trembling little boy toward the passenger door. But he kept his eye on Ruth Ann. Her eyes were sad and rounded.

The little boy stopped crying at that and looked up at Clyde. He said solemnly, "I get to sit in the front seat with my mama."

Clyde's smile was more genuine this time. "That's right," he told the boy. "We're just gonna drive to McDonald's and you can sit in her lap while we all chat and get to know each other. Okay?"

The boy thought a moment. He hopped into the front seat and Clyde and Jared slid into the back next to the little girl who was pressed against the other side of the car. Her eyes were round and scared. Then the boy said, "Do we still get to have ice cream?"

27

That day in the attic kept buzzing in his brain like one of those wasps that stung him and Rooney. It was a dangerous place. It was a dangerous place in many ways. He was seven years old and he lacked for something "to do" and was too old to ask his mother, "What can I do?" and too young to figure out anything very specific for himself. At such times occasionally he'd climb those treacherous wooden fold-down stairs into the musty overheated attic. Up here was one triangular window following the roof-line and going down roughly four feet so there was light near the window but then it petered out into the corners of the little attic room.

That's where that day he'd found a box that contained of all things his father's report cards. From thirty or thirty-five years ago. There had been six or eight of the small folded-over cards that his now-dead grandmother had assiduously saved and stowed away one by one into this particular box. Seven-year-old Clyde started pawing through the box as if he'd found a treasure. His own grades were above-average. He was only in second grade and got mostly Bs and occasionally an A if a teacher liked or felt sorry for him. Once he'd even gotten a gold star on one of his drawings. But as he opened his father's report cards one by one he saw in shock that his father's grades were another matter. Almost all his grades were F. An occasional D that Clyde thought probably resulted from a teacher liking or feeling sorry for his old man.

Clyde could barely imagine his father as a child. Of course he'd seen photographs. (A bony-headed and tough-looking kid.) But still. Something in Clyde was deeply gratified that his own grades were so much better. At the same time he felt an unwanted pity and mortification for his old man. Clyde knew that his grandfather was a mean old bird and that his father must have gotten a beating from hell for each one of those report cards. The thought of his father's fear in between the time that he got the card and the time he had to present it to Clyde's grandmother for her chicken-scratch signature buzzed at him like one of those wasps again. For Clyde's grandmother surely showed the cards to his grandfather and Clyde knew from family stories and just from the look of the older man in photographs that pure mayhem had ensued.

That day he was thinking about all this and going through the cards for the umpteenth time. English. History. Arithmetic. All Fs. There would be an occasional C in physical education. Once unexpectedly he got a D in social studies. But all the rest were Fs. Clyde was pondering all this when he realized Rooney had followed him up the attic steps and was looking around herself, though not delving the way Clyde always did inside the stacks and stacks of cardboard boxes. She was singing a little song that was just the repetition of *la la la* in high scarcely varying notes that got on his nerves. A kind of trilling. She'd walk around the attic behind him, running her hand along the sides of the boxes to no purpose and singing that little trilling song that had no melody or charm but was merely a small child's tune that he most definitely did not like. It bugged him. It buzzed in his head. *La la la.* And many repetitions of that.

She was four years old.

"Shut up," he said but she couldn't hear him or didn't bother to listen. She would run her hand along the window frame in a pointless triangle while doing the little trill and occasionally pausing to swat a fly or even a wasp out of her way. Clyde's insides clenched. His insides burned. How and why had his father been so stupid? The school his father had attended was the same one Clyde attended now and he knew the readings were simple and the tests were easy. You could get the answers just by common sense even if you hadn't read anything in the book at all.

Clyde had never understood his father. Why he was so mean.

Nor did he understand himself or if he really wanted to hold these nice people at gunpoint.

Kidnapping. Home invasion. Those were his crimes for today. He added them in his mind to a long list and then stopped thinking about that. Thinking was a luxury he couldn't afford at the moment.

⌘

They were exiting their cars in the parking lot. The golden arches loomed above them.

"See?" Clyde said. He nodded his head toward the boy, who had run to his mother. "Safe and sound."

Mother and son were hugging. "Thank you," Ruth Ann rasped out.

The McDonald's was the usual affair of scooped-out plastic orange seats and exhausted-looking counter kids who spoke to you without any humanity in their voices or on their faces. Clyde thought that if he had to work at a McDonald's there would be the option to shoot himself. But he knew he'd never need the gun in his pocket for that or any other reason.

They ordered Big Macs and Cokes and ice cream cones for the kids. Some of the tension he'd felt in the lot outside Walgreens had evaporated now that they were eating. They even had some normal conversation of a sort.

Ruth Ann said: "Where—where's your wife?"

"Must of left," Clyde said. "Is the food good?"

"Yup," the boy said. His mouth was covered with ketchup. He'd foregone a burger and had only wanted fries and the ice cream cone. He stuffed fries in his mouth with one hand and then would lick the cone he held in the other.

Clyde couldn't help laughing.

"You're a character," he said.

Then the girl piped up. "I am too," she said uncertainly.

Clyde laughed again. "I reckon you are." Then he added, "Honey-bunny."

Jared and Ruth Ann were both smiling their vague and waxy

smiles. Jared's smile had a touch of sullenness like that of any teenager. It occurred to Clyde that Jared was growing up right before his eyes. When they'd started this journey days ago he'd been just a kid but now he was a teenager with a menacing look to him. You could even say he was becoming a man although that might be taking it too far.

"Jared?" he said. "You're not eating that burger."

Jared gave him a cold look. "Not hungry. Remember I had that Whopper a while ago."

Clyde gave Ruth Ann a tilted half-smile. "We've been driving for days; actually, we've been driving at night. We've eaten a lot of hamburgers…"

"Yeah," Jared said. "It's a wonder we don't look like hamburgers by now."

The little boy laughed at this. "You don't look like no hamburger," he said.

Clyde made a face. He said, "My tongue's the burger and my lips are the buns," and he put his tongue out between his lips.

The child laughed in delight. His sister smiled as if wanting to be convinced that Clyde was funny. She wasn't quite there.

Clyde noticed that Ruth Ann kept glancing nervously at her watch. "We really ought to get back," she said, as if she were in charge of things.

"That so," Clyde said. "But the kids aren't finished eating."

"We can take some home," she said without meeting his eyes.

"And miss out on the delightful atmosphere of this place?" This joke wasn't very funny and nobody laughed.

But after another minute or two Clyde relented and said, "Okay. Let's get going."

"Can I finish my ice cream in the car?" the boy asked. The girl had already devoured hers.

"Sure thing," Clyde said.

The boy nodded and took another bite of the ice cream that was starting to melt down his hand. "My daddy says that," he said. "Sure thing."

Clyde stood and the others started gathering their remaining food together. "Well," he told the boy, "you should always do what your daddy says."

For some reason Clyde glanced over at Jared. He looked like he had at that barber shop they'd visited—like he wanted nothing more than to throw up.

28

Rooney would not stop singing that song. It was not even a song. Just a trilling to herself for her own amusement and giving no thought to how it got on her older brother's nerves. *La la la.* He could pull out his dick and start playing with it and she wouldn't notice. She was that caught up in her own little world. Following her big brother up the attic stairs to no purpose except that she likewise needed something to "do" and their mother was out back clipping shirts and sheets along the clothesline (Clyde could see her from the attic window) and there was no one to keep Rooney away from him.

He thought: She's like one of those wasps. He was digging around in box after box looking at his parents' mementoes and he supposed there had been yearbooks and photographs and old letters—and he thought he remembered an old stamp collection—and all manner of such but for some reason all he remembered with any detail were the old man's report cards. His father had failed in school just like he'd failed in life. Living on "disability" from the government because his doctor had prettified the diagnosis of "alcoholism" and made it "chronic depression" and that was that. His grandma, his mother's mama, had money but wouldn't give a cent to Clyde's mother because she had married his worthless old man. So his mother got disability too. A bad knee, supposedly. A bad back. Using these two checks that arrived every month from good ole Uncle Sammy his mama and old man raised these kids and kept the household going. Soon enough there would be another disability check too.

Clyde dropped the report cards back into the box. At last his sister said something to him and seemed to come out of her reverie.

"Whatcha doin'?"

"None of your damn business."

"Clyde..." she whined.

"Clyde..." he mocked her back.

That's when she sealed her fate. She seemed to reenter her dream world again. She was wearing an old dress that must have been one of Billie's from years ago with stains that looked like grape juice down the front. Her skin was doughy. She wasn't fat but she was doughy. Clyde understood that he couldn't stand the look of her. And now she'd started that odd singing again *la la la* as she ran her hand along the triangular window. Then she just started wandering around the attic. Aimlessly. Pointlessly. Her hair was a brownish tangle and her face was rounded and Clyde's mama probably hadn't made her brush her teeth in a week or more. She smelled bad. She smelled of her body at only four years old for she was large for her age. Now she was wandering over toward the big squarish hole in the floor where the steps went down and she dragged her feet along *la la la* and seemed to have forgotten that the two of them had been conversing. Was she stupid? Was she retarded? In his corner of the attic he raised up and told himself that he could not bear to hear that *la la la* one more time but there she was with her tongue halfway lolling out of her mouth and singing that song so he eased up behind her.

Put the palm of his hand against the flat of her back. Even her back was doughy and she felt nothing. He felt the need to push. (Why?) Push.

Because he wanted to.

She tumbled head over feet down the stairs and she was screaming and he thought that probably he'd never hear *la la la* again. That was over. Her childhood was over. She was a lumpen mass at the bottom of the stairs. Ma had heard her and came running in. Pa was out somewhere with Billie.

He didn't want to think about the rest of the story. He supposed he'd come clambering down the stairs saying that Rooney had tried to jump across the opening in the attic floor but she missed and came crashing down. He worked up a few tears.

"I shouldn't have let her. I should have stopped her…" That's when Mama slapped him. She bent down and turned Rooney gently so that the milky unmoving whites of her eyes were showing. "Mama? I shouldn't have let her. It's all my fault!"

"Shut up, you! I told you two not to mess around up in that attic!"

She'd gathered Rooney close to her oversized bosom and began rocking her. "Now go call like we taught you. 911. Understand me?"

"Yeah. 911." Clyde spoke dully.

When he got to the kitchen phone and dialed the number the woman said, "Where is your emergency?"

Clyde said, "My sister done fell down the stairs."

"Thanks for having us over," Clyde said pointlessly. Without irony.

Ruth Ann was sitting in one shabby wingback chair and Clyde in the other. Jared sat on the sofa looking apprehensive. The children were lurking behind their mother's chair. Every once in a while the little girl would say, "Mama, why are they here?" and Ruth Ann would shush her.

Involuntarily Clyde thought *Rooney/Ruth Ann*. How similar the names were. But he wasn't going to hurt Ruth Ann. Not at all.

"You're welcome," Ruth Ann finally said.

Suddenly Clyde felt the need to pee. Something fierce. But he didn't want to leave these people who were all against him— yes, even Jared—alone in one room. Was Jared really against him? He could not read the look in his eyes. They were glazed over and just about expressionless. They gave nothing away. But Clyde figured the boy would run out of the house yelling bloody murder if given half the chance. Oddly he'd brought that flaking old school satchel from the backseat with him, as if he might feel the urge to read a book or work his Rubik's cube, but the satchel stayed beside him and he did not reach inside.

"Listen," Clyde said abruptly. "Do you care if I use your bathroom? Jared, don't you need to go?"

"No," Jared said as if offended.

The little girl, who wasn't as shy as her brother, pointed to a door that led to the hall. "It's that way," she said. "The bathroom."

The air in the room was still and strained. Clyde glanced around and found the telephone on an end table next to the sofa. The phone had the look of being little-used. He didn't think any of them would reach for it once he went to the bathroom. But still. He saw to his relief that it was one of those new cordless phones and he walked over and picked it up. The eyes of the others all followed him.

"I need to make a call," he said.

"While you're going to the bathroom?" the little girl said.

"Julie, hush," Ruth Ann said. Her face had a waxen look.

"That's all right," Clyde said. He tried to smile at Julie and then at her mother. The smile wasn't a success.

To Clyde's surprise the little boy piped up. "Mama, when are they leaving?"

"Benjamin, hush," his mother said.

"Benjamin," Clyde said. "That's a mighty big name for such a little boy." He grinned and this time he felt it was authentic. "We won't be staying long," he added.

"Okay," Benjamin said.

So he went to the bathroom and came back to the living room to ponder his next move and a couple of minutes later the police siren was blaring. Clyde took out his gun. Ruth Ann's hands were shaking but then women tended to react that way to guns. They never handled or even saw them so they were "exotic" to them and purely dangerous. Clyde wished he could convey to her that he'd only wanted the car and that he'd never harm a hair on her head and certainly he wouldn't hurt the children. But at the moment it suited his needs for her to think otherwise.

And before hearing the sirens he'd planned to tell her: Say

a word to Odessa police and I'm coming back for you all. You don't want that.

Within a second of first hearing the siren, Clyde glanced at Ruth Ann and then he thought of Nina. He thought: Women. You could not trust them. Which one had summoned the cops? He'd been in the bathroom no more than sixty seconds but that's all it took for a woman to shaft you. There could be another cordless phone in the kitchen maybe that matched the one Clyde had taken into the bathroom. But of course he hadn't incapacitated the line. That was his own stupid fault.

But, no, he could tell Ruth Ann hadn't moved. It was Nina for sure. She couldn't have just gone back to Georgia and kept her mouth shut. Had to come back for this baby boy of hers.

"My wife called them," he told Ruth Ann. "But I'm wanted for something I didn't do."

"You did it, all right," Jared said. Clyde looked over, annoyed. It wasn't like Jared to pop off that way. Something was happening with that boy. He seemed larger. Angrier.

"I'm scared," Julie said out of nowhere. She held her ears against the noise of the siren.

"It'll be all right, Julie!" her mother cried.

"Don't worry," Clyde said. He held the gun down to his side. "See? No danger." His hands were shaking but not too bad. He could handle this. He could stay in control of this. "Nobody will get hurt. Nobody but those goddamn cops will get hurt."

"Don't hurt *anybody*," Jared said.

Out of instinct Clyde pointed the gun at him.

"Oh my God…" Ruth Ann was whimpering.

Jared didn't look scared. He just gave Clyde a sour look.

They heard heavy footsteps on the wooden porch. At Clyde's instruction Ruth Ann went to open the door and when the officer said, "Something wrong, ma'am?" she said, "Sorry. False alarm."

There was a screen door between them. Ruth Ann was shaking like a leaf. Goddamn her.

"Mind if I look inside?" the officer said.

"Um. I guess," Ruth Ann said. Over on the couch Jared and the little kids were huddled in a small group. On the table next to Jared was his idiot satchel with its books and games and such. Clyde reckoned he was through with all that.

"Come on in!" Clyde cried. He was suddenly jovial. He was going to play a part and he'd play it well.

"Sir?" the portly officer said. "Ya'll having some kind of trouble here?" His Texas drawl was thick as cow dung. Clyde smiled.

"Just a little argument but all is A-OK now," he said.

The officer looked at Jared and Ruth Ann and the kids. None of them looked happy. Clyde's hand was behind him which didn't please the officer.

"Hands where I can see 'em," the officer said.

Clyde raised his eyebrows as if he didn't understand and then he shrugged and said, "Sure thing" and pulled out his revolver and shot the officer square in the chest. The older man fell heavily.

"Clyde! No!" It was Jared.

Ruth Ann kept saying, "Oh my God…" Little Julie had started crying.

"Shut up," Clyde said. "All ya'll."

"Stop it, Clyde!" Jared said.

The officer was lying on the floor next to the coffee table. He was twitching and moaning and trying to reach for something. His radio. His gun. He was an overweight grizzled man in his fifties and they never should have sent him alone. But maybe Nina had minimized what was happening or else hadn't been clear. She'd written down the Mustang's license plate number and told the police a maniac killer was going to kill four people or some shit like that. Or maybe she hadn't explained what was happening at all and just provided the license number and the dispatcher presumed it was a routine domestic call. What the hell difference did it make?

Clyde went to the officer's side and took out his gun and put it next to the officer's forehead. Clyde said, "Bye bye."

That's when Clyde felt the worst pain of his life. His throat burned like holy hell. There was blood and heat as though someone had drawn a knife blade jaggedly along his throat from one side to the other. And that's more or less what had happened. Jared had taken that old box cutter of his and, with all his strength, had cut his uncle's throat. He wasn't going to let him execute that innocent officer Clyde supposed in a dying swoon. One of his last perceptions was the gold glinting on the officer's wedding finger. So he had a wife. A family. Jared was such a good kid, Clyde thought snidely, and wasn't going to let this officer who'd wandered into their mess get killed. He wasn't going to allow it. That was all. And that was all.

BOOK THREE

PART SEVEN

JARED

29

August 18, 2005

Dear Mama,

It was good to get your birthday card, even though you didn't say very much. I'm glad, though, that you're "feeling okay" and that the folks at the clinic there appear to be treating you well. And I'm so glad you found that job! I don't think you'd have been happy in Atlanta, or really anywhere else but there in the house where I grew up and where you lived happily with Daddy, at least for a time.

As you might know, I communicate with Aunt Billie quite a bit on the telephone and through letters (she hasn't yet mastered email, I'm afraid), and she very kindly reaches out with news each time she visits you.

I'm also glad that you're continuing to work part-time. Though it's been such a long time since Clyde and all the rest, I think you still need some more time to recuperate. I know those many years in the hospital cannot have been pleasant, and I'm glad at least that you're out of there.

Everything is going fairly well here. You asked me to tell you about my "life." Well, my life is a matter of strict routine, which I find comforting. I get up every morning at seven o'clock, without exception, then I shower and have some oatmeal and get dressed in the "uniform" they have us wear to work—plain black pants, white short-sleeve shirt bearing a pin with my name on it, so no one, including me, forgets who I am. (Smile.) Then I get in my black '98 Cougar, a car you've never seen, and drive the 3.7 miles from my apartment over to the supermarket in Brookhaven.

It occurs to me that I've never told you very much about where I work, or about my co-workers. I guess that's because they are nothing out of the ordinary. All supermarkets are alike, after all, except for size, and the one where I work is a medium-sized one. It's a Publix, and the other people who work there are for the most part very nice. Most of them work hard, and have families, and I know few of them well except Ernest (he's the one who sold me, for fifty bucks, this old computer I'm using), whom I've befriended to a degree. He lives a life similar to mine, except that he inherited some money not long ago and has a nice condo in midtown Atlanta, about a six-mile drive from my place. Usually on weekends we meet at the condo, and have a couple of beers, and talk about what guys like us would normally talk about—our co-workers at the store, our families, our plans for the future. Or maybe that isn't "normal"—for instance, we don't talk about sports or, much, about the opposite sex.

I did tell him that I still have a kind of crush on Linda, though it's been years now since I've seen her. Does Kay ever talk about Linda to you? I haven't seen Kay in more than a year, I'd guess—the last time she came into the store. All I know is that Linda "went off to college" somewhere in Alabama, and met someone, and lives in a tidy subdivision outside Birmingham. But when I think of her, I'm still filled with an emotion I can't quite define.

Thanks again for the card, Mama. I hope you're having a pleasant summer.

Love,

Jared

&

He lives in a large apartment complex just a few blocks off Interstate 85, and sometimes he goes out onto the balcony and sits in the aluminum lawn chair he inherited from the previous owner and watches the traffic flow by. It drifts along in an endless stream, though naturally the stream is more congested in the evening, between five and seven, which is the time he usually sits out here. He gets off work at three, so thankfully he's home before "rush hour," and he'll sit with a beer or a glass of iced tea and watch idly as all the cars—most of them black, silver, red, white—inch along toward their destinations in the suburbs. Sometimes he'll fix on a specific car, catching a glimpse of the man or woman driving it, and wonder idly at this person's life. Was he happy? Was she miserable? Once in a great while a driver will glance up to where Jared is sitting, eyes fixing on those of the comely dark-haired young man in his lawn chair, and even less frequently the driver will wave, or smile, and Jared will wave or smile back. But truthfully, this does not happen very often.

Jared usually sits there only for half an hour, at most an hour, and then he'll go inside to fix his dinner. He'll grill a burger, or heat up some chili and rice, and usually he'll have some ice cream for dessert. Then he'll read or watch TV until it's time to go to bed. He rarely calls anyone, and rarely does the phone ring for him, unless it's a telemarketer. Then he hangs up. He has no desire to speak with strangers about things he does not want to buy.

His life is quiet, mundane, harmless. Just the way he likes it.

Sometimes in bed at night he'll think about Clyde, and everything that happened back in his teenage years, but he tries to avoid such thoughts, which agitate him and which serve no purpose, after all. More often he thinks about his mother.

Neither of them was arrested, of course, the mitigating factor being self-defense in his case, and simply being "not guilty"—of being an accessory after the fact—in hers.

Nina had gotten better so slowly that at first her doctor told him frankly she might never be the mother Jared had known. She had suffered from severe depression, suicidal ideation, and a form of psychosis that had her drifting in and out of touch with what a psychiatric expert they consulted confidently termed "reality." Listening to this, Jared gave an inner sneer, but made sure his face stayed expressionless. Nina, he thought, had endured more "reality" than this psychiatrist with his gray silk suit and natty red bow tie would ever encounter in his life.

And her baby was stillborn—was it callous of him to think this had been a kind of blessing? Jared had gone home with Billie, who was given legal custody of her nephew, and Nina had stayed in the hospital, where her sister-in-law and son visited her on a biweekly basis. She was always the same, essentially. She'd grown out her light-auburn hair and had cut it short to remove any trace of the whitish blond that must have represented to her Clyde's criminal depravity and the worst time of her life. Her face for a long time had been pale and slack, and since she declined to do the physical exercises recommended by the hospital she had gained some weight, especially around her stomach and hips. She did not say much, not to Billie and not even to her only child whom she'd once professed to love so much. Quickly enough the visits to see her in the hospital became a matter of routine, of asking the same bland questions and receiving the same bland responses. More than once Jared noticed that his mother didn't quite meet his eyes.

When he turned eighteen, he got the job at Publix and moved into his apartment, much against the wishes of his aunt Billie. She believed he was too young, too "traumatized" to live alone; and she told him so, face to face. But of course he did not listen. Fortunately Nina had improved. She'd moved from the hospital, to a "halfway house," and finally back home where she worked on renewing her nursing license and recently had gotten her new job at a clinic on the outskirts of town.

As for him, he seems to have turned into an ordinary young man of his time and place. The younger George Bush is president now, and he reads the newspaper and watches the TV news enough to know that the country is being led by an idiot. At least, he thinks, no future president could be worse than this one. Politics is only one of the topics he talks about with his friend Ernest and co-workers at the grocery store. They talk about movies, less often about music, almost never about books. Though Jared usually has a paperback suspense thriller splay-backed on his night table, Ernest does not read much and most of his co-workers not at all. They are ordinary people, and

Jared had the idea that ordinary people do not read. Nor, in the age of email, do they write letters, though Jared continues to write to his mother who, like Billie, has a stubborn aversion to computers and can be reached only through the mail.

❧

August 25, 2005

Dear Mama,

I hope you are well. Though you didn't answer my last letter, Aunt Billie says you're taking your new medication regularly and that it's helping a lot. Nowadays whether a person has heart disease or cancer or plain old depression, there is a pill that will cure it, or at least lessen the symptoms, and as we used to hear all too often, we all have to "take our medicine."

Not much has changed here. I notice that the school buses are back in business and the apartments in my complex with kids in them run according to a routine as strict as my own. A big old yellow dented bus appears at one corner of the parking lot every morning at 7:15, about the time I'm shaving and getting ready for work. I can just see the bus with the kids climbing inside from my bathroom window. It makes me think of Sacred Heart School and the nuns who taught us there (most of whom, to be honest, I didn't like) and old Father Brody and young Father Zach. You'll be surprised to hear this, but Father Zach came to see me this past week—he'd gotten my address from Aunt Billie—and we had a short visit. Did you know he had left the priesthood? It was startling to see him in walking shorts and a polo-style shirt, but otherwise he looked pretty much the same. We talked for maybe twenty minutes and then he left. He lives here in Atlanta now, and I got the uncomfortable idea that he wanted us to be friends, which would be strange not only because of our age difference but because of everything else.

Otherwise not much has been happening. I have some close friends here—well, at least one, his name is Ernest, and I think I told you about him in a previous letter. He has the kind of lively, smiling disposition that results from a normal childhood and adolescence. (I don't mean that to sound resentful, but maybe to your ears it does, inevitably. I'm sorry if that is the case.) He's always telling me to "smile," to "cheer up," and when I tell him I feel fine and don't need any cheering up, he cants his head to one side with a skeptical look. I guess he thinks I'm too "serious" for my age, and maybe I am. Everything is relative, I tell him. And everybody is different.

I've never told him or any of my other acquaintances what happened to me as a teenager, and I don't intend to. I think that's best, don't you?

Well, as usual I'm rattling on too long. Please have a happy week and don't forget to take that medication. It's very important. I take mine, and I don't want to think what my life would be like without it. Though I guess I would survive. At least, I hope I would.

Much love,

Jared

‎❧

It was rare that the doorbell rang, so he almost didn't answer. He feared it was a door-to-door salesman or somebody from Jehovah's Witness. Creeping to the window near the door and peeking out the Venetian blinds, he could just see the front porch, where a familiar-looking man in his thirties was standing. He had nothing in his hands. No clipboard, no religious pamphlets.

Jared opened the door and his heart thudded at the sight of Father Zach.

"Hi, Jared," he said.

He'd aged very little, just a few smile lines at his eyes' corners. Still the dark hair sprinkled with silver (a bit more silver, now) and the same slender long face and pleasant but hesitant smile.

"Gee, Father Zach," Jared said, swinging the door open. "What a surprise."

"I hope you don't mind my barging in like this. Your aunt

gave me your address, but I forgot to ask for the phone number. I didn't want to call back and bother her again."

He came inside the living room, shyly, glancing around as if impressed though Jared's ordinary two-bedroom apartment was very minimally furnished and decorated.

"Nice place," he said. "Can't believe you're living here on your own."

"I'm twenty-eight," Jared told him.

"Oh yes, yes…"

Jared motioned him to the couch, where they sat, each turned slightly in the other's direction.

"I hope you don't mind my—"

"You've already said that, Father." Jared smiled.

They both laughed, uneasily.

"Oh, so I did. Except you can drop the 'Father' now, if you like. I've left the priesthood. Did your aunt tell you that?"

"She did. I was surprised."

Father Zach splayed his hands outward, a meaningless gesture. Jared knew he must be past forty, even forty-five, yet his gestures were those of a much younger man. He seemed unsure of himself, as if not accustomed to being an ordinary man wearing ordinary clothes.

Jared did not know what to say to him.

"What brings you over here…shall I call you Zach?"

"Yes, yes. Zach is fine." The former priest grinned. "Just wanted to touch base, I suppose, see if you needed anything. Once you're 'in charge' of someone, it's hard to let go of that shepherding instinct. Do you understand?"

"Of course," Jared said.

There was a brief, awkward silence. Then Zach added, "And I guess I've been a bit lonesome, since moving to Atlanta. It's an awfully big city, and though I grew up here, most of my friends have fled the roost. That's the way Atlanta is, somehow."

"Yeah, everybody is from someplace else. Native Atlantans are rare."

"That's true," Zach said.

Another silence.

Zach rubbed his hands together, and for a second Jared had the idea that the man was about to rise and flee. But he stayed seated.

"Oh, and I also wanted to say—to tell you I was sorry to hear about your aunt Maureen."

"Thanks," Jared said, smiling awkwardly. He didn't know what else to say. Several months ago, Rooney had developed a lethal brain tumor called a glioblastoma—Jared had thought the word one of the ugliest he'd ever heard. *Glioblastoma*. They treated her in the usual way, with chemo and radiation, and had been pondering surgery when Rooney died one night in her sleep. Jared had attended the funeral, though he hadn't wanted to re-enter that church where he'd spent so many boring and pointless hours during his childhood. He supposed that one more hour wouldn't matter much in the scheme of things, and of course Aunt Billie was pleased to have him there. (His mother, to his disappointment, did not attend.) The casket had been placed near the altar, an open casket (upon Billie's instructions); but Jared had not approached it. He did not want to see, once again, that fleshy, childish face, and wonder about what she had suffered in her life at Clyde's hands, and subsequently. So he stayed in the pew, hands folded in his lap like a child's. The hour passed quickly and painlessly and Jared had made a point of not listening to a word of the priest's sermon. The man was a middle-aged paunchy Latino gentleman named Father Luis; he had taken over the parish after Father Brody died several years ago.

Jared added, "You must have been sorry to lose Father Brody. I mean, the two of you must have been...close."

Zach was already shaking his head. "No, not really," he said. "Generation gap and all that. We were friendly colleagues, but not really friends."

"I see," Jared said.

Once again there seemed nothing left to say.

Zach was glancing around the room. The only furniture besides the sofa was a pair of wingback chairs, a coffee table, and some small occasional tables, which held lamps. On the coffee table was a plant, a fern, that looked like it could use a good watering. Jared noticed this with some embarrassment—was he really so self-centered? But Zach seemed to look around vaguely and if he was having the same thought, he kept it to himself.

"Yes, a nice place," Zach said. "Do you ever—ever have dates? The apartment, if you don't mind my saying so, looks a bit—spartan. Like it could use a woman's touch."

So maybe the man was more observant than Jared thought.

"No, no dates," Jared said quickly. "I really don't have time."

This lie was so blatant that neither man took it up.

"I see," Zach said.

Jared thought for a moment and then asked, "What about you? Do you allow yourself to—to date?"

Zach laughed. He splayed his hands backwards again and the knuckles cracked.

"Oh no, not since high school," he said. "I think I've forgotten how."

Jared liked this answer so he said, "Me too. I've forgotten how."

Zach laughed again. "We're quite a pair, aren't we?"

Jared didn't reply. Zach was looking at him in a way that made him uncomfortable.

"If you don't mind, Jared, I'd like to keep in touch. Maybe we could grab dinner some evening."

The idea sounded preposterous, which both men seemed to recognize even though they were nodding vigorously.

"Sure, I'd like that," Jared lied. He'd recently gotten "Caller ID" on his telephone, so he simply wouldn't answer if the man called.

That settled, Zach clasped his hands together once more and this time rose from the sofa. "Well, it was good chatting with you."

They walked to the door in that slow, foot-dragging way of people who know they'll never meet again.

"Yes, I appreciate your stopping by," Jared said.

A suddenly serious and almost frowning look came over Zach's face. "And listen, if you ever need to talk to somebody about what—what happened to you…" His voice trailed off and he didn't seem to be able to finish this thought.

"Yes," Jared said quickly. "I prefer not to talk about that, but I appreciate the offer."

Zach closed his eyes briefly, as though relieved. Then he said, "All right, then." He reached into his pocket and pulled out a piece of paper and handed it to Jared. It had Zach's name and phone number printed in large block letters. "I'll hope to hear from you," Zach said.

"Sure thing," Jared said.

Truly there was nothing left to say, so Zach nodded and went out the door. "See you soon!" he called over his shoulder.

"Sounds good," Jared said. Something icy-cold had grabbed on to his heart, impelling him into the kitchen where he opened the lower cabinet and gently dropped the paper with Zach's phone number inside the trash can. The cabinet door shut with a sound of finality, and Jared thought, in exactly these words: *That was that.*

30

Self-defense—he spent much of his time pondering this term. He went back to that moment when he understood that Clyde was going to shoot and kill the sheriff's deputy, who likely had a family at home; and that once the officer was dead, Clyde was going to understand that Ruth Ann and the children were witnesses and they'd be next. Jared had come to intuit how Clyde's brain functioned, if you could call it functioning. And what about himself? Would Clyde consider Jared a potential witness, and "off" him—a term he'd once heard Clyde use while they were watching a TV detective show in one of their dismal motel rooms—so Jared couldn't testify against him, either?

One time in high school they'd read a play, a tragedy. Their teacher, Sister Angela, had joked that at the end of the play, which had been written by Shakespeare five hundred years ago, the stage was "littered with corpses." Everyone in the class thought her phrasing was funny, and they all laughed, including Sister Angela. He'd noticed that she wasn't above making a joke now and then; she liked to get a rise out of her students. Jared had wondered, only seconds after jaggedly slitting his uncle's throat with the box-cutter, what she might have found to laugh about in this case. Half a dozen bodies "littering" a stage were somehow funny; one man gasping and twitching on the floor in his own blood was not funny—not at all.

Jared had stood there with the box-cutter in his numbed hand, not knowing what to say or feel. He couldn't imagine what expression had overtaken his face.

Later his mother said tensely, "It's all right, Jared. You had to."

The pale-faced sheriff's officer, whom they'd helped to the

couch while they waited for the ambulance, had managed to
say, "You did the right thing, son. You did."

No one had used the term *self-defense* then but months later,
at his court hearing, he'd heard the phrase often. The county
prosecutor had insisted that Jared be remanded to the youth
detention center, but the slick-looking lawyer hired by Billie had
pointed out that he was a good kid, he'd never been in trouble,
he was no threat to society, and so forth. So the judge had followed Jared's lawyer's recommendation that he be placed into
the custody of his aunt, Billie McCune Fair. He'd slammed his
gavel down much harder than they did on TV.

Jared had flinched, and that was that.

It was a phrase that entered his head often lately. *That was
that.*

Of them all, Jared knew that Clyde was the lucky one. Jared
never saw his uncle's dying eyes, and he felt they must have
been filled with pain and outrage, but only for a few seconds.
The man had not suffered for very long. Quickly enough he was
a corpse littering the room. It seemed only seconds, though it
must have been several minutes, before two uniformed sheriff's
officers arrived to take photographs of Clyde, and of Jared.
They asked Jared to remove his shirt and his pants, and the officer whose life Jared had saved protested this wasn't necessary,
but his colleagues muttered, "You know it's procedure. Won't
take long."

Jared didn't mind. In fact, it didn't take long.

Once the hearing was over and the judge's decision rendered,
Jared felt he had aged many years in just a few months. But his
mother seemed to regress. She could no longer do the simplest
things. Her eyes looked vacuous, stunned. Jared, of course, did
not know what to do. Soon enough it was summertime, and
he resumed sacking at the grocery store where he'd worked
before. When summer was over Jared went back to school, and
then another summer arrived and that one passed quickly, too.
He was sixteen, he was seventeen. He did not "date" and he

had few friends. Occasionally he thought of calling Linda, but she and her mother were still living peaceably (he assumed) in Atlanta, and he did not see why he should bother them. Jared was different, now. He had blood on his hands. He thought, Why should he bother anyone? By the time Nina was admitted to a psychiatric hospital, Jared's isolation was almost complete. When he turned eighteen, he made a brief embarrassed announcement to his aunt and uncle (how much embarrassment there was, in all this!) that he was moving to Atlanta; he'd driven there one weekend and secured the Publix job and, with part of his savings, rented the apartment in which he'd live for the next decade. And those years, too, began to pass. Quickly. Vertiginously. Simply walking from his bedroom into the kitchen late at night he'd feel, in fact, as though he had vertigo, as if the floor were about to disappear beneath him; but then he always caught himself, just in time. He never fell. Some of these were close calls, but he never fell.

His mother got better, slowly. She began to reply to Jared's letters more frequently and in a more fulsome way.

Darling, I think about you so often and wish everything had worked out differently, who knows once you start a family how it will go, what turns life will take, how horrifying it might all become? It's been like that night at the amusement park when Rooney suddenly stood up in the Ferris wheel and I thought something terrible would happen, that she might fall or jump, and I remember standing down below, watching the three of you swaying over earth in the night sky with the carnival music and the winking mocking multicolored lights all around, and nothing I could do. I feel that way now, honey, like I'm in a Ferris-wheel car high above the earth and the car is swaying, rocking, and I wonder from one moment to the next what will be my fate? Do you have such thoughts, honey? Wondering what will be your fate? I wish you happiness and love and a long, peaceful life from now on, but still I'm worried. Still I worry if our swaying car will abruptly descend and bring us all crashing back to earth.

Or has this already happened?...

The letter had disturbed but at the same time comforted him. Only a few years ago she could barely write at all, it seemed, and now she could express herself so beautifully. He knew he could never write like that. He knew he could never have such thoughts. Maybe the time was yet ahead when his mother would resume guiding him, and they would be restored to their rightful places in their family, and there would be some kind of happiness in that. In fact, maybe the time was near. He hoped that this was so.

About a month after Zach's visit, Jared was absorbed in stocking jars of jam and preserves on aisle three of Publix when he was startled by someone touching his forearm. He looked over and saw Kay Hanratty. As usual, compared to the other customers in the store she looked "dressed up," a red dress and a brightly printed scarf around her neck, some gold earrings that twinkled under the fluorescent lights, a perfectly made-up face. Occasionally she ran into Jared in the store—she had moved to a nearby apartment—but as he'd told his mother, it had been at least a year since the last time.

"You look wonderful!" she cried, patting his forearm as though he were still fourteen. Instinctively Jared withdrew his arm, though he knew she meant nothing untoward by touching him. That was simply her way. Yet he did not like to be touched, not by men and not by women. At the touch of another, his skin would be covered with pinpricks of distaste and panic. Even now, in this public place, on this bright Sunday afternoon, he felt himself in a place of potential darkness and had a strong impulse to flee.

But he did not flee. He simply folded his arms, looked her up and down, and said, "Thank you."

The woman smelled of flowers. He remembered that about her—she'd always worn perfume, or else a floral-scented cologne. Clyde had once said something about her "stinking up the place" but Jared felt differently. He liked that she troubled to dress nicely, to brush her hair to a shine, to carefully apply make-up. And to put on cologne, so that others might be pleased.

"So *tell* me," she said, out of nowhere.

"Tell you...?"

She made a broad grimace. "About you, your life... Are you dating someone, by now? Are you married, or—?"

"No, not married," he said quickly. "Like I told you before, I'm just—just alone, I guess."

He shrugged and looked off, but Mrs. Hanratty's gaze was fixed on Jared.

"A handsome young man like you! Alone!" she cried.

Jared could feel warm blood creeping upward to his face.

He said, "Well..."

She was nodding, vigorously. "I know, I know. It's not easy finding someone, is it? The right person?"

"I guess not," he said, though he was hardly looking for anyone. He hoped she would change the subject.

"Gosh," she said, abruptly, "I'm being rude. I haven't even invited you over! I thought of that the last time I ran into you. Well, there's no time like the present! Can you stop by this evening, maybe around seven? We can have a glass of wine, talk over old times..." Then she frowned, as if understanding this had struck the wrong note. "We—we can talk," she added hesitantly.

To his surprise, Jared heard himself say, "Seven o'clock? Sure, why not," and then quickly, as if the "why not" had sounded rude, "I'd enjoy talking with you, Mrs. Hanratty. It's been a long time."

She nodded. "It surely has." She pulled a card from her purse. "Here's the address.

And please call me Kay, won't you? We're both grown-ups now, unfortunately for you." She gave her hectic smile.

"All right. Kay," Jared said.

"That's better. Much better," she said.

ે

That evening he arrived promptly at seven, and he was touched that she'd prepared for his visit—not only had she changed into a navy-silk dress that fitted her voluptuous figure well, but she'd clearly spruced up the apartment. Everything was immaculate, and the dining room table held a large vase of flowers—iris, chrysanthemums, a few pink roses. Jared felt vaguely uncomfortable that she'd gone to such trouble for him. Though now twenty-eight, as he kept reminding himself and others, he often felt like that fourteen-year-old boy who had gone with Clyde and Nina on their doomed journey out west.

"Everything looks—terrific," he stammered, coming inside.

"Oh, it's nothing," Kay said.

They sat, much as he and Father Zach had sat on Jared's living room sofa, legs primly held together and facing each other, yet not quite facing each other. Jared kept looking around the room, as if to avoid looking at this attractive woman, who must be in her fifties.

"It all looks great," he repeated. "You shouldn't have gone to any trouble."

She waved her hand as though dismissing a gnat. "Don't worry," she said. "I like to keep the place looking nice."

"It reminds me of your other house—the furniture is the same, I guess that's it."

"Yes, everything is the same. Except that I'm all alone now," she said.

He blushed slightly at this indirect reference to Linda.

"How—how is she doing?" he said. It was inevitable that they talk about her, he thought, and there was no sense putting it off.

"Fine, fine." Kay smiled. "She graduated college with a 4.0, did I tell you? And she likes her job. She works for some kind of marketing firm, I couldn't even tell you exactly what she does." Kay laughed. "But she loves it," she insisted.

"That's good," Jared said, though this didn't sound quite right. Linda had been interested in literature and philosophy, and now she was working in…a marketing firm? He didn't understand, but he decided not to question Kay about it. If Linda was happy, that's what mattered, surely.

"But you know what?" Kay said, with what Jared thought

was a rather sly look in her eyes. "She just broke up with her boyfriend. Her third one in a year."

"Oh, sorry to hear that." Jared glanced away.

"She can't seem to find the right one." Kay paused. "You know, she was always very fond of *you*, Jared."

"Oh. Well…"

"No. She really was."

Jared smiled at Linda's mother, shyly. "That's nice to hear," he said.

When he thought back to his teenage years, the thought of Linda was the one thing that comforted him. "I—I was fond of her too."

Kay's legs were crossed at the ankles, girlishly, but now she uncrossed them and bent toward Jared. She clapped her hands, in an almost childlike way. "I know!" she said. "Why don't we call her?"

"Call her?" Jared said. "Oh, I doubt she—"

"She'd *love* to talk to you," Kay said brightly. "You know, I've been trying to talk her into moving back home—back to Atlanta, I mean. I know she could get just as good a job here. Maybe you could help me talk her into it."

"Well, Kay, I don't think—"

But now that Kay had seized upon the idea, she would not let it go. Jared saw, nervously, that Kay's cell phone rested on the coffee table, and within seconds she had lifted it, punched a few numbers.

"She'll be so thrilled to hear your voice!" Kay cried.

"Really, Mrs. Hanratty, I don't think—"

"Nope. Kay," she said. "Remember?"

"Kay," he repeated.

The woman was frowning slightly in the way people do when on the phone, trying to make a connection. Then she smiled. "Linda honey?" she said. "Just thought I'd give you a call."

Kay made a bit of small talk with her daughter while Jared sat fidgeting.

"Listen," Kay said, "before we go any further, I wanted to

let you know that I've got someone here. Somebody who wants to talk to you." There was a brief silence and then Kay said, "Well, you'll just have to find out for yourself."

Then Kay held out the phone to Jared.

For a moment, he thought he might stand up and flee the room, flee Kay and Linda's lives forever. But even as he had this stray, unpleasant thought, he knew that he would not stand up, no. He would do exactly as Kay Hanratty instructed him.

He nodded, giving her a strained smile, and he took the phone.

"Hello…Linda?" he said.